"I didn't know you were pregnant until it was too late."

"But you knew," Kathleen whispered.

Jett hesitated, wondering what would happen if he lied. But then he realized it was too late for that. "I knew."

Her face crumpled slightly, as though she had been hoping for some other answer. Then she sighed, closing her eyes. "Strangely enough, it doesn't even matter anymore. Just go away, Jett, all right? I'm tired of talking about the past. I'm just tired of everything!"

She turned away from him, kneading the back of her neck with slender, strong fingers. And suddenly he could remember the touch of those fingers. Could still feel the way she used to trail them delicately down his bare belly until—

"It matters," he g

Dear Reader,

It's summertime, and the livin' may or may not be easy—but the reading is great. Just check out Naomi Horton's *Wild Blood,* the first in her new WILD HEARTS miniseries. In Jett Kendrick you'll find a hero to take to heart and never let go, and you'll understand why memories of their brief, long-ago loving have stayed with Kathy Patterson for sixteen years. Now she's back in Burnt River, back in Jett's life—and about to discover a secret that will change *three* lives forever.

We feature two more great miniseries this month, too. Cathryn Clare's ASSIGNMENT: ROMANCE brings you *The Baby Assignment,* the exciting conclusion to the Cotter brothers' search for love, while Alicia Scott's THE GUINESS GANG continues with *The One Who Almost Got Away,* featuring brother Jake Guiness. And there's still more great reading you won't want to miss. Patricia Coughlin's *Borrowed Bride* features a bride who's kidnapped—right out from under the groom's nose. Of course, it's her kidnapper who turns out to be Mr. Right. And by the way, both Alicia and Patricia had earlier books that were made into CBS TV movies last year. In *Unbroken Vows,* Frances Williams sends her hero and heroine on a search for the heroine's ex-fiancé, a man hero David Reid is increasingly uninterested in finding. Finally, check out Kay David's *Hero in Hiding,* featuring aptly named Mercy Hamilton and enigmatic Rio Barrigan, a man who is far more than he seems.

Then join us again next month and every month, as we bring you more of the best romantic reading around—only in Silhouette Intimate Moments.

Yours,

Leslie Wainger

Leslie Wainger,
Senior Editor and Editorial Coordinator

Please address questions and book requests to:
Silhouette Reader Service
U.S.: 3010 Walden Ave., P.O. Box 1325, Buffalo, NY 14269
Canadian: P.O. Box 609, Fort Erie, Ont. L2A 5X3

Naomi Horton

WILD BLOOD

Silhouette®
INTIMATE™MOMENTS®

Published by Silhouette Books

America's Publisher of Contemporary Romance

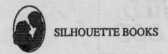

SILHOUETTE BOOKS

ISBN 0-373-07721-1

WILD BLOOD

Books by Naomi Horton

Silhouette Intimate Moments

Strangers No More #323
In Safekeeping #343
Dangerous Stranger #425
Hell on Wheels #505
Born To Be Bad #543
*Wild Blood #721

Silhouette Desire

Dream Builder #162
River of Dreams #236
Split Images #269
Star Light, Star Bright #302
Lady Liberty #320
No Walls Between Us #365
Pure Chemistry #386
Crossfire #435
A Dangerous Kind of Man #487
The Ideal Man #518
Cat's Play #596
McAllister's Lady #630
No Lies Between Us #656
McConnell's Bride #719
Chastity's Pirate #769
What Are Friends For? #873

Silhouette Books

Silhouette Christmas Stories 1991
"Dreaming of Angels"

Silhouette Romance

Risk Factor #342

*Wild Hearts

NAOMI HORTON

was born in northern Alberta, where the winters are long and the libraries far apart. "When I'd run out of books," she says, "I'd simply create my own—entire worlds filled with people, adventure and romance. I guess it's not surprising that I'm still at it!" An engineering technologist, she presently lives in Nanaimo, British Columbia, with her collection of assorted pets.

Special thanks to:

Leslie Wainger, for her support and encouragement,
even in the darkest days. Edna, who asked exactly the
right question one day, and Vanessa, who owes me big
time for stating the obvious in such a way I couldn't
ignore it. Bonnie, Lynn, Kathi and Nancy, for their
friendship and invaluable insights into the mysteries of
motherhood. Maureen and her newfound daughter,
Amy, for the magic they have rediscovered and have so
generously shared. Jennifer and Sabine, for reminding
me why I write. Marty, Barry, Nev, Donald, Brian and
David, for providing me with enough material to keep
me writing for decades. Annette Broadrick, for being
there. And Sharon and Colin, whose wisdom, laughter
and love I shall treasure always.

Chapter 1

Kathleen saw Jett Kendrick's son a little after three in the afternoon about sixty miles south of Burnt River, and for one mind-spinning moment she thought that she'd just gone back through time.

Maybe it had happened when she'd come off the interstate. Maybe there had been some sort of time warp back at that last cloverleaf that had shot her sixteen years into the past and she was fifteen again and so much in love she was dizzy with it.

Except . . .

Slowly, still breathless with surprise, she eased her breath out and stared at the kid standing hunch-shouldered under the overhang by the door of the gas station café. Except time warps didn't happen in real life, she hadn't been fifteen for a decade and a half, and the kid by the café was *not* Jett Kendrick.

He already had the height—and those wide Kendrick shoulders—even though he couldn't be much over fourteen. When he filled out, he was going to be the spitting image of his father, right down to the cleft in that strong,

stubborn chin and the tangled cowlick of unruly black hair
that no amount of cajoling or combing would ever control.
It was probably the bane of his life, as it had been the bane
of his father's, and had every girl in a hundred mile area
dying to run her fingers through it.

And Jett?

Mouth and throat suddenly dry, Kathleen looked around
nervously, trying to catch a glimpse of the boy's father before *he* saw *her*. That would be Jett's style, spotting her from
a distance and coming up on her when she was least expecting it.

She couldn't stop here, obviously. She'd pulled in off the
main road to get gas, but she could just keep going until—

Until she ran out of gas and had to walk the last sixty
miles, she realized with a sinking heart as she stared down
at the gas gauge. The needle was already below the empty
mark.

Damn. She wasn't ready for this. Wasn't ready for Jett.
She took another deep breath and looked over her shoulder, unable to see a thing through the rain coursing down the
rear window. Why did she feel as though she was walking
into an ambush? Jett didn't know she was coming back to
Burnt River. And even if he had found out, he would hardly
be waiting out here in a no-name gas station on the off
chance she'd come wandering in.

Swearing at her own cowardice, she took her foot off the
brake and swung her rental car alongside the nearest pump,
gritting her teeth as she cut the engine. She was committed
now. No quick getaways should he suddenly come looming
out of the rain toward her, chiseled face grim as stone.

In spite of herself, Kathleen had to smile. Who was she
kidding? All this unresolved-anger-from-the-past baggage
she was still hauling around was in her own mind, not Jett's.
He'd probably forgotten about it by now. Had probably
forgotten *her*.

There was a sharp rap on the side window, and she
jumped like a startled cat.

"Hey, lady." A rain-blurred face peered at her. "D'ya want gas or what?"

She closed her eyes for an instant, trying to get her heart beating somewhere near normal, and lowered the window a crack. "Fill it, please."

The man nodded and hustled around the rear of her car, shoulders rounded against the pelting rain. She heard him fumble with the tank cap; then the pump came on with a hum, and she forced herself to relax. Just a few more minutes and she would be moving again. And Jett wouldn't even know she'd been here.

The boy was still standing hunched in the lee of the small café, looking even wetter and more miserable than when she'd first spotted him. He was sporting a wide strip of adhesive tape across his nose, but it wasn't until she noticed the cast on his left forearm that she made the connection.

Groaning inwardly, she looked for the other signs.

And there they were. Lying in a heap at his feet, safely out of the rain even though it meant getting wet himself. Even at this distance she recognized the saddle and rigging, the spurs, the fringed leather chaps.

Bronc rider. Just like his father, he was riding rodeo.

It made her smile again, wondering why she was surprised. His grandfather was Wild Bill Kendrick, five times saddle bronc world champion. And before he'd quit rodeo to take up ranching, his father had won enough money to turn pro.

A tap on the glass made her glance around, and she lowered the window to hand the attendant her credit card. He made a dash for the office, skating through puddles and mud, and as she watched, the kid said something to him, gesturing stiffly toward her car. The attendant just shook his head and went inside, and the boy settled back to his vigil again, hugging himself and stamping his feet, collar turned up, hat pulled low to shield his face from the blowing rain.

The gas attendant sprinted back to the car, and she opened the window before he got there, taking the dripping clipboard he shoved at her. "That boy standing over there..." She nodded toward the café. "He looks familiar."

"That's Jett Kendrick's boy, Jody."

"He looks like his dad."

"Spittin' image." The man looked at her with sudden respect. "You know Jett?"

"Once. A long time ago." *A lifetime and a million dreams and a broken heart ago,* she felt like adding. She looked at Jody again. "He looks a little worse for wear."

"Kid wants to be a champion rodeo pro like his grandpa. Spends all his spare time at every rodeo he can get to. Pretty good, too, from what I hear. Though it looks like he ran outta luck this weekend."

He tore off Kathleen's copy of the credit card slip and handed it to her. "Got busted up pretty bad. His old man's gonna be raisin' hell about that arm, I can tell you. He don't want the boy wastin' his time rodeoin' when there's work to be done."

He looked at Jody thoughtfully. "Came through here on Friday on his way to Silver Meadows, full of spit and vinegar, just enough cash in his jeans for the entry fee and a coupla hot dogs. Planned on winnin' enough to get himself a bus ticket home." He laughed and gave his head a shake. "Kinda looks like his best friend died and someone ran over his dog, don't he?"

Kathleen had to smile. "So his dad's...not here?"

"Nope."

She hoped the man wouldn't see the relief on her face. "You said he has no money. Is Jett coming out to pick him up?"

Her confidant gave a snort. "Boy'd crawl through broken glass before he'd call his daddy. Been standing there close to an hour, hopin' for a ride." His gaze turned suddenly shrewd. "His dad's spread is the Kicking Horse Ranch, about ten miles this side of Burnt River. Any chance you could give him a lift? You're headed in the right direction."

"Oh...no. I...it..." Caught by surprise, she flailed around for a reasonable excuse. "That is, I'm not going that way. I'm...I'm turning off at Tall Pine Road."

He gave a grunt. Kathleen shoved her receipt into her handbag and turned the key in the ignition, then put the car into gear and started to pull away from the pumps.

She had every intention of wheeling around and heading back out onto the highway, but to her annoyance she found herself pulling up in front of the café instead. A sandwich, she told herself. Knowing that Jett wasn't lurking just around the corner had taken some of the pressure off, and she was suddenly hungry. She would grab a sandwich and a cup of coffee to go and wouldn't have to stop again until she got to her father's house.

Besides—and there was no point kidding herself about this—she was just masochistic enough to want a close look at the boy. He'd been born only a few months after she'd given birth to *her* baby, the same wild Kendrick blood flowing through his veins, the same wild Kendrick sire.

Difference was, Jody was standing here tall and healthy and alive, while her baby had died minutes after he'd taken his first breath. And while she'd lain weeping in Baltimore all those years ago, bereft and stunned with grief, Jett's new girlfriend was already pregnant.

Kathleen fought down a jolt of automatic anger. Pulling her jacket collar tight around her throat, she pushed the car door open and sprinted for the café, catching her breath as the wind slapped a fistful of rain square in her face.

She pretended to have trouble with the door, trying to get a good look at the boy without being too obvious about it. He had his head tucked down against the wind-lashed rain, and all she could see from under the wide rim of his Stetson hat was a strong, firm mouth that was almost but not quite Jett's.

And then, just as she realized she was behaving like an idiot and went to step by him, he lifted his head and looked squarely at her.

And Kathleen's heart nearly stopped on the spot.

Jett's eyes gazed directly into hers, so heartbreakingly familiar that they took her breath away. Even half expecting it, it caught her so badly off guard that she simply gaped at him, mind wheeling and utterly blank.

Jody smiled ruefully, obviously misinterpreting her shock. "Looks worse'n it is."

Kathleen blinked, struggling to regain her equilibrium. To her surprise, she found herself smiling back. His face was a mess, both eyes bloodshot and puffy, the skin around them already a violent shade of purple. He'd split his lower lip, too, and his smile was crooked.

"I'd like to see the other guy."

He gave an embarrassed shrug. "Weren't no other guy. Just a horse. I was six seconds into my best ride all day when she bucked me off. It knocked the wind outta me and I didn't get clear in time, and she stomped on me a couple times." The smile widened into a sheepish grin. "The medic said my nose is broke clean, but both my eyes'll be black for a coupla weeks."

Without even intending to, she reached out and put her fingers under his chin, turning his face slightly and eyeing his broken nose. "It'll heal fine, but you'll have an interesting little crook in it." *Just like your father's.*

He looked mildly alarmed at the prospect, and she laughed out loud. "Don't worry about it. You'll be back to your handsome self, breaking hearts from here to Billings, in no time."

Kathleen was amused to see his cheeks color under the bruising. Not quite his father's son, then. Even at fourteen, Jett had been a ladies' man, lethally aware of the effect his dark good looks had on any female who came within range.

There wasn't much else to say. Kathleen suddenly felt awkward, guilty about having ulterior motives in talking to him in the first place. He was just a kid, unaware of what he represented. Of the heartbreak and broken dreams he stood for.

"Well, I hope you have better luck next time around." She smiled at him, her heart aching only a little as she thought of what it would be like to have a son like this. Of what her life might have been like if only Jett had truly loved her sixteen years ago. If... if...

"Thanks." He grinned again, wincing a little as the split in his lip pulled. "Figure it can't get much worse."

One last smile and she stepped past him and into the welcoming warmth of the café. He was still there when she came out a few minutes later with her coffee and a couple of sandwiches, and she gave him a polite smile as she walked resolutely by him and through the rain toward her car, telling herself she was *not* going to offer him a ride.

And yet, even as she started the car, she knew she was only kidding herself. She never had been able to resist that Kendrick charm.

She brought the car to a purring stop in front of him and rolled down the window. "The waitress says you're looking for a ride back to the Kicking Horse. I'm going right by it..." She left the sentence hanging, half hoping he would turn her down.

But he didn't. He stared at her for a startled moment, then nodded fiercely. "Yes, ma'am!" He pulled open the rear door and tossed his saddle and gear onto the back seat, then hurried around and slid into the passenger seat, filling the car with rainwater and broad Kendrick shoulders and the scent of horses and cold mountain air.

"Thanks a lot! I was beginnin' to wonder if I was ever going to get home."

"I thought all you rodeo cowboys learned early on to keep a couple of dollars in the bottom of your boot to get you home?"

He pulled off his hat and held it so rainwater sluiced onto the floor, then ran his fingers through his wet hair. "I had just enough for the entry fee. I was hopin' to—" He smiled ruefully. "Guess my dad was right again. Hope don't get the dog fed."

"Your dad sounds like quite a philosopher." Kathleen said it lightly, checking for traffic before pulling out onto the highway. That was something new. The Jett she'd known hadn't had a thought in his head that didn't relate directly to horses, women or a good time.

Jody rearranged his long legs under the dash and wiped his wet face with his sleeve, then settled his left arm gingerly in his lap, wincing slightly. "Oh, he's okay, I guess. He just doesn't want me riding rodeo."

Kathleen glanced at him. "Did the doctor who set your arm give you something for the pain?"

He nodded offhandedly. "Yeah, but it don't hurt too bad."

The tightness around his mouth told her otherwise, and Kathleen shook her head wearily. "Save all the macho heroics to impress your favorite girl. That arm hurts like blazes, and your head feels like someone's been kicking it around the back pasture for a day or two, am I right?"

He nodded after a moment. Gingerly.

"There's hot coffee in that bag by your feet. And a couple of sandwiches. Dig out one of those painkillers the medic gave you and wash it down with coffee, then eat something. If you can't afford a bus ticket home, odds are you haven't eaten since last night."

He gave her a sidelong look. Then, finally, he managed a sheepish smile. "The waitress back there snuck me a piece of apple pie when the owner wasn't lookin'."

"Then eat," she said more gently.

He toyed with the idea for a minute or two as though he didn't care one way or the other, trying to play it cool, trying not to let on how hungry he was. But then his stomach got the better of him, and he pulled out one of the sandwiches and downed it like a young wolf.

Then, too tired and hurt to even pretend to tough it out, he dug the bottle of painkillers out of the pocket of his jeans and struggled to open it, hampered by the cast and childproof cap. Not saying anything, Kathleen reached across and took it from him. She snapped the cap off and handed it back to him, and he downed two without being told again.

"Finish that other sandwich if you want," she said after a few minutes. "I thought I was hungry, but I'm not."

"Are you sure?" He looked at the bag hopefully.

"Positive." Laughing, she looked at him. "My name's Kathleen—" She caught herself just in time. There was probably no need to lie, but still . . . Heaven knew what Jett had told his son about her father. About her.

"Pleased to meet you." Nothing wrong with his manners. "I'm Jody. Jody Kendrick."

"Yeah, I know. You look just like your father."

"You know my dad?"

"A long time ago," she said lightly, not daring to look at him. "Before you were born."

"You're not from around here." He was looking at her curiously, undoubtedly trying to fit her into the community he knew. Into his father's life.

Not anymore, she nearly said. Instead she just shook her head, concentrating on her driving. She wanted to ask him a thousand questions but didn't dare. One or two, maybe, but more than that and he would start wondering who she was, what she wanted, why she was so curious about his father.

For that matter, she wasn't sure herself. It wasn't as though she wanted anything to do with Jett. He'd poisoned any feelings she'd had for him a long time ago.

She smiled humorlessly, staring through the rain at the wet pavement glistening ahead of them. While she'd been banished to her aunt and uncle's in Baltimore, fifteen and pregnant and still foolish enough to think he loved her, Jett had lost no time getting himself invited into Pam's bed.

And here *she* was, sixteen years later, Kathleen taunted herself, driving back into Burnt River with *their* son beside her, trying to pretend she didn't care.

Jody dozed off finally, long legs akimbo, head at an awkward angle, clearly exhausted and worn out by pain and disappointment. Kathleen found herself glancing at him again and again, thinking of the first time she'd met Jett.

He'd been older than Jody, but not by much, and was already being touted as one of the best up-and-coming saddle bronc riders around. She and a couple of friends had gone to the local amateur rodeo for lack of anything better to do one Saturday afternoon, and there had been Jett, tall and rangy and handsome as sin.

He'd won every event they'd thrown at him and was loving the attention, carrying himself with the natural arrogance of a sixteen-year-old who hadn't met anything yet he couldn't ride. He was still calling himself Jett Walking Tall back then, half-blooded Sioux and proud of it, a beaded choker around his throat, raven hair long and loose except for one strand he'd braided with a buckskin thong and a single eagle feather.

She'd sat there mesmerized in the dust and heat, unable to take her eyes off him. Other riders came and went, but she barely saw them, eyes on the milling crowd of cowboys and handlers down by the chutes, rewarded now and again by a glimpse of *him*.

And then, much later, she'd walked to the concession stand for a soft drink, and there he'd been, leaning indolently against the counter as though waiting for her, six-feet-plus of more trouble than any girl needed.

Except he'd barely even noticed her that day. He'd turned his head to look at her when she'd walked up and had let his eyes drift over her speculatively. Then he must have realized how young she was and turned back to finish his conversation with the giggling girl at the counter.

Miffed, Kathleen had ignored him pointedly a few minutes later when he'd said something about the sunburn across her cheeks. He'd laughed at her, a low, husky sound that even back then had made her toes curl, and there had been something taunting and even a little dangerous in his eyes.

She hadn't realized just how dangerous until a couple of years later. She'd been not quite sixteen then, and he'd come into Vic's Café, where she and a bevy of girlfriends were comparing boyfriends over hamburgers and soft drinks. The entire group had gone silent when he'd come sauntering in, all tight jeans and broad shoulders and attitude, radiating sex like heat.

He'd sprawled on a stool at the counter and ordered coffee, then casually turned the stool to look them all over, dark eyes insolent. And then, with a hint of derisive amusement, he'd just turned his back on them.

To this day, Kathleen could remember the irritation that had flooded through her. She was Judge Nelson Patterson's daughter, pretty and rich and privileged, and she was *not* used to being so cavalierly dismissed by the likes of Jett Walking Tall. Most boys considered themselves lucky simply to get a smile; he didn't seem to think she was worth his time.

Piqued, she'd gotten up from the table and walked across to the counter, pretending she wanted another soft drink. Waiting for the waitress to get it, she'd leaned against the counter, the picture of pretty and bored, and glanced idly at Jett.

He'd looked back, eyes narrowed against the steam from his coffee. "See something you like, Slick?"

"Excuse me?" Caught, she pretended that she hadn't been looking at him at all but at something out on the street. "Did you say something to me?"

"Your daddy know you're down in this part of town?"

"What's wrong with this part of town?"

"Not the part you rich kids hang out in, for one thing." He took a swallow of coffee. "Or are you and your friends just lookin' for a little excitement?"

"My friends and I are having something to eat," she said icily. "Not that it's any of your business."

His mouth canted aside in a lazy smile, and he ran his eyes over her brazenly, taking his time, deliberately letting his gaze linger on her breasts.

She stood utterly motionless, refusing to let him bait her. "See something *you* like?"

"Maybe." Grinning insolently, he lifted his gaze to meet hers. "Can't tell from just lookin'. Woman's kinda like a buckin' bronc—sometimes the best-lookin' ones aren't worth throwing a saddle on."

Kathleen went stiff with indignation. She curled her lip and started to turn away. "Too bad you'll never find out."

"Oh, I figure if I wanted to find out bad enough, I wouldn't have much trouble convincing you to show me."

She gave a sputter, knowing she should just cut her losses and leave with at least some of her pride intact, but hating to let him have the last word. "I can't imagine why you think I'd be interested." She gave him a cool smile designed to cut him down to size. "I've heard all about you rodeo cowboys—you make love like you ride rough stock, hard, fast and done in eight seconds."

He gave a snort of laughter. "What the hell do you know about makin' love? You're what—fifteen?"

"Sixteen," she snapped. It seemed important, somehow, that he thought her sixteen.

"And never been kissed, I'll bet."

"Wrong again." She gave her head a toss, sincerely wishing she'd never started this but not sure how to retreat without making a complete fool of herself.

"Not by much." The grin faded, but he continued to look at her, eyes narrowed slightly. "You want to be careful playin' with fire, Slick. You could get burned real bad." He swung the stool away from her and planted his elbows on the counter, losing interest. "Come back in a year or two and maybe I'll take you up on your offer. And it'll take longer than eight seconds, darlin', I can guarantee that. A lot longer."

There was a husky undertone to the words that made her breath catch, and she opened her mouth to shoot back some smart-aleck reply, then caught herself. Sometimes it paid to just quit while you could. Biting her tongue, she picked up the soft drink the waitress had put in front of her and started to turn away.

"Tomorrow night."

He said it so quietly that she didn't realize for a moment that he was talking to her. She paused awkwardly. "W-what?"

"You heard me." He blew across the surface of his coffee, still not looking at her. "If you're not too scared, meet me here tomorrow night. Eight o'clock. I'll take you to a movie, and we can grab a burger after. And maybe," he added with a faint smile, "I'll give you your first kiss."

"It wouldn't be," she said a little breathlessly. It wasn't a lie, but somehow she had the feeling that kissing Jett would be unlike anything she'd ever experienced before. "But I—I couldn't get away that late. It's a school night and—" She bit off the words, nearly dying of embarrassment at sounding like such a prude.

He shrugged carelessly. "Suit yourself."

"I'd have to be home by eleven-thirty," she said all in a rush.

"I'll have you home by eleven-thirty."

"I..." She was out of excuses and simply stood there, heart hammering, suddenly scared to death but not wanting to show it. "I—I'll see." She swallowed, trying to look nonchalant. "If I don't have anything better to do, maybe I will."

"Like I said, suit yourself. You're more trouble than I need anyway."

"And what is *that* supposed to mean?"

He turned his head and met her gaze evenly. "I'm Wild Bill Kendrick's half-breed bastard, and you're Judge Patterson's little girl. If your old man knew I was even talkin' to you, he'd have me gelded with a rusty razor."

"Don't tell me my father scares you," she taunted.

"Not half as bad as you scare me," he said very softly, his dark eyes holding hers. "You're trouble, honey—I can tell that just from lookin' at you. I reckon a man could get hurt real bad gettin' too close to you."

"Then why are you asking me out?" she asked irritably.

He paused for just a heartbeat of time, and Kathleen held her breath. And then, abruptly, he gave a snort of laughter and turned away again. "Hell, honey," he drawled, "trouble's my middle name."

An eighteen-wheel transport went roaring past just then, spray flying. Kathleen's rental bucked in the backwash of wind and muddy water, jolting her back into the present. The wipers struggled to clear the windshield, and she squinted through rivulets of water, heart hammering.

Not long now, she realized. Stumpy Jones's old lopsided barn still marked the county line, roofline canted across the sky at a gravity-defying angle. How it hadn't tumbled in on itself years ago, she didn't know.

She and Jett had made love there once or twice, hidden away in the loft on a bed of clean straw and blankets, so lost in the delights of each other that the place could have fallen down then and there and they wouldn't have noticed.

She *had* met him that night sixteen years ago, probably more to her own surprise than his. Although nothing much had happened. He'd taken her to a movie and then for a hamburger, and they'd talked a bit, both of them still wary, still prickly, and then he'd driven her home in his old battered-up blue Chevy truck.

He'd parked in the deep shadows under the massive oak tree by the side of the house, just out of sight of the front door, and when he finally turned and reached for her, she slipped into his arms as naturally as breathing.

She hadn't been too sure what she'd been expecting, but it hadn't been such gentleness—he scarcely brushed her lips with his. She shivered slightly, and he smiled, kissing her again, still lightly, sliding the tip of his tongue between her lips. And then he settled his mouth fully over hers, lips warmly parted, and in the next instant his tongue was against hers, moving, coaxing, sliding wetly, and she melted against him, dizzy and breathless as something hot and urgent blossomed inside her.

He'd touched her breast that night, no more than a feather touch of his fingers, and she'd gasped something, so startled by the electric sensation that shot through her that she felt dazed. Then he moved gently against her, and she realized that he was as turned on as she was, his body graphically aroused, and she shuddered at the touch of him, terrified and delighted at once.

Laughing softly, he took her hand and pressed it against himself without embarrassment, and she held her breath with shocked delight, too unnerved to do more than blush.

"What...what should I do?" she finally whispered, mortified at being so inept, and he just laughed again and meshed his fingers with hers and took her hand away, kissing her lightly.

"Get out of here before I do something your old man'll shoot me for," he whispered against her ear. Teeth gritted, he leaned past her and opened the truck door, pushing it open.

Cool night air swirled around them, and Kathleen shivered again. "Will...I see you again?"

"Count on it," he growled, kissing her swiftly again with such searing intensity it made her heart almost stop. "Now get out of here before I—"

There was no need for him to finish the thought. Kathleen slipped out of his arms and out of the truck, and a few moments later he eased back up the lane, headlights off, engine just a muted growl. She watched until she couldn't see the truck anymore, then hurried inside, sneaking in the back door and up the stairs. No one had even realized she was gone.

Four months later she was pregnant with his child and on a plane to Baltimore. And not long after *that* Jett was sleeping with Pam Easton, and things had just gone downhill from there.

She shook off the feelings, annoyed at her wandering thoughts, and glanced at Jody. He was still sound asleep, looking about six years old under the bruises and adhesive tape, and she reached over and shook him gently.

"Jody? We're almost at the ranch."

He sat up groggily, wincing in pain.

"It'll get worse," she said cheerfully. "Have a long, hot bath tonight, and then take a couple of days off."

He managed a humorless laugh and retrieved his Stetson from the floor, groaning. "I don't figure my dad'll take kindly to that idea. I was supposed to be stringin' barbed wire this weekend, not headin' down to Silver Meadows for the rodeo. He'll be spittin' nails by now."

"You've got to let that arm heal properly. Your dad will just have to string that fence by himself."

Jody managed a ghost of a smile. "Guess maybe you don't know my dad very well after all."

It made her smile, although it had about as much humor as Jody's. "No," she said, more to herself than to him. "The truth is, I didn't know him half as well as I thought I did."

Even waiting for it, she felt her heart do a flip-flop when she came around a long curve in the road and saw the ranch gate looming out of the rain and mist. Sixteen years ago, when Jett's grandfather had run the Kicking Horse spread, there had been just a low gate here, with the ranch name and brand painted on a flat board. There was a full-fledged timber arch here now, with Kicking Horse Ranch—J. Kendrick And Son carved into a thick plank that hung suspended on two short lengths of chain.

"You can just let me out here and I'll walk in."

"It's nearly a mile," Kathleen said quietly. Jody gave her a curious look, as though wondering how she knew that, but didn't say anything as she flipped on her turn signal and slowed to make the turn.

She could handle this, she told herself calmly as she turned off the highway, the car bouncing across the Texas cattle gate set in the road. She was thirty-one years old, a successful attorney, respected among her peers. She'd handled the death of her baby, law school, a career...she should sure as heck be able to handle one worn-around-the-edges cowboy with no trouble at all.

Chapter 2

Barbed wire. God, he hated barbed wire!

Jett swore under his breath as he tried to set a staple in the fence post, shaking his head to get the rainwater out of his eyes. He hit the staple off center, and it flew out of his cold-numbed fingers, and the coiled strand of barbed wire he was trying to hold taut slipped free and whipped past his face like a snake.

He snapped his head back, but not before one of the razor-sharp barbs caught him across the cheek, and he snarled an oath of anger and frustration, wiping the back of his gloved hand across his cheek. It came away smeared with blood, and he muttered another profanity and turned the collar of his denim jacket up against the pelting rain.

Time to call it a day.

Wearily, he walked across to his pickup truck and tossed the hammer into the toolbox behind the seat. The coil of barbed wire could stay where it was. It and Jody were going to be on a first-name basis by the time the week was over.

Jett swung into the truck and slammed the door shut, then started the engine and headed back to the ranch. He was going to wring that kid's neck one of these days. This wasn't the first weekend he'd gone off to ride in some small-town rodeo instead of staying home and doing his chores. It had been like this for almost a year now, ever since the kid had gotten it into his head that he wanted to be a champion bronc rider like his granddad.

Jett shook his head. He'd figured it wouldn't last. That after Jody had gotten thrown and stomped and slammed into the chute rails a few times, he'd decide ranching wasn't half bad after all. But he'd figured wrong. Riding the rodeo circuit was all Jody dreamed about these days.

Jett parked beside the big ranch house, pulling the truck in under the pines where it was sheltered. Thinking—as he had at least a million times in the past eight years—that one of these days he had to get around to building that garage he kept talking about. Time, that was what it always came down to. Somehow he'd figured that when Jody got older and took on more of the day-to-day work, there would be more time to get things done. But it didn't seem to be working out that way.

Especially now. The kid wasn't here half the time, and even when he wasn't off riding in some rodeo, his head was someplace else. You had to tell him everything twice, and even then he didn't hear you half the time.

Shaking his head in weary disgust, Jett slid out of the truck, ducking against a blast of wind and rain. He was halfway to the house before he realized a late-model gray car he didn't recognize had pulled in around front. And as he walked toward it, the passenger side door opened and who got out but Jody, moving so slowly and stiffly that Jett groaned inwardly.

Jody pulled the rear door open and started to pull out his saddle and duffel bag, and it was only then that Jett saw the cast on his son's left forearm.

He swore under his breath and started toward the car. "It's about time you decided to come home."

Jody looked up guiltily, and Jett got a clear look at his face. He swore again. "What else did you break?"

"Nothin'," Jody muttered sullenly. "Don't worry, I can still do my chores."

"Damn straight you can still do your chores. That fence down by the creek's been waiting all weekend—you can get started on it as soon as you put your gear away."

Jody's head came up, and he stared at Jett defiantly. "How am I goin' to string barbed wire with my arm in a cast?"

"Guess you'll figure out a way. Maybe you should have thought of that before you ran off to play rodeo hero."

Jody stared at him, mouth and chin stubborn. And then, very suddenly, all the fight went out of him. His shoulders sagged, and he just nodded and bent to pick up his gear, moving so slowly and painfully that Jett winced, remembering all too clearly what it felt like to come out on the losing end of a no-point ride.

He opened his mouth to tell Jody to leave his gear and get inside where it was warm and dry, then shut it again. No point wasting sympathy on him. The kid knew better, damn it.

"You're being awfully hard on him, aren't you?"

The woman's voice made Jett look up. He hadn't even realized that the driver had gotten out of the car, and he turned to give her a hard look, drawing a breath to suggest that she might want to consider minding her own business.

It was the hair he noticed first, a wind-tangled mane the color of spring wheat that fell just to her shoulders, aglitter with rain. Dark-lashed eyes met his evenly across the roof of the car, as blue as a summer sky, and he frowned slightly, an echo from his past making the hair along his arms stir.

The woman stood looking at him, a hint of humor warming a mouth as sweet and kissable as any he'd ever known. The cold had rouged her pale cheeks, and he swallowed, disbelief curling up through him as rank as smoke. He was wrong, he told himself calmly. Wrong as could be.

She would never come back here. Not after what she'd done to him.

"Hello, Sundance."

Her voice was silken, and it was that—hearing his name from her mouth, the nickname she'd given him all those years ago—that made his heart career to a stop.

And time along with it. He simply stared at her, his eyes telling him everything his heart refused to contemplate. The hair, the eyes, that creamy pale skin...the same. All the same. Even that amused tilt of her head, the full sweep of her mouth, the dimple in the middle of her chin.

"What the hell are you doing here?" His voice was so rough with shock he scarcely recognized it.

She smiled and rested her arms on the roof of the car. "You never did waste time on small talk, did you?"

Mind still reeling, he started breathing again, ice cold and half sick. He clenched his fists at his sides, fighting for control. "Jody, get in the house."

"But—" Jody looked at him, then at Kathleen. "But I—"

"Get in the damn house!" Jett growled. "Now!"

Jody opened his mouth to speak, then saw something on Jett's face that made him close it with a snap. He started backing toward the house, mumbling something to Kathleen.

She smiled warmly at him. "Take care of yourself, Jody. It was nice meeting you."

Jody mumbled something else, then turned and headed for the house, limping badly. Only when he was safely inside and the door had banged closed behind him did Jett turn to look across the car at Kathleen again, teeth clenched so hard his entire jaw ached.

Her smile had faded, and she was looking across at him, face pensive. "It's been a long time, Jett."

"Not half long enough. What are you doing back here, Kathleen? What do you want?"

"Want?" She frowned, feigning innocence. "I don't want anything. I was just giving Jody a ride home."

"Sure you were." He said it derisively, fighting to look like a man who didn't give a damn one way or another. Like a man who was on top of things and had it all under control. "What did you tell Jody?"

"I told him I'd known you a long time ago, but without the gory details. What on earth do you think I told him?"

"And?" The fear was like something alive, and it kept trying to claw its way free, but he fought it back, knowing if she caught even a hint of weakness it would be all over.

"And nothing!" More than simple cold colored her cheeks now, and she tipped her chin up in a gesture so familiar it made him dizzy. "I know it's been sixteen years, Jett, but I don't know why you're turning this into a federal case when all I—"

"I'll turn it into whatever you want to make it," he said defiantly. "But I'll tell you one thing, lady—that deal I made with your old man still stands, and if you try breaking it, I'll fight you all the way to hell and back." He jabbed his finger at her. "Now get off my ranch and stay off. And stay away from Jody, or you'll regret the day you ever met me."

Then he turned on one heel and stalked back to the house, so filled with rage he could scarcely see straight. He took the front steps two at a time and stormed across the wide veranda and into the house, slamming the door solidly behind him.

Safe. He stood there for a moment, breathing hard, his back crawling. For the moment, anyway, he was safe.

He drew a deep, careful breath and unclenched his fists, trying to relax the taut muscles across his shoulders, heart still hammering against his ribs. Damn it, where the *hell* had she come from? He should have known. Should have guessed. Should have been ready for her...

For years after he had fought old man Patterson into a corner and made the bastard sign that agreement, he'd expected a double-cross. Patterson was too powerful, too important, too *rich,* to take something like that sitting down. Jett had spent years looking over his shoulder, waiting for

the trap to close. But it never had. And after a while he'd
relaxed a little, thinking maybe he'd gotten away with it after all.

When Patterson had died a year and a half ago the fear
had started again. Fear that there would be something in his
will, in his other papers, that would tear the whole thing
wide open again. But nothing had happened. And finally
Jett had convinced himself that nothing would. That it was
over. That the whole matter, like Patterson himself, was
dead and buried.

But then, a few months after Patterson had died, Kathleen's brother, Gordon, had moved back to Burnt River to
settle into the family home with his family. That had been
suspicious enough, but then Gordon had joined Cliff Albright's small downtown law practice, and Jett had spent
weeks bracing himself for the phone call, the friendly visit,
that would tear his life apart.

Because Cliff had been in on it right from the start. He
knew everything, and it seemed a hell of a lot more than
simple coincidence that Gordon should just *happen* to join
his law firm.

But again, nothing had happened. Gordon was friendly
enough the few times they'd seen each other on the street,
but casually so, not seeming too interested. Showing no
signs he knew the truth. That he was up to anything.

Then Cliff had died, and Jett had spent another uneasy
month or two, wondering what papers *he'd* left behind. But
still, nothing had happened. And finally Jett had managed
to convince himself that this time it really was over. That the
Kendrick secret was safe.

And now . . .

Now Kathleen herself was back in town, gorgeous and
composed and cool-eyed. How the hell she'd tracked Jody
down so fast was anyone's guess. Unless Gordon had been
doing the groundwork all along, of course. Quietly.
Stealthily. Getting the facts straight before he and Kathleen
came in for the kill.

Jett swallowed and wiped at the sweat beaded on his forehead, his hand shaking slightly. He had to think. Had to come up with some sort of plan.

Still badly rattled, he walked down the central corridor of the old house toward the kitchen. The smell of fresh, strong coffee wafted toward him, and he followed it down to the kitchen and stuck his head through the door. Angel Mc-Lean, his stock foreman, and one of the young hands they'd hired on last week were sitting at the big maple table, mugs of coffee cupped between cold hands, talking quietly.

Angel lifted his mug. "It's hot and black, boss."

"Did Jody come through here?"

"Just poked his head in, then hightailed it upstairs. He, uh…" Angel paused, as though trying to judge Jett's mood. "We might want to think about hiring on another hand for a few weeks. Until we get the rest of those early calves in for branding and cutting, anyway. It's lookin' to be mighty busy around here, and with Jody havin' only one good arm…"

"He'll manage," Jett said tightly. "And don't you go making things easy for him, either. Maybe this'll teach him to think twice before takin' off again."

"He's just a kid, Jett," Angel said quietly. "Barely even halter broke yet. Why don't you cut him a little slack?"

"He's fifteen," Jett said from between his teeth. "Isn't there something you two should be doin'?"

Angel's nostrils flared, and he glared at Jett for a moment; then he scraped his chair back noisily and stood, reaching for his hat. "Come on, Billy," he said to the kid. "Let's get back to work. Colder'n a witch's backside in here all of a sudden."

The kid swallowed a gulp of coffee as he scrambled to his feet. He grabbed his hat and shoved it down over a tangled nest of hair the color of copper wire, giving Jett a nervous glance as he trotted out the back door at Angel's heels.

Jett swore wearily. Angel hadn't deserved that. He'd hired on three weeks after Jett had taken over the Kicking Horse and eight years later was almost like a brother. He'd always spoken what was on his mind, and Jett liked that. Had learned to value and trust it.

Except when it came to Jody. There, he and Angel had a definite difference of opinion.

Jett paused at the bottom of the stairs leading up to the second floor of the big ranch house, wondering about the best way to handle this. One thing was certain: he had to get it right from the get-go. Jody was as cantankerous as a bull calf these days, as likely to argue that white was black as not. There was no telling how he was going to react to things, a good-natured boy one minute and a sullen, half-grown man the next, angry for no reason, storming out in fits of temper that had no cause.

Just a phase, the twice-weekly housekeeper, Mrs. Wells, kept saying. Wild blood, Angel kept saying. Just like his old man...

He heard the angry footsteps pounding across the veranda just as he planted his foot on the bottom stair, and stopped dead, the back of his neck prickling. Motionless, barely even breathing, he listened as whoever was out there stormed across and wrenched open the screen door. There was a barrage of furious hammering on the inside door.

"Jett! Jett Kendrick, damn you, open this door and talk to me!" It was Kathleen's voice, no doubt about it, muffled by three inches of solid pine but vibrant with fury. "Jett, you open this door and let me in!"

So angry she was practically incoherent, Kathleen hammered her fist against the door again. Like the three generations of Kendrick men it had sheltered, the thing was tall and wide and as solid as stone, impervious to her most determined pounding.

"Jett!" She gave the door another blow, then grabbed the brass knob and rattled it furiously. "Jett, if you think for one minute that you can—"

"I told you to get the hell off my land!"

The door was wrenched inward so abruptly that Kathleen nearly fell forward. A solid wall of blue denim loomed over and toward her, filling the entire doorway, and she held her breath for an instant, actually afraid he was going to strike her.

He didn't, but the expression on that hard, cold-eyed face made it pretty clear that he would like to. "Get back in your car and—"

"Don't you try to bully me, damn it!" More angry than scared, she planted her feet and glared up at him, hands on hips. "If you think you're going to get away with treating me like this after all this time, you—"

"I've got nothing to say to you," he said in a low, tight voice. "It's done. And there's nothing you *or* your brother can do about it now."

It didn't make any sense: not the anger, not the words, none of it. Struggling to contain her own anger, she took a deep breath. "Jett, I have absolutely no idea what you're talking about. I don't know anything about any business dealings you had with my father, and I don't *want* to know. All I—"

"You're lying," he said with flat, cold conviction. "You were in on it."

"Oh, for—" Kathleen caught the anger before it got away from her, took another deep breath and started all over again. "Jett, before he died, my father and I hadn't traded more than a dozen civil words in years. And he certainly never discussed business with me. If the two of you had some sort of arrangement that went sour, it's news to me."

She half expected him to argue with her, or at least call her a liar again. But to her surprise, he didn't say anything. Just continued to stare down at her with those obsidian eyes, face as hard as carved stone. There was a fresh cut along the high, wide plane of his left cheek, and rainwater had smeared a thin trickle of blood down the skin. Not deep enough to leave a scar, she found herself thinking inanely.

Although it wouldn't have mattered. He had the kind of face that bore scars well: the vee-shaped nick in his chin where an iron-shod hoof had clipped him when he'd been seventeen, the furrow bisecting his right eyebrow where he'd been hit with a flying stirrup a year later. There were oth-

ers, faint badges of cowboy courage he could probably cat-
alog by date and event.

Sixteen years. It was hard to believe it had been that long.

Each of those years had left its mark on that lean, handsome face, but he wore it well, sculpted features still clean-
cut and strong. He'd filled out, his shoulders nearly filling
the doorway, chest solid with muscle. A man now and not
the eighteen-year-old boy she'd once loved. A stranger, almost.

"Look, Jett," she said quietly, "I didn't come out here
to cause trouble. I simply gave Jody a lift because he had no
money and no way to get home and—"

"He knows how to use a phone."

"Oh, right. The kid's going to call home, collect, to listen to you lecture him on how irresponsible he is."

She must have hit pretty close to home, because a flush
settled across Jett's handsome features and his mouth got all
hard and stubborn. In spite of herself, she had to smile. "He
doesn't need you to tell him he screwed up, Jett. He went out
there and did his best and got nothing for it but some bruises
and broken bones, knowing you were going to give him hell
when he finally dragged himself home. Trust me, Sundance—he feels bad enough without you ragging on him
some more."

"Don't tell me how to raise my son." His voice was ice-
cold.

"I gave up trying to tell you anything sixteen years ago,"
she replied in a voice that was just as cold. "You didn't listen to anything you didn't want to hear back then, and
nothing I've seen today makes me think you've changed."

"What the hell's that supposed to mean?"

"You figure it out. You always had all the answers." Not
even bothering to wait for a reply—if he even had one—she
turned and stalked across the veranda and down the steps.
At the bottom, she paused and looked around. "Not that I
think you give a damn, but I was sorry to hear about Pam.
As far as I'm concerned, she deserved a hell of a lot better."

It was a cheap shot, but it seemed to be that kind of a day. Not feeling very proud of herself, but too angry to care, she turned and walked down the wide flagstone path to the driveway, back rigid against the almost palpable heat of his stare. She turned her coat collar up against the rain and pulled the car door open, daring to glance back up at him.

He was still standing in the doorway, as though barring hearth and home from a marauding army, and she fought down a sudden shiver.

Not a marauding army.

Just her.

She started the car and then dared another quick glance back up at the house. Jett had gone back inside, but she thought she saw the lace curtain in the living room window move just slightly. Saw—or imagined she saw—a tall shadow there, all but invisible through lace and rain.

She shoved the car's heater control to the highest setting, then headed back to the main road, chilled to the bone.

That deal I made with your old man still stands....

Deal. She found it almost impossible to believe that Jett and her father could have seen eye-to-eye long enough to have signed some deal. They'd hated each other on principle sixteen years ago; how in God's name had they ever bridged that gap? The only thing they'd ever had in common was her.

Just thinking about it made her go cold. She'd found out she was pregnant on the tenth of August, and two days after that she had made the mistake of telling her mother.

She'd planned to tell Jett first. But he'd been riding in the State National Rodeo Finals that week, and she hadn't been able to get hold of him. And the secret was too big to keep, too important. Foolishly, she'd thought her mother would understand. That when she explained how much she loved Jett and how much he loved her, her mother would be on their side.

But she hadn't been. She'd given her head an annoyed shake and had wondered aloud what on earth had possessed Kathleen to get herself pregnant by the likes of Jett

Walking Tall. "He's probably a very nice boy," she'd added as a vague afterthought. "But really, dear, he's a *half-breed*. What *were* you thinking?"

But it hadn't even been Jett's half Sioux parentage that had annoyed her mother as much as the timing of the whole thing. Judge Patterson's name was being mentioned officially as a possible candidate for the state Supreme Court and, as Kathleen had been reminded icily, if people found out that he had an unwed and pregnant fifteen-year-old daughter on his hands, it could all be over before it even started.

"Why now?" she'd asked Kathleen impatiently. "For heaven's sake, why did you have to do this *now?*"

Bad timing. That had been her greatest error in judgment.

Kathleen had to smile at the absurdity of it.

Her father had handled the problem with his usual take-charge efficiency. A week after Kathleen had found out about the baby, she was on a plane to Baltimore. She'd tried to get hold of Jett, but no one knew where he was, and she'd finally just left a message with his grandfather.

A few days at the most—that was how long she'd figured it would take him to come after her. Each night she'd fallen asleep knowing he was on his way, that he would come striding into her uncle's house and sweep her up into his arms and carry her out to his banged-up old Chevy pickup, and then they would head back to Montana, so much in love it hurt to breathe. They would get married and raise their son—she'd never doubted it was a son—and she would never have to set foot in her father's house again.

Except the days had turned to weeks, the weeks to months, and Jett never arrived. There had been no phone call explaining the delay, no letter telling her that he loved her and would be there soon. Just silence. She called him countless times, but he was never there; she wrote letters by the dozen, but never got a reply.

Then a girlfriend had dropped her a note. It had been full of gossip and news, but it had been the last bit that had stabbed Kathleen right through the heart. The part that said, "Jett sure doesn't seem too broken up that you're gone. He and that Pam Easton can't keep their hands off each other. Of course, she'll do it with anything in jeans, but it's pretty obvious that Jett can't get enough of her, either."

That was why he hadn't called. Hadn't written. Hadn't come to take her back to Burnt River and marry her. He'd been too busy with Pam Easton.

And the "deal" he and her father had put together?

She didn't know, and at the moment, frankly, she didn't give a damn. Land, taxes, legal wranglings . . . it could have been any of a dozen things. The only thing she *did* know for dead certain was that it would have been in her father's favor, which probably explained at least some of Jett's foul temper.

But whatever it was all about, it had nothing to do with her. Jett didn't believe that, obviously, seeming to think that one Patterson was pretty much like any other. Maybe he thought she knew about the mysterious "deal" and was planning to use it to get back at him for abandoning her all those years ago. Maybe he thought she was going to hurt him through Jody, using his own son in some bizarre scheme for revenge. Maybe . . .

Oh, hell, she thought wearily, there could be a thousand reasons for Jett's behavior. They'd both been hurt sixteen years ago. Who knew what he thought she was up to? If she decided to stay in Burnt River, she would deal with it later. Until then, she'd just stay as far away from the wretched man as possible.

Jett stood silently in the door of Jody's bedroom and watched his son struggle to pull on a pale denim shirt, wondering a bit wistfully how the two of them had wound up so far apart. They'd been best buddies once, Jett scarcely able to move without falling over the boy dogging his heels.

Now they barely spoke to each other unless they were trading hostilities.

Something tightened in his chest, and he took a deep breath to shake it off. Fear. Fear of doing it all wrong, of making one mistake too many and losing his son once and for all. He thought of his own father, of the unbridgeable distance still between them even after all these years. They were speaking to each other now, at least, but the tension was still there, the awkwardness, the awareness of too much of one thing said and not enough of the other. Both needing to be right, neither able to forgive.

Jody had all but given up trying to get the shirt on and was just pulling it around his shoulder, having trouble with even that much. Not surprisingly. Jett winced as he looked at the vivid bruising covering his son's slender back.

"Looks like she stomped on you a couple of times after you hit the dirt." He said it casually, trying to keep any hint of criticism out of his voice, and strolled into the room.

Jody looked around, startled.

"Ribs okay?"

Jody nodded warily, as though sensing a trap. "They took X rays. Said everything's fine."

"I'll dig out a plastic bag to wrap around that cast so you can have a shower."

Jody nodded again, even more suspicious now. "I was going to head out and have a look at that fence," he muttered, turning around and limping across to the dresser. He eyed himself in the mirror, gingerly touching the tape across the bridge of his nose.

"Forget it," Jett said quietly. "Angel and Billy can take care of the fence. You're in bad enough shape as it is without getting mixed up with a bale of barbed wire."

"I said I'd do it," Jody muttered again, casting Jett a defiant look. "I'll be fine in a coupla days."

Jett bit back an impatient reply, taking a deep breath instead; then he released it, pretending to examine the shelf where Jody kept his rodeo trophies. There were more than he remembered.

"That arm needs some rest if you want it to heal right," he said mildly. He glanced around. "Besides, you can use the time to hit the books. Your civics teacher called me on Friday.''

Jody winced. He turned away, trying to look unconcerned. ''What's she on my case about now?''

''That essay project you haven't handed in yet, for one thing. She says it's worth half the year's mark, and she's willing to give you another couple of weeks to get it done. Asked me if you were having trouble with it.'' Jett kept his voice neutral. ''I told her you hadn't said anything to me about it.''

Another careless shrug. ''It's just about government and law and stuff. I don't need to know about that stuff to ride broncs.''

''Maybe not, but you need it to get into college.'' Jett heard the anger creeping into his voice in spite of his best efforts.

Jody gave him a defiant look. ''I want to ride broncs for a living, not spend my life with my face in a book.''

''No reason you can't do both. You can ride the college circuit *and* get an education, and maybe even pick up a scholarship or two.'' It was an old argument, and Jett could hear himself start into the same litany he'd been through a dozen times before. For a change, he decided to let it go. ''You need a hand with that sling?''

Jody shook his head, dropping the strap of the sling around his neck and fumbling ineffectually with it with his one good hand. The skin around his lips whitened with pain.

Swallowing a smile—having been there himself more times than he liked to remember—Jett stepped across and expertly slipped the cradle of the sling around the cast. Then he tugged Jody's shirt closed and did up a couple of the buttons.

Jody mumbled something that sounded like *thanks,* looking suddenly awkward and very young, and Jett found himself wondering as he often did these days how the hell this tall, wary-eyed young stranger could possibly be his son. Another couple of inches and he would top out at six feet, although Jett could swear it had only been a handful of months ago that he'd been a scrawny kid scarcely belt-buckle high.

"They give you some painkillers when they set this arm?"

"Yeah. I took a couple in the car. Kathleen said I should," he added quickly, as though afraid Jett might think it had been his own idea.

Jett wondered what else she'd been saying. "The two of you seemed to hit it off pretty well. How did you happen to meet her?"

"I caught a ride with a trucker as far as Doomey's gas station down by Big Elk turnoff, and I was trying to hitch a ride home when she came in."

Jett frowned. It sounded plausible enough, at least on the surface. Until you remembered that Kathleen was a Patterson. And what was at stake.

She could have followed Jody all the way down to Silver Meadows. Could have stayed there all weekend, watching him. Waiting for a chance to make her move. Hell, maybe the whole thing had been planned. She might have hired that truck driver to take Jody as far as Doomey's and then come in a few minutes later to pick him up. They'd been in the car together for a good hour or more. More than enough time to tell him anything she wanted him to know.

"So, what did you talk about?"

"Nothin' much. You, mostly. Then I fell asleep."

Jett's gut tightened. "Me?" He struggled to keep his voice disinterested. "What did she say about me?"

"She just said she knew you from way back." Jody's mouth curved in a speculative smile. "You used to get it on with her back then, or something?" He said it jauntily, but Jett could read the uncertainty under it, as though he wasn't any too sure of his father's reaction.

And suddenly Jett felt weary and old. How long *had* it been since they'd joked around like this, relaxed and comfortable together? So long they were both out of practice, both rusty, both afraid of giving offense at every word.

"That's a hell of a question to ask your old man." He reached out to rumple Jody's tangled hair, ignoring a sudden rush of all-too-vivid memories of silken flesh and breath-caught whispers and that certain little shivery way she'd moaned his name at just the right moment. "I just wanted to know if she said...anything, that's all."

Jody ducked away, grin widening. "Nothin' incriminating, if that's what you mean."

"So she didn't say anything about me or your mother or anything?" He was pushing too hard, asking too many questions, Jett knew, but he couldn't seem to stop himself. The fear in his belly had turned hard and cold, and he tried to ignore it. Tried to pretend there was nothing behind his words but idle curiosity about a woman he'd once known.

Something shadowed Jody's face, and his smile faded. He dropped his gaze, shaking his head, apparently distracted by a loose button on his shirt. "I already said we didn't talk about nothin'. Why should she ask me about Mom?" He glanced up, eyes sullen again. "Did she know Mom?"

Jett paused just a heartbeat. "Yeah. She knew your mom." Which wasn't even a lie, he reminded himself, when you cut through all the complications and untruths and heartbreak.

He opened his mouth to say something to tease Jody back into laughter, then caught himself. The mood was broken. Jody had retreated into himself again, putting distance between them.

"Look, I, uh..." Frowning, Jett found himself wanting to say something, though he had no idea what. "I, uh, I'm glad you're all right," he finally said lamely.

Jody gave him a long, wary look. "I'm okay."

Jett stood there for an awkward moment, then nodded and headed for the door. Then he paused and looked back. "I never did ask how you made out. Before..." He nodded toward Jody's arm.

"I didn't do too bad." Jody said it carelessly, as though it didn't matter one way or another. But then he grinned. "Pretty good, actually. Got a seventy-six-point ride on Crop Duster."

Jett gave a quiet whistle, not having to pretend to be impressed. "That's one rank little horse. She's busted a lot of dreams in her day."

Jody beamed at the praise. "Then I drew Shameless Lady, a new horse brought in by some outfit down by Billings. She's only been rode once so far this year."

He paused expectantly, and Jett had to grin, feeling a jolt of the old excitement. It had been fifteen years since he'd tested his mettle against a wild bronc, but he could still feel the sweet rush of adrenaline at just the thought of sitting in the chute in those moments before the gate opened and all hell broke loose. "And?" he urged.

"I rode her." Jody's face lit up like a kid looking at a Christmas tree. "Seventy-nine points, and the announcer told everyone to keep an eye on me 'cause I was already ridin' like my grandpa, Wild Bill Kendrick. He mentioned you, too." Jody's face grew more serious, and he looked across the room at Jett, gaze steady. "He said you were one of the best anyone had ever seen. That you had the world by the tail when you just up and quit and never competed again."

Jody's voice and eyes were filled with questions Jett couldn't answer. He just shrugged, not wanting to think about it too much. "Guess I just had better things to do."

"Ain't nothin' better than rodeo," his son replied firmly.

"You look worn-out," Jett said quietly. "Why don't you catch some shut-eye before supper?"

Jody looked startled. "But I got chores to—"

"You can skip chores tonight." Jett gave him a faint smile, then turned and walked through the door. "Anyone who can get a seventy-six-point ride on a cyclone like Crop Duster deserves one night off."

"Hey...Dad?"

The hesitant voice caught Jett at the top of the stairs, and he paused and looked around.

Jody was sitting on the end of his bed, shoulders slumped, tugging at one of the buttons on his shirt. "I..." He frowned, then looked up to meet Jett's gaze, gnawing the inside of his cheek. "I'm sorry for taking off like that. With no warning or nothin'. But I knew if I asked first, you'd say no, and we'd wind up arguin' and—"

He let his gaze slide away from Jett's, shrugging. "I figured it would just be easier, that's all. That if I did good and came back with some winnings, you'd..." Another shrug. "I just want you to be proud of me, that's all," he said in what was almost a whisper.

Chapter 3

Something caught in the back of Jett's throat so fiercely he had to fight for breath. His mind flung itself backward twenty years, and he was standing in front of Wild Bill Kendrick again, wanting nothing more in this world than to have him say how proud he was and how much he loved him....

"There's never been a day I haven't been proud of you."

"But you don't want me riding rodeo." Jody looked up, expression miserable. "You get mad when I—"

"I get mad when you sneak off without telling me where you're going," Jett said more roughly than he intended. Jody's face went sullen and closed off, and Jett swore at himself, at his impatience. "Let's talk about this later. Now isn't a good time."

"It never is," Jody muttered, kicking at the rug.

Jett eased his breath out noisily. Damn it, they should give you a manual when your first kid is born! You couldn't even buy a television set these days without getting fifty pages of instructions along with it, so how come kids came with nothing but a lot of high hopes?

He'd thought it would be easy, once. He'd figured all he would have to do was the opposite of what *his* father had done and everything would be great. And for a few years that had worked fine. Then, suddenly, he couldn't do anything right. Couldn't say a word that didn't have the opposite effect of what he'd intended.

"It's just that riding professional rodeo is a hell of a hard life, Jody. Maybe one out of a thousand cowboys actually makes enough to live on, and the rest—" Jett caught himself abruptly, having to laugh in spite of himself. "Damned if I don't sound just like Grandpop Kendrick! Now *that's* something I never thought I'd live to hear."

Jody didn't say anything, and after a moment Jett walked back to the bedroom door, hands shoved into the back pockets of his jeans. "When I was your age, Grandpop used to tan my hide for not gettin' my chores done. I'd sneak off to wherever the circuit was that weekend and get all busted up, then come creeping home, hoping to get past him. But I never did."

Jody still didn't say anything, but he was listening curiously.

"He'd start whalin' on me, yellin' that he wasn't going to stand by and let me turn into a rodeo bum like my old man." He grinned suddenly. "Guess I shouldn't be surprised you want to ride broncs. You're a Kendrick. Wild blood, Grandma called it. Swore we never got it from *her* side of the family."

Jody nodded slowly, looking thoughtful. "So he didn't want you riding at all?"

"Nope. He wanted me to settle down and help him with the ranch, the way *his* son—your grandfather—was supposed to. But Dad took off to ride the rodeo circuit when he was seventeen and never came back to the Kicking Horse except to visit now and again. When he was broke, mainly." Jett leaned one shoulder against the door frame, knowing Jody had a right to know all this but not liking the remembering it required.

"Even after you were born, he never came back?"

Jett's eyes narrowed, and he stared at the trophies lined up on the shelf across the room. "No."

"Not even to marry your ma?"

It would be easy to just say no and turn and walk away, leaving it at that, Jett thought. Jody wouldn't bring it up again. But there was no reason not to talk about it. And there wasn't a lot to tell.

"He never even knew her name," he said quietly. "She was just a pretty girl he'd met at a rodeo one weekend. I reckon he'd pretty much forgotten all about her until he came home one day and discovered she'd come around a couple of months earlier to drop off a little surprise package for him."

Jody smiled. "You."

"No one ever saw her or heard from her again," Jett said evenly. "All I know about her is what Dad could remember, and that wasn't much. Just that she was full-blooded Sioux, from somewhere in North Dakota."

Jody nodded slowly. "And she never came back to see how you were doing or nothin'? She never even wrote, just to make sure you was all right?"

Jett felt the muscles along his shoulders tense up and forced himself to relax. "No."

Jody met Jett's gaze, rock steady. "You'd think a mother would want to know what happened to her baby, wouldn't you?"

Jett stopped breathing for an instant, wondering what lay hidden behind the question. It was almost too casual. Too careless. He shrugged offhandedly. "You'd think so."

It seemed to satisfy the boy. He nodded again and got to his feet painfully, wincing as he put his weight down wrong and some bruised muscle he didn't even know he had complained bitterly.

"I'll bring the bottle of liniment up later and you can slap some on those sore muscles or you won't be able to get out of bed in the morning."

"Can't reach half of 'em," Jody muttered. "I've been throwed before, and I've even been stomped on before, but I don't ever remember nothin' hurtin' this bad before."

Jett found himself laughing without even meaning to. "Hell, this is just a taste of what it's like. If you're serious about riding rodeo, you'd better get used to hurtin' most of the time."

"I'm serious about *ridin'*, I'm just having some second thoughts about the fallin' off part." Jody managed a painful, lopsided smile. "You got any tips about how to stay on more than you get throwed?"

Jett let his breath out, mouth half open to tell him that the best way not to get thrown was not to get on in the first place. But Jody didn't want to hear that. No more than *he'd* wanted to hear it when his father had told him the same thing.

"I don't know how much my advice is worth. It's been a long time since I threw my leg over a bronc for money and time." Jett intended to leave it at that, but Jody was watching him so hopefully that he felt his resolve crumbling even as he stood there. "Yeah, maybe I've got a tip or two I can pass on. But later. Right now you need rest more than advice. Mrs. Wells left fried chicken for supper. I'll give you a shout when it's ready."

It was twenty-six winding country miles from the Kicking Horse to the big house up on Deer Jump Road where she'd grown up, and Kathleen drove most of those miles lost in troubled thought. It was only when she swung the car around the last curve and the house loomed into view that she was finally able to shake off her confrontation with Jett, but even then, it was with an effort.

Here, too, the past was strong.

The Oaks. The pretentiousness of the name, of the house itself, didn't fit here in Montana ranch country. Her mother had seen a picture in a magazine and handed it to the architect, and The Oaks had been born. The massive, redbrick plantation manor sprawled across the hillside, looking as though an errant tornado had picked it up just outside Charleston and deposited it here, complete with six white pillars marching across the front.

Even now, it stank of money and privilege and power.

And memories.

Driving the last few hundred feet under the familiar archway of luxuriant oak and maple trees, Kathleen took a deep breath. She hadn't been back since her father's funeral nearly eighteen months ago, and she was surprised now at how little emotion she felt. Anticipation at seeing Gord and Sherry and the kids again, true, but under that there was nothing. No grief, no sadness, no fear. None of the turmoil she'd half expected.

He was gone, she found herself thinking calmly as she looked up at the house. The father she had warred with for most of her life was dead. There would be no more cold looks of disapproval. No more reproving silences. No more razor-edged critiques of her choices in colleges, clothes, careers, men. There was nothing here anymore except memories and maybe a few regrets here and there. Nothing she couldn't handle.

Maybe moving back to Burnt River wouldn't be that hard after all. When she'd called Gord a couple of months ago to tell him she'd quit her job with one of the top law firms in Baltimore, he'd promptly offered her a partnership. He'd spent the past two months trying to coax her into moving back here and finally, unemployed and at loose ends, not knowing *what* she wanted, she'd given in and agreed to come out for a couple of weeks to look things over. No promises, no commitments.

And here she was. Already up to her neck in a past she'd sworn to put behind her!

Smiling to herself—*at* herself—she pulled the car around to the side of the house and parked it under one of the huge oaks. Jett used to park under this same tree when he brought her home, usually well after her curfew. And here, out of sight, they would spend a fevered last few minutes trying to satiate themselves, drunk on sex and each other.

Once they'd even made love out here in silent, desperate urgency. She'd been wearing a full denim skirt, although by that time it was up around her waist somewhere, and finally, too far gone to even care if someone saw them, Jett had peeled her out of her panties and she'd been astride him in no time flat.

She could still remember his gratified groan as she'd settled over him and around him, how he'd let his head fall against the back of the truck seat, the sweet, salty taste of his hot skin as she'd kissed his throat.

Terrified of being discovered, already out of her mind from his all-too-skillful caresses, she'd let herself go that night, moving on him with utter abandon, desperate for the release she still only half understood and that eluded her most times.

But not this time. This time it had burst up and through her like a molten explosion, and Jett had reached up and pulled her mouth down over his and kissed her hard and deep to smother her outcry of pleasure. Then, laughing and breathless, he'd gripped her hips with his hands and moved like a stallion under her, wild, strong, whispering things that took her breath away. In only moments he arched his back and thrust hard and deep against her with an explosive groan, and then they'd collapsed in each other's arms, spent and dazed.

Gasping for breath, she'd eased herself off him and hurriedly pulled on her panties, then slipped out of the truck and into the house and up to her room, weak-kneed and still dizzy with the scent and taste of him.

Only later did she discover the imprint of his belt buckle embossed on her inner thigh, and she'd gone to bed that night smiling with the thought of carrying his mark on her, like a brand. Jett Kendrick's woman, she'd thought as she'd slipped toward sleep, unaware then that she was already three weeks pregnant with his child. I'm Jett Kendrick's woman....

Kathleen shook off the memory impatiently and looked up at the house. Time she got rid of those memories, too.

It had stopped raining, but water was still pattering off the maples, and she turned her collar up as she slid out of the car and walked around to the huge double front door.

Muddy handprints clustered around each brass knob, and the top step was littered with plastic toys. A tricycle lay on its side in the nearest flower bed, and Kathleen had to grin. If anyone needed proof that Judge Nelson Patterson was dead, they didn't have to look farther than right here.

Still grinning, she reached out and gave the huge brass lion's head knocker a couple of solid raps. She could hear kids shouting somewhere far inside, assorted crashes and thumps, then rapid footsteps clattering on marble.

The door swung in, and Sherry glared out at her, looking frazzled and out of sorts, jeans rolled up to mid-calf, feet bare, sloppy sweatshirt smeared with jam and heaven knew what else.

She blinked, then broke into a huge smile. "Kathleen! I thought you were the plumber—he said he'd be here three hours ago!" She stepped forward to give Kathleen a hug, then stopped, gesturing at her sweatshirt. "Better not, unless you want to get marinaded with peanut butter."

"I can think of worse things." Laughing, Kathleen gave her sister-in-law a quick—if cautious—hug. "Plumber?"

Sherry rolled her eyes. "Shaun tried to flush his teddy bear down the upstairs john. I just got the last of the water mopped up, but teddy's still jammed down there somewhere."

Kathleen couldn't keep from laughing, Jett's hostility and her own strange moodiness suddenly gone. She gave Sherry another reckless hug, peanut butter be damned. "Gosh, it's good to see you! It's always so...so *normal* around you."

Sherry gave a peal of merry laughter and made a wide gesture that took in the entire house. "Honey, if this strikes you as *normal,* you obviously need a strong shot of whiskey!" She slipped her arm through Kathleen's and pulled her inside, shoving the door closed with her foot.

"Trust me, this is the closest thing to normal that this house has ever seen." Kathleen looked around her as they walked past the huge double sweep of the split staircase. "Maybe if Gordo and I had stuffed a few teddy bears down the john when we were kids, things would have been . . . different."

Sherry gave a snort. "It would have taken a lot more than some bunged-up plumbing to have made this place normal when you two were—" She snapped her mouth shut, cheeks coloring. "Sorry. That was way out of line."

"It's true," Kathleen replied quietly. "And it's refreshing to hear someone say what they think, for a change." She gave Sherry a quick grin. "When Gord and I were growing up, denial was the rule of the day. Everyone knew our mother was a discreet but dedicated drunk and our father was a cold, unemotional man who loved power and money and little else, but no one ever *said* it."

Sherry looked so shocked that Kathleen had to laugh out loud. "Hey, it's okay! He can't hear us." Grin widening, she pulled Sherry to a stop in the center of the foyer and tipped her head back. The cupola that had been her mother's pride and joy arched thirty feet above them, windows aglow with watery late afternoon light.

"Did you hear that, Dad?" she shouted with sudden, heady recklessness. Echoes rattled back, and she laughed, feeling giddy with daring. She'd never shouted in this house. Had never slid down these wide, polished banisters. Had never left dirty handprints on the doors or crumbs on the carpets or toys on the floor. "I'm not afraid of you anymore!" She gave a whoop of defiance and laughter, astonished at how wonderful a childish outburst could feel, how exhilarating the sense of freedom.

"Me, neither!" Sherry's voice rose to join the echoes, laced with laughter. "I spilled a soft drink on the carpet and Chelsea threw a baseball through a bedroom window, and we have a *puppy!*"

"A puppy?" Kathleen looked at her. "You guys have a puppy?"

Sherry grimaced. "Yeah, and it peed on the rug in the dining room. I just hope the cleaners can get it out."

Kathleen felt a grin start to take hold. She met Sherry's gaze, and after a moment Sherry's mouth twitched, as though she were holding back laughter.

Giggling, she slipped her arm through Kathleen's, and they both looked up. And, in unison, shouted at the top of their lungs, "The puppy peed on the carpet!"

They collapsed against each other, helpless with laughter, when a slight noise behind them made them both whirl around, Kathleen's heart nearly stopping on the spot.

It wouldn't have surprised her if her father *had* been standing there, that familiar look of thunder on his face. But it was just Gordon and the two kids, mouths agape in astonishment.

Kathleen gave a sputter of laughter and walked across to him. "Relax, Gordo! We were just exorcising a few ghosts."

Gordon blinked, then grinned and embraced her awkwardly. "Yeah, I know what you mean. Every now and again I find myself doing something crazy just for the hell of it. Just because I *can*." He stepped back and let his arms fall to his sides again, as though not too certain what to do with them.

Another inheritance from their father, Kathleen thought sadly. Hugging had never been big in the Patterson household.

"Hi, Aunt Kathleen!" Chelsea grinned up at her, revealing a gap where her front teeth used to be. "'Member me?"

"Well, I don't know. Let me think..." Kathleen squatted so she was eye level with her niece and pretended to give it serious thought. "Short person with no teeth and a dirty face...hmm. Could it be? Is it? My gosh, it's Chelsea Anne Patterson!"

Chelsea gave a squeal of laughter and launched herself at Kathleen. No inhibitions there. Kathleen returned the hug, breathing in the scent of baby shampoo and peanut butter. "It's good to see you again, sweetie."

"Guess what! I got two whole dollars from the tooth fairy and Daddy says I can have a pony for my birthday and Shaun flushed his teddy down the pot and it flooded all over! And, and—you know what?'' She was practically incandescent with excitement, eyes shining like stars. "We got a puppy!''

''An' it peed on the carpet,'' came a whisper from somewhere behind Gordon's legs. A head peeked cautiously around, and serious blue eyes met Kathleen's from under a tangle of flaxen hair.

"Well, hi, Shaun. Do you remember me?''

He nodded shyly. "Uh-huh.''

"You're practically all grown up!''

He giggled.

"Can I have a hug?''

He stepped around Gordon's legs and into her arms with no hesitation, planting a noisy damp kiss on her cheek.

"Wow.'' Kathleen gazed at him, then at Chelsea, who was leaning against her, one small arm draped around her neck. Something tugged at her heart just a little, and she swallowed. "You two are really something else, you know that?''

She gave both children one last ferocious hug, then stood, inadvertently intercepting a look of sympathy—pity?—passing between Gord and Sherry. Pretending not to notice, she smiled brightly and tried not to think what they were obviously thinking. Tried not to think of her own baby, dead before she'd even held him.

Might as well try not to think of elephants in a room filled with them.

Shaun's small hand slid into hers, and she smiled down at him, throat tightening. Then she slipped her arm through Gordon's and hugged it. "So, big brother, what's it like? Setting up shop in town, living out here at The Oaks—with a *puppy,* no less! Facing the good folk of Burnt River every day.''

"Easier than I'd anticipated in some ways, harder in others. Half those good folk routinely remind me that I'm not the man my father was, and the other half are afraid I might be.''

"But you're happy you came out here? You don't ever think of moving back to Sacramento?"

"No way." He shook his head firmly.

"The weather's the pits," Sherry put in with a laugh. "The first time it snowed, I was ready to go back to California, but Gord and the kids thought they'd gone to heaven. Gord stayed home, and we all went tobogganing up by Deer Jump Creek. I've never been so cold—or had so much fun—in my life!"

"Stayed home?" Kathleen feigned astonishment. "Gordon Patterson, the quintessential workaholic, stayed home to take his family tobogganing?" She looked at him suspiciously. "Who are you, and what have you done with my brother?"

"I keep working on him," Sherry said dryly. "Yesterday he came home early to help Chelsea build a doghouse."

"Good grief!" Kathleen gave her a look of horror. "And the roof didn't cave in?"

"It trembled a little, but it held." Sherry gave her husband a nudge in the ribs and grinned up at him. "Another year or two with me and he'll be going around unshaven on weekends and belching at the table."

Gordon winced. "Now there's something to look forward to."

Sherry laughed good-naturedly and patted Gordon's shoulder. "How about grabbing Kathy's bags out of the car and putting them in—" Sherry looked at Kathleen. "I was going to put you in your old room, but maybe you'd prefer one of the others?"

Kathleen hesitated, then shook her head. "My old room is fine, Sherry. There are no boogeymen in this house, just a few bad memories. And it's time I exorcized *them,* too."

"Mommy exorcizes every morning," Chelsea piped up. "She's got a exorcize bike in the bedroom, and she gets on and says bad words and everything."

"I'm trying to exorcize away about ten pounds," Sherry said with a laugh.

"You wanna come and play with the puppy?"

"Your aunt's going to be staying for a good long while, so there's no need to wear her out in the first five minutes. Shaun, it's *long* past your nap time."

"Ahhh." Shaun shuffled and frowned, small face pursing. "Do I hafta? I'm too old for a nap."

"You're never too old for a nap. Upstairs, kiddo."

"But I wanna show Aunt Kathleen the puppy!"

"The puppy's asleep," Gordon said gently, bending to scoop up his son. Two small arms went around his neck instantly, and Gordon smiled like a kid himself as his son nestled against his shoulder. "You, too, Chelsea. I'll read you both a story."

Chelsea broke into a radiant smile and skipped along beside her father, sparing Kathleen a wide grin before reaching up to hold her father's hand.

Smiling, Kathleen watched her brother walk slowly up the stairs, then followed Sherry toward the kitchen. "You really have done wonders for that guy. He used to be so uptight he squeaked. He looks happier than I've ever seen him."

"Well, I think moving back here helped a lot. There were things he'd never dealt with, things about your mom and dad he'd never faced. It's as though he had to come back here to make peace with that part of himself."

"Yeah, I know what you mean."

Sherry flashed her a sympathetic smile and reached out to squeeze her arm. "I'm really sorry you and Brice broke up."

"Don't be. Brice was a mistake. I'm just glad I figured that out *before* I married him."

"You had Gord and me worried, if you want the truth. When we met him at your dad's funeral, I got the impression he was more interested in marrying you for the connections the Patterson name would give him than any undying passion."

"Undying passion? Brice?" Kathleen gave a snort.

"Well, you can always move back here and find yourself a good-lookin' cowboy." She grinned at Kathleen over her shoulder. "I'm sure there's an old boyfriend or two around who'd love to catch up on old times."

The image of Jett's darkly handsome face flickered across Kathleen's memory, and she shook it off. "No, I don't think so. There's been a little too much water under *that* bridge."

"Supper's not going to be for hours, thanks to the teddy bear crisis. How about a chicken sandwich and a slab of cherry pie to tide you over? Oh, and that coffee's fresh—help yourself."

Gratefully, Kathleen walked across to the coffee maker and picked up one of the mugs sitting on the counter. "Sounds wonderful, but don't go to any trouble."

"No trouble. Of course, there's always Jett Kendrick."

Kathleen spilled hot coffee and swore under her breath, looking around for a cloth to wipe the counter. "Jett Kendrick?"

"From what Gordie says, you two had quite a thing going." Sherry stepped past her with a sly smile and wiped up the mess expertly. "What a hunk! I see him around town now and again, and I'll tell you—if I weren't happily married to that brother of yours, I'd be tempted to take a run at him myself." She glanced at Kathleen. "You *do* know that he's single again? His wife died about six years ago—some sort of car accident."

Kathleen added cream to her coffee and studiously avoided looking at her sister-in-law. "Mmm," she finally said, opting for noncommittal. "This is really good coffee. Do you grind the beans yourself?"

"Picked and roasted 'em just before you got here," Sherry said dryly. "If you don't want to talk about Jett Kendrick, we won't."

"It's not that I don't want to talk about him, it's just that I can't imagine why we…why I…why…oh, hell!" Kathleen gave up finally, laughing. "Yes, Jett and I did date for a few months, but it's ancient history. I doubt he even remembers me." Thinking, as she said it, of the sultry anger in Jett's eyes when he'd faced her down barely an hour ago.

"So you don't want me to invite him for supper?"

Kathleen nearly spilled her coffee again. "Don't even joke about it."

"I guess the history's not as ancient as you'd like me to think." There was a hint of amusement in Sherry's voice.

"No." Kathleen's voice was slightly rough. "That's not it. It's..." She frowned. "Gord told you that my dad sent me to Baltimore to live with my aunt and uncle when I was fifteen, and I guess he told you why."

Sherry nodded, her eyes filled with sympathy.

"But I guess he *didn't* tell you that the baby's father was Jett Kendrick."

"Oh, Father Christmas!" Sherry's cheeks turned scarlet. "No, he didn't, or I'd never have—oh, I can't believe I—"

"Forget it," Kathleen said with a laugh. "That *is* ancient history. But I think you can see why inviting Jett to dinner might not be a good idea."

"Consider it forgotten!" Sherry managed a quiet laugh. "But I have to tell you, if Jett was even half as cute and sexy then as he is today, I can sure see why you wound up...compromised."

"Oh, honey!" In spite of herself—in spite of the memories—Kathleen couldn't hold back a whoop of laughter. "You have no idea! He had this raven-black hair that hung halfway to his waist, and he'd wear this beaded choker and a beaded denim vest with nothing under it but muscles, and tight jeans and...oh, man!" She fanned herself with her fingers. "He looked like he'd just stepped off the cover of a romance novel. One look at him, and I was ready to be compromised on the spot."

Sherry gave a sputter of delighted laughter. "You were all of fifteen. Your dad must have had a fit!"

"That was half the attraction. At first, anyway." Kathleen smiled reminiscently. "But after that first date..." Her smile turned wistful. "I know people don't think a fifteen-year-old girl knows what love is, that it's all just hormones and infatuation. But I really did love the guy, Sherry."

"No hormones?" Sherry raised one eyebrow skeptically.

"Plenty of hormones! But there was more. I've never—" She shook her head. "I know it sounds crazy, but I've never felt that way about anyone since. Maybe that's why I'm still single. Maybe I'm still looking for the same kind of magic that I had for those four months when I was fifteen. Pretty silly, huh?"

Sherry didn't say anything. She looked at Kathleen thoughtfully, then walked across and poured herself a cup of coffee, taking her time adding cream and sugar. "I think it's time you moved back here to Burnt River," she finally said. "I think it's time you put Baltimore and the baby and your father and everything that happened sixteen years ago behind you, and got on with the rest of your life."

The plumber arrived just as Sherry was pulling cold roast chicken out of the fridge. Kathleen sent her upstairs to help rescue Shaun's teddy bear and set about making her own lunch, musing that she felt more at home here now than when she'd actually lived here.

And a couple of hours later, after the plumber had left and the bear had been hung up to dry and Sherry had disappeared to shower and change, Kathleen ran lightly up the winding staircase leading to the second floor. Here, the past was stronger, each step upward like a step back through time, the house enveloping her with sudden, unexpected memories. Her mother walking down these same stairs, wreathed in expensive perfume and silk. Her father striding down them, tailored and perfect and remote, never relaxed, always impatient.

She could remember sitting on these same stairs as a child, hoping that sooner or later one of them would notice her. And they always did, although more often than not it was only to tell her to go outside and play, and for heaven's sake, didn't she have anything better to do than get in the way?

Thinking about it made Kathleen smile humorlessly as she turned at the top of the stairs to walk down the long corridor to her father's study. She'd grown up here, had lived here, but this big, coldly elegant house had never truly been a home. It had been a showcase, a place where wealthy people gathered to talk business and investments, where powerful men drank coffee and plotted political futures.

A place with no room at all for a pregnant fifteen-year-old.

She gave the door a couple of raps with her knuckles and pushed it open. Gord was sitting behind her father's massive walnut desk, frowning over a scattering of papers. He looked up when she poked her head in, then leaned back in the leather chair, grinning, when he saw it was her. "Hey. Come on in."

"Kids asleep?"

"Finally."

"I have to tell you, big brother, they are really something else. You've made me a very happy aunt."

Gord's grin widened with pleasure. "Move back to Burnt River and you can play aunt to your heart's content."

"I haven't said no yet," she reminded him with a laugh.

"It feels right, Kathy. Being in Burnt River. Practicing law here. It feels *good*. At Dad's funeral, when Cliff Albright first asked if I was interested in moving back here, when he'd said that he was getting old and needed a partner, I thought he was nuts." He gave a quiet laugh. "Now you couldn't get me out of town with dynamite. It's a good place to live, Kathy. You'd be happy here."

Kathleen just nodded again, thinking, fleetingly, of Jett. Of what he'd say if she announced to all and sundry that she was thinking of staying. "It's tempting, I won't deny that. To get back to someplace where the words *values* and *integrity* still mean something."

She realized Gordon was looking at her curiously and managed a rough smile. "When I told you I'd quit Adams, Caldwell and Associates, I wasn't quite lying. But it wasn't the whole truth, either. It was a . . . mutual decision."

Gordon just smiled. "I didn't think you'd walked away from one of the most prestigious law firms on the East Coast because you just got bored one day, Kathy. I figured there had to be more to it."

"When they hired me six years ago, I thought I had it made. That all I had to was work hard and make partner, and my life would be perfect. But with every day that passed, I found myself liking it less. Liking *myself*—what I was becoming—less. I was turning into someone Dad would have admired, and it scared me."

"I've been there," Gordon said quietly.

"I know. That's what gave me the courage to finally walk away." Kathleen wandered across the room and dropped into one of the chairs. "We were in the middle of one of the biggest cases of the decade, representing a pharmaceutical company in a huge class-action suit worth millions. It was starting to look really bad for us, and I was told to lose a critical piece of evidence. I refused. Adams, Caldwell and sundry Associates suggested I might be happier continuing my law career elsewhere. I concurred."

"Cliff Albright ran a straight-up law office, and so do I. Come on as my partner and you'll never feel compromised again, I promise you that."

"An honest lawyer? You're going to give the profession a bad name."

"Come in with me, Kath. I can get a new shingle made up in a day—Patterson And Patterson, Honorable Attorneys At Law. We Ain't Our Old Man."

Kathleen laughed. "And you think people will believe us?"

"Some people in town have made it plain that they'd crawl through broken glass before they'd hire a Patterson to do their lawyering for them. But there are plenty of others who love the irony of watching one of Nelson Patterson's kids working *for* the little guy instead of trying to stick it to him. Having both of us in town will double their fun."

"And there's enough work for two of us?"

"There's enough work for *six* of us," Gord said with feeling. "I'm the only game in town, now that Cliff's gone. I'll be honest with you—moving back here would be good for you, but it's mainly *me* I'm thinking about. You're a damned good attorney, and I think we'd make a great team.''

''I won't deny it's tempting.''

''Burnt River's a long way from Baltimore, I'll admit that,'' Gordon said grudgingly. ''It won't be life in the fast lane, that's for sure.''

''Life in the fast lane's not all it's cracked up to be.'' Kathleen gave him a half smile. ''And Baltimore was never *my* choice, remember. Baltimore just . . . happened.''

A flicker of something darkened Gordon's face. He shoved the chair back almost roughly, walked across to the walnut liquor cabinet and poured himself a long shot of Scotch whiskey. ''I should have killed Jett Kendrick sixteen years ago.'' He held the bottle up with a questioning look at her.

Kathleen shook her head. ''Killing Jett wouldn't have helped. I was already three months pregnant by the time you discovered the real reason I'd run off to Baltimore in such a hurry.''

''It might not have helped you, but it would have made *me* feel better,'' Gordon muttered. ''Still would, come to think of it.''

''Forget it.'' Laughing, Kathleen leaned well back in the chair and put her feet on the coffee table. ''Why are you making such a big deal out of it now? You never said much back then.''

''That's why,'' he said quietly. ''I let you down back then, Kathy. You were my kid sister. I should have come back here and beat the hell out of Kendrick, but I was—'' Shrugging, he dropped into the chair again. ''I was twenty-one and too busy with law school and girls to even care. Burnt River was a bad memory, one I didn't even want to think about. So I did nothing.'' He shook his head, tight-lipped with anger. ''It was like something out of a Gothic novel, the way Dad hustled you and your shameful little secret out of town.''

''It was the best thing that ever happened to me. Mac and Leah are generous, loving people, and they made me feel as though I was one of their own kids. It was the first time in my life I felt as though someone actually *cared*. And after the baby died, I—they took care of me, Gord. Emotionally, I mean. If it hadn't been for them . . ."

"I should have been there for you then, too." Gord swirled the liquor in the glass, not looking at her. "I didn't know you'd lost the baby until nearly a month later. I was too busy partying to keep track of when you were due, and Dad didn't let me know." He gave his head a shake. "I've always felt guilty about that."

Kathleen had to laugh. "Come on, Gord, lighten up. There was nothing you could have done."

"I could have come down to see you. I could have phoned you. Could have written. Sent *flowers*. Done something. I mean, hell, even *Dad* flew down to be with you."

"Dad came to Baltimore to talk me into giving the baby up for adoption," Kathleen said bitterly. "He didn't give a damn about me *or* the baby. He just didn't want me coming back to Burnt River with Jett Kendrick's mixed-breed mongrel brat in my arms."

"The miserable old—" Gord bit off the rest of the sentence. "It was always about him. His career, his reputation, his future. The rest of us were just . . ." He made an angry gesture. "Window-dressing. Props to make the Honorable Judge Nelson Patterson look like the caring family man Supreme Court nominees are supposed to be."

A log popped on the fire, the sound like a pistol shot, and they both jumped, staring at each other a little wide-eyed. Then, abruptly, they both started to laugh.

"I didn't sleep for five nights straight after the funeral," Gord said, still laughing. "I was sure he was going to come back to tell me everything I'd done wrong, how disappointed he was that I couldn't handle even a simple burial without screwing up."

Kathleen nodded, not saying anything. She looked around the big, fire-warmed study, remembering being summoned here to face the music for some transgression or other. Throwing a ball in the house, galloping down the stairs too noisily, forgetting to hang up her coat.

And talking back, of course. Her natural gift for argument made her a formidable opponent in the courtroom, but back then it had done nothing but get her into trouble.

The room hadn't changed much. Dark paneling, acres of law books, wing-backed chairs in burgundy leather, plenty of brass and polished hardwood. The big grandfather clock in the corner still ticked loudly, filling the stillness with the passage of time, a reminder to all who entered of how valuable it was to the man who used to sit here, how little he appreciated having it wasted.

He used to sit behind the massive desk, papers laid out in front of him in precise formation, nothing out of place, not a hint of clutter....

A chill stole down Kathleen's back as she defied the past, daring it to scare her. She'd stood in front of this desk for the last time sixteen years ago, fifteen and pregnant and defiant to the end. That defiance hadn't kept her father from shipping her off to Baltimore, but it had changed something between them.

It was on that day that she'd stopped being afraid of him. Fear had been changed to something else that afternoon, something hot and fierce and vital. And she'd never been afraid again.

"You never came back, did you? Except for Mom's funeral."

"Once or twice." Kathleen smiled faintly. "There never seemed to be much point. Dad and I couldn't talk to one another for more than five minutes without arguing, and he always made me feel as though I was taking up his time. He never hid the fact that he was relieved when it was time for me to leave, so after a while I just stayed away. It seemed easier on both of us."

"Yeah, I know what you mean. I tried a few times, but... hell, let's face it, he didn't give a damn. After a while, neither did I." He finished the whiskey in one swallow and set the glass down. "He gave us brains, good educations and the ability to take care of ourselves. I figure we should thank him for that and let the rest go."

"Amen," Kathleen said quietly. Another ghost down. Maybe that was the end of them.

Chapter 4

Vic's Café hadn't changed much in sixteen years.

Which wasn't saying much, Kathleen thought as she stood on the sidewalk in front of the place and perused it distastefully. The big front windows were dirty and fly-specked and covered with painted signs advertising cheap breakfasts and great hamburgers, and even out here, the air was redolent with hot grease.

There was still a rickety screen door you had to pull hard to open, the frame filthy with a thousand handprints and peeling stickers advertising soft drinks and candy bars. The floor was still green linoleum, the stools still chrome and red plastic, the countertop still pale green Formica, dotted here and there with plates of sugared doughnuts and pies covered with plastic domes.

Another time warp.

She'd spent the morning wandering around town, marveling at how any place could change so much and still be the same.

Like her.

Smiling at her own sense of drama, she slid into one of the booths along the wall, wondering if Vic was still running the place. But it was a statuesque blonde who trotted across with a smile and a menu, and for some reason, Kathleen didn't even ask. If she decided to take Gordon up on his offer of a job, she would have plenty of time to catch up on old times. But for the moment she was enjoying being anonymous, a stranger passing through.

She ordered coffee and flipped idly through the small jukebox mounted on the wall. The names of the groups were different, but the flavor of the music was pretty much unchanged: still lots of broken hearts and teenaged angst and cowboy laments about love gone wrong.

She looked around the place curiously. A couple of farmers in feed store hats were sitting at the counter drinking coffee and smoking unfiltered cigarettes, and two young women shared a Formica-topped table, laughing over grilled cheese and fries, while a baby cooed happily in a carrier beside them. Four men—ranch hands, by the looks of them—were crowded into one of the booths, talking and laughing while sliding speculative glances her way.

Just like old times.

The waitress came across with two cups of steaming coffee just then. She set one in front of Kathleen with a smile, then took the other one to the next booth. All Kathleen could see of the occupant was a battered cowboy hat, but when he thanked the waitress, the voice was too familiar to ignore.

She slid out of the booth and walked around to look at him. "Well, hi. How are you feeling this morning?"

Jody Kendrick lifted his head painfully, both eyes swollen almost shut. The skin around them had turned a sulphur yellow that clashed with the purple bruising across his high cheekbones. "Hi," he croaked, trying to smile. "Been worse, I guess."

"Not in this lifetime, I'll bet."

He managed another crooked smile, pleased at the attention.

"Mind if I join you? It's nice to see a familiar face," she said.

"Yeah, sure!"

Kathleen picked up her coffee and slid into the seat across from him, smiling as she saw the pile of school books spilled carelessly across the table. "Cutting classes?"

He gave her a startled look, then ducked his head, looking almost ridiculously guilty. "Not gonna tell my old man, are you? He's on my case all the time as it is."

"I doubt I'll be seeing your dad anytime soon," she assured her dryly. Idly, she picked up the nearest book. "Biology. Hope you're doing better in it than I ever did."

His shoulders slumped again, and he stared into his coffee morosely. "Squeakin' by, I guess."

She set the biology text aside and picked up another one. "Algebra. Now that's something I could have lived without."

"No kiddin'."

Kathleen took a sip of hot coffee to hide her smile. "That bad, huh?"

He nodded, looking as though someone had just died. "Don't know why I hafta learn all that stuff anyhow. Got nothin' to do with what I want. Got nothin' to do with rodeo."

"I have to admit it didn't make much sense to me when I was your age, either." She paused, then laughed. "Come to think of it, it still doesn't make much sense. Especially algebra." She made a face. "Who in their right mind needs *algebra?*"

"No one I can figure out."

"Is that the only class you're flunking?"

He lifted his head and stared at her. "How'd you know I was flunkin' algebra? Dad don't even know. Yet."

"Lucky guess," she said dryly. "What else?"

He shrugged, just a little too carelessly. "Chemistry, I guess. All them formulas and stuff to remember." He frowned and gave the sling on his left arm a hitch. "What'm I gonna need chemistry for, anyhow? Don't need chemistry to stay on a saddle bronc for eight seconds. Don't need chemistry to figure out my winnin's." He let his shoulders slump, eyes bleak. "I just can't figure this stuff out! It's too hard, and if I ask Dad, he gets mad and jumps all over me and—ah, what's the use!"

He dropped his head into his hand and stared unhappily into the coffee. "Soon as I can, I'm quittin' school. Figure I can get a job with one of the rodeo stock contractors until I'm old enough to join the Professional Rodeo Cowboys Association, then all them X's and Y's won't matter. Nothin'll matter except staying in the saddle long enough to get me into the money."

Oh, boy. Kathleen looked at him, trying to figure out what to say. He didn't want to hear all the usual platitudes—he'd heard them a dozen times by now. And they wouldn't carry any more weight with him than they did with any other fourteen-year-old boy who saw no relevance between school and his dreams.

"What does your dad think about that?"

"I don't guess he cares," Jody said in a sullen mutter. "He figures I'm gonna flunk out anyway. Keeps sayin' if I do, he ain't keeping me on rent-free. That I'll have to work for my keep like the rest of the hired hands."

"Don't be too hard on him," Kathleen said mildly, feeling an unexpected surge of sympathy for Jett. It sounded as though he was doing his best to keep Jody in school, even if his best meant driving the boy in the opposite direction. "Subtlety never was your dad's strong suit." Even in bed, she found herself thinking irrelevantly. Maybe especially in bed, where his lack of subtlety had once had its own benefits.

Jody gave her a frankly curious look, and Kathleen avoided his eyes. There were some things a fourteen-year-old boy did *not* need to know about his father's past. "Have you talked to your teachers about the difficulty you're having with algebra and chemistry? I'm sure they could arrange special tutoring or—"

"Ain't just that." Jody's shoulders slumped even lower. "It's Miss Cameron's civics class. Even if I pull my marks up in them other things, I'm *never* gonna make civics." He gave her a look of pure despair. "I got this paper to write. It counts for half the year's grade, and I..." He shook his head. "It was supposed to be handed in last week."

"And you haven't even started it yet."

"Oh, I started it." Jody looked up, face miserable. "I started it three or four times. Miss Cameron says she'll give me more time, but that won't help. I gotta write twenty pages on the Constitution. *Twenty* pages. That's...that's a whole *book,* practically! How'm I gonna write twenty pages about the Constitution, you tell me that?" He stared into the coffee as though it might have the answer he needed. "Twenty pages..."

Kathleen had to bite her lip to hide her smile. She'd been there. "What kind of extension did you get?"

"Two weeks." It was little more than a whisper. "But I don't figure two *years* would help me any. I may as well just drop out now and save 'em the trouble of kicking me out. I'll get a job. I'll do something...."

"Jody, you're fourteen," she said gently. "You can't just—"

"Fifteen," he said stubbornly.

Kathleen felt something twist inside her, and she just stared at him. Fifteen! That—that meant Pam had gotten pregnant at almost the same time she had.

Kathleen closed her eyes, feeling dizzy with shock. Jett had been sleeping with both of them. Slipping out of one pair of arms and into the other with hardly time to catch his breath between.

"Well, damn him," she heard herself whisper, not realizing until too late that she'd said it aloud. She looked at Jody quickly, but he was still staring glumly into his coffee mug, too lost in his own misery to hear hers.

It was silly to be reacting like this, she told herself calmly. It was an old betrayal, after all. And just one of many. So why was she taking it so hard?

Because there was still a tiny part of her that cared, she realized with a sinking heart. A tiny part that still loved the man, that had been harboring the secret hope that she'd been wrong all this time, that he *had* loved her, and it had all just been some kind of mistake. . . .

She gritted her teeth and let herself fantasize for one brief moment about driving down Main Street and spotting Jett crossing in front of her. Oh, it had been a terrible accident, she would tell the police. She'd *meant* to step on the brake, but her foot had slipped and hit the accelerator instead. Poor Jett, she would say, feigning tears. He hadn't stood a chance. . . .

She found herself smiling a little malevolently. "So your dad's already convinced you're going to flunk school this year."

Jody nodded unhappily.

"It sure would be nice to prove him wrong, wouldn't it?"

"Yeah. But what chance have I got to—"

"Twenty pages on the American Constitution? That's all?"

"The *underlying principles,* Miss Cameron said. Whatever that means."

"It means you're the luckiest kid in the country," Kathleen said with feeling. "I think what you want is a comparative study of the original premise behind the Constitution and how it's being interpreted on a day-to-day basis."

Jody looked dazed. "I . . . guess," he managed to whisper.

"I did a thesis on just that topic in college. Got a darn good grade, too." She laughed quietly. "I just might be able to help you out, Jody Kendrick."

"You . . . you mean you'd write it for me?"

"I most certainly will not! But I *will* help you research it. What would you say to a few days of tutoring on the Constitution, along with a look at our legal and judicial systems, the evolution of the law, rulings that have changed how we think about our rights and liberties . . . the whole nine yards?"

He was staring at her in awe. "You know all that stuff?"

"You'd be amazed at what a few years of law school can do for you. And what I don't know, my brother does. He loves this sort of thing."

"You're a *lawyer?*"

"Sure am."

"And you'd do this? For me?"

She grinned, feeling almost ebullient. "Darned right. It's not as though I've got anything better to do for the next couple of weeks." Except figure out the rest of her life, she reminded herself wryly. But that could wait. Heaven itself could wait if it meant getting a chance to make Jett eat crow. Plenty of crow. "Algebra's still a mystery to me, but my sister-in-law said something about being a math whiz. Maybe we can recruit her."

"But why would you do this? For me, I mean?"

"I'd just love to help you prove your dad wrong, that's all," she said, not even lying. "Besides, one of the best ways to work your way up to professional rodeo is through high school and college competition. It'll keep your dad off your back *and* give you a shot at your dream."

"Yeah." Brightening, he sat up, shoulders squaring. "He couldn't keep me from ridin' if my marks was good."

"Well, it would punch a good-size hole through the best part of his argument." She glanced at her watch. "It's almost two o'clock. Why don't I drive you to school and talk with the school nurse about giving you a medical absence slip for the day? It won't make up for the classes you missed, but at least it will keep them off your record."

"You mean it? You think she'll go for it?"

"I think one look at that face of yours should convince the most hard-nosed school nurse that you're not faking it."

He managed a sheepish smile.

"We can drop by my brother's office and see what reference books he's got lying around that you can borrow. Then I'll run you out to The Oaks, and we can spend the rest of the afternoon putting together a game plan for this paper.

And maybe Sherry will have some ideas on how to get your algebra mark up."

He blinked. "The Oaks?"

"That big, redbrick monstrosity up on Deer Jump Road."

"B-but that's the Patterson place, ain't it?"

Kathleen gave him a rueful smile. "I guess I never did introduce myself properly yesterday. I'm Kathleen Patterson, and my brother's Gord Patterson—his law office is just up the street. He and his wife, Sherry, live out at The Oaks. I'm staying with them for a couple of weeks."

His eyes widened visibly behind the bruising. "You're related to old man Patter—I mean, Judge Patterson?"

"He was my father," she told him quietly.

"Oh, man." He glanced around nervously. "If my old man finds out I've even been *talkin'* to you, he'll tan my hide good."

"Your father told you about me?" Kathleen's voice was cool.

"He said you and him went out together a long time ago, but he never said you were Judge Patterson's daughter. I didn't even know Judge Patterson *had* a daughter." Jody was looking more apprehensive by the passing moment. "He told me I wasn't to have anything to do with the Pattersons—ever. I was seven when we moved back here to Burnt River from where we lived in Arizona. And I remember both Mom and my old man sayin' over and over—I wasn't to have *nothing* to do with no Patterson."

A jolt of raw anger went through her, and she narrowed her eyes slightly. "I'm sorry to hear that, Jody. Because—" And then, abruptly, she caught herself. Getting Jody embroiled in the feud between his father and the Pattersons wasn't going to accomplish anything; it was hardly his fault that his father was acting like a prize idiot.

"Your dad and I dated one summer," she said mildly. "And my father was anything but happy about it. He didn't like your dad and . . . well, the feeling was mutual. My father said some things that made your dad pretty mad, and I guess when you moved back here, he still had some strong feelings about it.''

Jody nodded. Kathleen half expected him to say something, or at least to ask some questions, but he didn't say a word, just looked thoughtful.

"Under the circumstances, it's probably better if you don't come out to The Oaks. Or into Gord's law office. I can pick out some things I think will be helpful and drop them off here at Vic's, and you can pick them up when it's convenient. Your dad will never have to know you've even been talking to me.''

"No.'' Jody sat up straight and looked at her evenly. "I ain't goin' to sneak around like I'm doin' somethin' wrong. My old man and your old man might have hated each other, but that's got nothin' to do with me. Besides, he's always on at me about gettin' my marks up. I don't guess he can complain much if that's what I'm tryin' to do.''

Stubborn, Kathleen thought. Although heaven knew he came by it honestly. Those Kendrick bloodlines ran as deep as bedrock. "I don't want to get you into trouble with your father, Jody.''

"Heck, I'm always in trouble one way or another.'' He flashed a cocky, devil-may-care grin that made him look so much like Jett that it made Kathleen's heart turn over. "You're still goin' to help me get outta school this afternoon, ain't you?''

Kathleen reached across and gave his hat brim a rap with her finger to knock it over his eyes. "Don't make the mistake of thinking I'm a pushover, hotshot. I'm going to make you work like you've never worked before.''

He just grinned cheerily and pushed his hat back where it belonged. "Can't be worse 'n stringin' barbed wire. And if I was home right now, that's what I'd be doin'.''

"Don't bet on it,'' Kathleen assured him with a laugh. "Barbed wire is my middle name.''

* * *

Vic's Café hadn't changed much in sixteen years.

Which wasn't saying much, Jett thought as he pulled the old wooden screen door open and stepped inside.

He didn't come in here much anymore. The past seemed too close here, too real, as though at any moment the years might ripple and shimmer and fall away, and it would be that summer again. He'd been eighteen and fearless, and the whole world had been his.

And Kathleen. Oh, yeah, Kathleen had been his, too.

He gave his head a shake and looked around the café impatiently, tired of the way his mind kept tossing the memories at him. There were too many things back there he didn't want to relive. And Kathleen Patterson, damn her, was one of them.

The place was all but empty. A couple of farmers drinking coffee at the counter nodded to him companionably through wreaths of cigarette smoke, and two pretty young women at a table stopped talking when he walked by, then went back to their conversation in hushed undertones and giggles.

The waitress spotted him and came sashaying over, hips swinging. "Well, well. If it isn't the Mystery Man himself. I thought you were going to call me, Jett Kendrick. Or is that what you tell every woman you—"

"I've been busy, Gretchen," Jett muttered, feeling himself flush. "I, uh, I meant to call you. But—"

She gave a ladylike snort and started picking up empty coffee cups from the red Formica-topped table in one of the booths along the wall. "Don't embarrass yourself, Jett. We both know you stayed over that night because you'd had too much to drink. And we both know that you had no intention of calling. So let's at least be grown up about it, all right?"

Jett winced. He'd almost have preferred it if she'd called him a few choice names or thrown things. "I, uh, I'm sorry, Gretch. I should have—"

"So, what brings you in here today?"

He bit back his unwanted apology. "Looking for Jody. The school principal called and told me he hasn't been in today."

"Doesn't surprise me. Poor kid looked like he had a head-on with a freight train. He should be home in bed, not sitting in school with his arm in a cast and his face swollen up like—"

"So he was in here?"

"Left about fifteen minutes ago." She smiled slightly, eyes cool. "With a woman."

Jett's heart tumbled to a stop. "A woman?"

"A *pretty* woman. Blond. Blue-eyed. Citified, by the looks of her. You can always tell, even when they wear jeans and cowboy boots. It's the fingernails, I think. City women always have nice nails." She held her own out to admire them. They were long and red and looked dangerous enough to require a carry permit.

Jett's chest felt so tight he was having trouble breathing. Kathleen. Kathleen had Jody. "Do you know where they went when they left here? A car . . . was she driving a car?" Gray, he thought dizzily. She'd been driving a dark gray four-door when she'd been out at the Kicking Horse yesterday. Fifteen minutes . . . she couldn't have gotten far in only fifteen minutes. He could call Sheriff Carmody and—

"I didn't notice." Gretchen pocketed a handful of change lying on the table. "I heard her say something about going by the office to pick up some books."

"What office?"

"How would I know what office?" she snapped. "And who died and made me your personal secretary, anyway?"

Jett gritted his teeth. "Gretch, I'm sorry. It's just important, that's all. Real important."

She looked at him impatiently, then sighed. "Jett, I don't know who she was or where they went. You might try Gord Patterson's law office, though—I heard her say something about him. And they were talking about the Constitution, if that's any help. Legal stuff, anyway. I didn't pay much attention.''

Legal stuff. His heart careened to a stop, then started up again at twice its normal pace. The law office. Cliff Albright's old office. Everything was still there. All the files. The papers. Everything.

"If you want, I can call and—"

But Jett was already through the door and out on the sidewalk, Gretchen's voice lost in the bang of the screen door behind him. No way, he told Kathleen in his mind as he took off up the street. No damn way are you getting my boy away from me . . .

In the end, Kathleen didn't need to resort to any courtroom theatrics to convince the school nurse to give Jody an absence slip. She simply introduced herself, and the Patterson name did most of it. Then the nurse took one look at Jody's face and another at the cast on his arm, and the rest was history. The woman gave her head a weary shake and muttered something about *rodeos* and *young fools* as she wrote up the medical slip without so much as a quibble.

While they walked through the corridors back to the front door, Kathleen drank in the familiar sounds and sights and pungencies of a small-town high school and tried to remember what it had been like sixteen years ago.

But it was too long ago. She gave up finally, and as she walked back out into the sunshine and cool mountain air, she reminded herself that she was grown up now, and that part of her life and all it had held were long gone.

But even having told herself that, she couldn't keep from glancing toward the parking lot as she walked down the wide front steps. Once, in that other life, Jett's blue pickup truck would have been parked right there in front, waiting for her. And she could still remember that wonderful, magical warmth that used to flow through her at just the sight of him.

He would be slouched down in the seat, one arm draped across the top of the wheel, Stetson hat pulled low, staring out across the mob of students flowing around him with the sullen arrogance of a young lord surveying the peasantry.

Then he would spot her and give that slow, incendiary smile that made her heart do double cartwheels, and he'd reach down and start the truck, gunning the engine just a little for effect. She'd say goodbye to her friends and stroll across to the truck, knowing that every female eye was on her, that every female heart was breaking just a little as Jett leaned across and pushed the truck door open so she could slide in beside him....

She had to laugh at herself as she strode across to her car. What a little fool she'd been back then. Not quite sixteen and green as grass, sure he was in love with her. Telling herself what she wanted to hear. Telling herself it was real.

She glanced at Jody, and suddenly the past seemed very far away. This was reality, she reminded herself. This tall, good-looking young man was the truth of what had really gone on back then. Jett had loved Pam. Had married her. Had given her a son. And nothing else really mattered. Then, *or* now.

It was after three by the time Kathleen finally got back out to The Oaks, and as she ushered Jody through the front door, she was beginning to think this whole idea had been one huge mistake.

The kid was scared to death. He stepped through the open door like a deer walking into a den of wolves, and he kept looking over his shoulder as though expecting to see Judge Patterson himself—or, worse yet, his own father—bearing down on him like an avenging angel.

It would have been funny if it hadn't annoyed Kathleen so badly. Heaven knew there were plenty of people around who hated the Patterson name and everything it stood for, but Jett had carried it to an extreme.

And he didn't have that right, damn it. It wasn't as though his life had been turned upside down sixteen years ago!

"Sherry? Are you home?" Looking around for her sister-in-law, Kathleen escorted Jody into the kitchen, inhaling the perfume of freshly baked Toll-House cookies. "Looks like our timing was pretty good."

"Kathy, gosh, I'm glad you're here!" Sherry came dashing through from the dining room, looking frazzled. "Can you watch the kids for about an hour? I have to—" She stopped dead when she spotted Jody, her mouth still open.

"Jody, this is my sister-in-law, Sherry Patterson."

Jody snatched off his hat. "Ma'am."

"I—" Sherry gaped at him, then at Kathleen. Back to Jody.

"This is Jody Kendrick, Jett's son."

"I...guessed as much." Sherry seemed to collect her wits and smiled at Jody. "Sorry. I knew Jett had a son, I just never expected him to be so... tall."

"I'm helping Jody with a school project. And I'll be glad to watch the kids."

Sherry nodded, still staring at Jody. "Yeah." Then she gave herself a shake and laughed. "I mean, that's great. Thanks. The coffee's fresh. Help yourself to the cookies, and I'll be back as soon as I can. You're a sweetheart!"

Jody seemed to have relaxed slightly, and by the time Kathleen plied him with milk and oven-warm cookies, he was almost smiling. Then Shaun and Chelsea crowded around, asking solicitous questions about the cast on his arm and the rainbow of bruising across his face, and growing wide-eyed with awe when he explained what had happened.

Chelsea touched his arm gently and asked if it hurt, and Shaun wanted to learn how to ride saddle broncs right then and there, and by the time Kathleen sat the two kids down in the dining room with coloring books and crayons, the panic had left Jody's eyes and he was almost at ease.

"I think you've got yourself a couple of fans," Kathleen teased. "Though I bet you have a few of those already. Buckle bunnies—isn't that what rodeo groupies are called?"

Jody grinned and blushed. "Yeah. I guess."

"Not that you pay attention to things like that, right?"

The blush deepened, and he shrugged carelessly. "Well... sometimes, I guess."

Kathleen had to laugh. "Anyone special, or are you still playing the field?"

He squirmed, cheeks aflame, long legs wrapped awkwardly around the legs of the chair. "Still playin' the field." He shrugged with exaggerated nonchalance. "Though I guess there might be this one girl in my class..."

Kathleen poured herself a cup of coffee, then pulled one of the chairs out and sat down. "I'd say that's another good reason to stay in school."

"Yeah, I guess." Then he gnawed the inside of his cheek, the picture of a fifteen-year-old with something on his mind. "I, uh..." He shifted uncomfortably in the chair, head hung so low she couldn't even see his face, a handful of raven black hair dangling across his forehead. "I, um..." And then, taking a deep breath for courage, he lifted his head and looked at her, eyes filled with desperation. "Can you teach me to dance?"

Kathleen blinked. "Dance? What kind of dance?"

His bravado was starting to slip, desperation turning to misery. "Slow, mainly. I—I can do some of the other stuff."

The light finally dawned, and Kathleen mentally kicked herself for being so slow. A girl. In his class. Spring prom coming up. Get with the program, Kathy!

"Of course I can teach you to dance, Jody," she assured him gently. "I'm not up on all the modern stuff they're doing these days, but I can sure enough teach you some old-fashioned, romantic slow dancing."

He grinned, looking relieved and embarrassed at the same time, as endearingly awkward as a young colt, all feet and clumsy shyness and limbs that went every which way. His hair needed trimming, his shirt and jeans could do with a wash, and his boots gave off the faint but unmistakably pungent perfume of horse manure, and Kathleen felt her heart go out to him with sudden and unexpected poignancy.

He needed a mother. Someone to make sure those jeans and shirts got tossed in the laundry now and again, and the hair got cut and the boots scraped. Someone to keep an eye on his schoolwork and spend some time with him on algebra and civics. Someone to sympathize over the bruises and tell him he would do better next time, and listen to his dreams and recognize the first hesitant, shy blossomings of love. Someone to teach him to dance...

She shook herself out of it firmly. "Actually, your dad's a pretty good dancer. Or he used to be, anyway."

It clearly surprised Jody, as though the possibility that his father could dance—*had* danced—was too bizarre to be real. Then he frowned, expression darkening. "I can't ask him," he said with a hint of sullen anger. "He'd just start ragging on me. Tellin' me I don't need to know how to dance to fix fences."

"You probably won't believe this, but your dad used to be quite a hell-raiser when he was young. All he was interested in back then was rodeo, girls, and having a good time."

Jody was looking at her curiously, and Kathleen realized she'd said too much. Sitting up straight, she picked up a book she'd scrounged from Gordon's library and opened it. "Okay, we'd better get started. First, how about giving me a quick review of what you've studied in civics class so far."

The afternoon went better than she'd expected. For all his disinterest in school, Jody had a mind as sharp and supple as a whipsaw. And he stuck with the lesson like a burr, that bred-in-the-bone Kendrick stubbornness keeping him at it even when he was close to tears of sheer frustration.

Kathleen had just glanced at her watch and was about to call it a day when someone hammered against the back door, making it rattle. "That's probably Sherry with an armload of groceries," she said as she got to her feet. "If you want to gather up all those books, I'll give you a ride home. There's no point in trying cover everything today.''

She walked through the mudroom, dodging kids' toys and discarded coats, and pulled the door open. ''If you'd given me a shout, I'd have helped you carry in the—''

But it wasn't Sherry. Jett Kendrick loomed through the doorway like a thunderstorm, hat brim pulled down, mouth thin and tight with fury. ''Where is he? What the hell have you done with my son?''

Chapter 5

Kathleen stared at him in shock. "H-he's in the—"

He shouldered past her roughly. "I warned you, lady. I told you to stay the hell away from him."

He strode into the kitchen without another word, and Kathleen scrambled to keep up with him. "You can't just come storming in here as though—"

"What are you doin' here?" Jody shoved his chair back angrily and got to his feet, fists clenching.

"What the hell do you think *you're* doing?" Jett's voice was vibrant with fury. "I told you never to come near this house or anyone in it. The truck's outside. Get in it—and I mean now!"

"You have no right coming after me!" Jody faced his father belligerently, dark eyes glittering. "I'm old enough to—"

"No *right?*" Jett's voice dropped to a deceptive whisper. "Did you just say I have no *right* coming up here to take my own son home? Just what the hell have they been telling you, anyway?"

"Nothing! She's helpin' me with my homework, that's all!"

Jett was glaring at Jody, nostrils flared, every muscle in his body as taut as wire. "I want you out of this house. Now."

But Jody didn't budge. He glared back at his father pugnaciously, feet braced, fists balled at his sides, flushed with anger and embarrassment and raw adrenaline. No longer boy to man in that instant, but man to man. Ready, finally, to stand his ground, to fight, his young blood hot with rebellion and a million years of instinct. In another time, he and Jett would have been at each other's throats, young challenger against herd sire, tendon to tendon, bone to bone, driven by laws of nature neither understood but both had to obey.

Kathleen understood. And so, finally, did Jett.

And—with an inherent wisdom that surprised her—he defused the moment with more grace than she would have given him credit for. Easing his breath out, he shifted his weight and moved back slightly, giving ground.

Without even thinking, Kathleen stepped across and put her hand on Jody's arm. "Do as your dad says," she said quietly. "This is my fault. I shouldn't have gone behind your father's back like this. I'll straighten it out, all right?"

Jett had his mouth open to tell her there was nothing to straighten out, that the whole damn lot of them could go to hell if they thought it was going to be this easy.

But not with Jody there.

Breathing heavily, Jett backed off another step, feeling trapped and harried and half wild with fear. This was the enemy stronghold, and they had the power here. She and her brother, both Pattersons, both attorneys, both as clever, as manipulative as their old man. And both with the weight of the Patterson name and bank account behind them, so even if the law didn't uphold their claim, they had other ways to get what they wanted.

Jody mumbled something and nodded, looking embarrassed and mad. He started gathering up the books and papers spread across the table, and Jett waited, silently, until he was finished. Jody grabbed up the last book, young face sullen, then sidestepped Jett without looking at him and strode toward the back door.

Jett waited until he heard it slam behind his son, then he turned and gave Kathleen a long, cold look. "I don't know what the hell you have planned, lady, but it won't work."

"Planned?" Kathleen's voice was too calm. Too quiet. "What I had *planned*, Mr. Kendrick, was to help your son get a passing grade in civics. And algebra. And maybe even chemistry. But you've screwed that up very nicely, not to mention embarrassing *him* half to death and making a complete fool of yourself into the bargain!" Her voice had been rising steadily, and by the time she got to the last word, she was practically shouting. It seemed to startle her, and she took a deep breath. "And dancing," she added out of the blue, her eyes still snapping.

"Dancing?" Jett's voice was little more than a yelp of frustration as he struggled to understand what was going on. "What in the *hell* are you talking about?"

"He wants to learn to dance!" she all but yelled at him. "He's got a girlfriend, and he wants to learn how to slow dance. And if you were any kind of a father, damn it, he'd be asking you to teach him instead of me!"

"A girlfriend?" Jett felt the whole thing starting to get away from him. Jody had never mentioned a girlfriend or dancing or any of it to *him*. "And what the hell do you mean, if I was any kind of a father?" he bellowed. "You've got no right coming into town telling me how to raise my son, lady! No damn right at all!"

"The kid's flunking, Kendrick! He can use all the help he can get!" She gestured impatiently, chest heaving under the thin silk blouse; then she blew her breath out and combed her thick hair back from her face with her fingers, looking suddenly subdued. "But . . . you're right. I had no business jumping in without talking to you first. I'm sorry."

As she pulled her hand away, her hair spilled back around her shoulders, distracting Jett badly. That mane of silken hair, the color of sun-ripened wheat, had driven him crazy once. He could remember burying his face in its scented depths once, could still taste it, could feel the weight of it in his hands, against his chest.

"And I apologize," she was saying, bringing him back to the present with a jolt. "That crack about you not being a good father was *way* out of line. I had no right saying that."

He shook off the tantalizing shadows of the past and glared at her, reminding himself of how much he had to lose. "Let's just cut the song and dance and get down to it, all right?" He stepped close to her, leaning into her space. "You walked out on me sixteen years ago, lady, and there is no damn way you're going to come back here now and—"

"Walked out on you?" Kathleen stared at him, mind reeling as she tried to figure out what this had to do with Jody and his civics project. Understanding suddenly that it had nothing at all to do with Jody. Or homework or girlfriends or any of it. This was about *them*. Had been about them right from the beginning. About them and sixteen years of simmering anger.

And just as suddenly, as though his words had somehow shattered some wall of restraint between them, she felt the anger explode up through her in a starburst of sheer rage that all but took her breath away. She planted both hands against his chest and gave him a ferocious shove, and he stumbled back a step or two with a startled expression. "*Walked* out? My father practically had to drag me onto the plane, and you never even—"

"Don't pull that holier-than-thou act on me," he snarled, his voice like a whip crack. "You were all over me when I had what you wanted, but the minute your old man caved in and let you move to the big city, you couldn't get rid of me fast enough."

Kathleen stared up at him, the fury pounding through her like heavy surf. Half blinded by tears of rage, she brought her right hand up without even thinking and slapped him across the cheek as hard as she could, the crack of flesh on flesh echoing through the room like a pistol shot.

Jett froze in astonishment, and Kathleen simply stared up at him in shocked disbelief, the room suddenly so deathly silent that she could hear the pounding of her own heart.

Breathing hard, she gritted her teeth together, fighting for control. "I loved you so much I was half crazy with it, and you threw it back in my face like it was nothing. Like *I* was nothing. I was fifteen, Jett. *Fifteen.* I would have done anything for you. I let you make love to me because I knew it was what you wanted—and I would have done anything to make you happy. I thought it meant something. I thought *I* meant something."

"Sixteen," he growled, rubbing his reddened cheek. "You were sixteen." He made it sound as though it mattered.

"Fifteen," she said with precision. "And stop making noises like a betrayed lover, Jett. I know all about you and Pam. Did you really think I wouldn't find out? The only question is, did you get her pregnant before or *after* you got me pregnant?"

"What?" His brows crashed together in a ferocious scowl. "What are you talking about *now?*"

"My dad *said* you were just sleeping with me to count coup. That I was a real prize, a rich white girl whose daddy just happened to be Judge Patterson. The same Judge Patterson who sentenced you to four months in a juvenile detention facility when you were fourteen." Kathleen lifted her chin, daring him to deny it. "He told me that I was nothing to you but a notch on your belt."

Jett didn't move so much as a hair, but the effort it took cost him every bit of self-control he had. "So that's the line you're going to take, is it?" He made it sound as though he couldn't care less what she did, as though she had no power to touch him, to hurt him.

But she did. The sheer immensity of just what she *could* do made him feel sick. It was just a line, all right, but a damned good one. With enough of the shadow of truth in it that she could make people listen if she tried hard. And she would try. He knew her.

Kathleen glared up at him for a moment longer, then turned away, poised and as remote as ice. "I didn't believe him at first. I told him that we loved each other. That you'd marry me as soon as I told you about the baby and there was nothing he could do to stop us."

He would beg if he had to, Jett realized remotely. He would do whatever it took to keep her from destroying his world.

Kathleen looked around at him, her eyes cold with fury. "That's how good you were, Jett—I really didn't have a clue it was just a game to you. I spent weeks—*weeks*—waiting for you to come after me." She took a deep breath, her gaze never leaving his. "And while I was sitting up in the tower spinning my pathetic little fantasies about happily ever after, *you* were back here screwing your brains out with Pam Easton!"

She turned and strode across to the window, fists clenched. "Don't think I came back here looking for you, Jett Kendrick. I got you out of my system long ago."

The room was so silent that Jett could hear the pounding of his own blood. Her anger confused him. He'd expected triumph. Even satisfaction. A cold smile when she told him that the agreement he'd had with her father was nothing but paper. An even colder one while she laid it out chapter and verse and told him how it was going to be. That her father was dead and Cliff Albright was dead and she was running things her way now.

She turned around suddenly, her eyes meeting his. They were glittering slightly, and he realized with a sense of shock that she was crying.

"Could you at least tell me one thing? Did you plan it right from the start—right from that first night when I walked into Vic's Café? Or did the idea of using me to get even with Dad come later? It doesn't matter, but I'd like to know."

"There was never any plan," he said, his voice as rough as splintered pine. "None of what went down between your old man and me had anything to do with you."

"Yeah, right."

"I didn't know you were pregnant until it was too late."

"But you knew."

Jett hesitated, wondering what would happen if he lied. But then he realized it was too late for that. "I knew."

Her face crumpled slightly, as though she had been hoping for some other answer. Then she sighed and reached up to rake her hair away from her face with her fingers, tipping her head back and closing her eyes. "Strangely enough, it doesn't even matter anymore. Just go away, Jett, all right? I'm tired of talking about the past. I'm tired of . . . I'm just tired of everything!"

She turned away from him again, kneading the back of her neck with slender, strong fingers. And suddenly he could remember the touch of those fingers. Could feel the way she used to trail them delicately down his bare belly until—

Roughly, he dragged his thoughts back to the here and now.

"It matters," he growled, surprised to discover that he was telling the truth. And in spite of himself, he found himself just standing there. Found himself talking again, as though he had no control over the words. "All I knew was that when I got back from the rodeo finals, you were gone. No one knew why. Just that you'd packed up and gone to live with relatives in Baltimore."

She didn't say anything, but Jett knew she'd heard him.

"I came out here looking for you, and your old man said you'd decided Burnt River was too small-town. That you wanted to get a head start on college by finishing school out east."

She glanced around, eyes wary and a little angry. But, to his surprise, she didn't say anything. Just stood there as though waiting for him to go on.

Although why he was even wasting his time, he had no idea. She didn't care about any of this. The only thing she cared about was the one thing he would never let her have. "He said you'd wanted to go to Baltimore for the better part of a year, but that he wouldn't agree to it. That you figured one sure way to get him to let you go was to start sleeping with me."

"That's ridiculous. He said no such thing."

But she didn't sound convinced. Not convinced at all.

"He told me you'd just been using me all along. That I was crazy if I actually thought I had a chance with you. That you had your future all planned out and sure as hell weren't going to waste your life on a backwater half-breed like me."

"That's not true." But she looked stricken, her voice little more than a whisper. "He wouldn't have said that."

Jett gave a snort of mirthless laughter. "Honey, that's maybe half of what he said. He called me a worthless, no-good punk and said the only thing keeping him from having me arrested for rape was the fact that he didn't want to ruin your prospects with the rich boys down east. But that if I ever tried to talk to you or see you, he'd hunt me down and bury what was left so deep even the coyotes wouldn't find me."

Somehow he managed another smile, though it hurt his mouth. "Come after you? Honey, I didn't even want to *think* about you."

Her face was oddly pale, and she stared at him as though trying to make sense of what he'd said. "I don't believe you," she whispered finally. But her eyes said otherwise. "I left messages. With your grandparents."

"I never got them." He bit the words out, not wanting to see the bewilderment in her eyes. Not wanting to think about the implications if she were telling the truth. "If you loved me so damn much, why didn't you come back? Why did you get rid of my baby?"

Kathleen looked at him for a long moment. "I didn't come back," she whispered, "because you were with Pam, and without you, there was nothing here for me. And your baby died, Jett. An hour and a handful of minutes after he was born."

An odd expression crossed Jett's face, half disbelief, half shock. Kathleen took a deep breath. "I heard him cry, then . . . they took him away. I never even got to hold him." Tears filled her eyes suddenly, and she blinked, fighting to keep her voice steady. "I loved you, damn it. And you broke my heart. So don't stand there telling me that I did something wrong. Don't stand there trying to tell me you were the one who got hurt!"

"What do you mean, he died?" Jett's voice was tight. "What the hell kind of story are you making up now?"

Kathleen eased her breath out, feeling the anguish stab through her as it always did when she thought of that day. "I don't know what happened." She rubbed her arms, chilled, although the room was almost too warm. "Everything seemed normal. I went into labor when I was supposed to and—" She shook her head. "I had the baby, and suddenly everything got really quiet, and one of the nurses looked at me—there was such pity in her eyes, I knew right away that something was wrong."

She closed her eyes, fighting the memories. "I started to scream that I wanted to see him, that I wanted my baby. But they took him away." She opened her eyes, still seeing that room, the white-robed figures bustling around, the hushed whispers. "Then I guess they gave me something, because I went to sleep, and when I woke up, my father told me the baby had died."

Jett was just looking at her, eyes narrowed and as cold as glass. She rubbed her arms again, feeling the disbelief radiate from him like deep cold. "They kept me in the hospital for days, and when it was finally time for me to go home, everyone seemed to take it for granted that I'd stay in Baltimore. Mom and Dad were busy with Dad's political career, and you were . . . with Pam. I'd been gone for almost seven months by then, and everyone here figured I'd spent the time sailing and playing tennis and going to parties. The thought of having to come back and pretend nothing else had happened . . ."

She shivered and turned away, then walked across to look out the window, not really seeing anything at all. Idly, she thought of what it had been like back then, and found the memories as cold as ashes.

"Were you telling the truth?" She turned to look at Jett. He hadn't moved, was still standing there like a figure carved of stone. "Did you really come looking for me?"

Even if he lied, it didn't matter. She just wanted him to say the words.

She thought for a moment that he wasn't going to answer. Then he shook himself lightly, like a dog coming out of the water, and rubbed his eyes with his fingers. "Like you said," he muttered, not quite looking at her as he turned and walked across to the door. "I don't think it matters anymore."

"It matters."

"No." He paused with his hand on the door, his back to her, not turning around. "No, it doesn't."

And then, just like that, he was gone.

She didn't know.

Jett wet his lips and swallowed, his heartbeat still erratic. He gave Jody a sidelong glance, half afraid the boy could read his mind. But Jody was slouched in the seat, staring out the truck window, his profile hard with anger.

She didn't know.

It didn't seem possible. And yet . . . damn it, it sounded exactly like something Patterson would do. Even to his own daughter. And, in a nightmarish kind of way, it even made sense.

Patterson's name was being tossed around for the Supreme Court back then. You didn't have to be a rocket scientist to figure out that a pregnant sixteen-year-old daughter—*fifteen,* God help him!—would be a definite liability for a man with political aspirations. Especially if the illegitimate baby she was carrying belonged to a half-breed rodeo rider with a juvenile record and a reputation for being a troublemaker.

So she didn't know.

The reality of it, the *immensity* of it, took his breath away. She actually had no idea that the baby boy she'd given birth to that cold April night a little over fifteen years ago was right here in Burnt River.

Again, he glanced at Jody, his gut tightening.

No one knew. No one but him, Patterson, Kathleen's uncle and Cliff Albright. And Pam, of course. Pam had known.

Jett's belly gave another unpleasant little twist, this time of guilt. After Kathleen had left, he'd started going out with Pam more out of anger than anything else. Then he'd found out about the baby, and things had gone a little crazy for a while. He'd gone after her, eighteen and green as grass, and that was when he'd found out they'd sold the baby—his baby—and had grown up fast.

His memories of those days were still fuzzy. And he never had known all the details, except that the original adoption had fallen through and there had been threats of legal action and counter threats of some kind. He hadn't cared. All he'd cared about was getting his son.

And he had.

With stipulations. Jett's fingers tightened around the steering wheel, and he took a deep breath to ease the knot of anger in his gut.

He'd agreed to the stipulations because there had been no other way, and he would have bartered his very soul if it had been the only way to get Jody. Then he'd married Pam because she loved him too much to care that he only needed a wife to look after his child. She had never stopped loving him, except maybe toward the very end, when his flat refusal to give her a child of her own drove her half wild with anger and grief.

He swallowed again. It had been his stubbornness that had killed her, as certainly as if he'd been at the wheel of the car that day. And his selfishness. If he'd relented and let her have a baby, she would probably be alive now.

But he hadn't wanted another child. Pam had been a good mother, but he'd feared that if she'd had her own baby, Jody would have become the outsider, the half sibling who suddenly didn't quite fit in.

Like *he'd* been, Jett thought bitterly. With absolutely no warning he found himself thinking of that hot August afternoon when he'd been thirteen and had hitchhiked down to Billings to be with his old man. He'd found him shacked up in a trailer park with a blowsy blonde and a couple of golden-haired, blue-eyed kids. Even now, a lifetime later, Jett could remember what it had been like, walking in there and realizing his father had a whole other life he'd never be a part of.

He shook the memories off impatiently. He hadn't thought of his father's betrayal in years, and he had no intention of thinking about it now. He took another deep breath, forcing it past a sudden tightness in his throat, very aware of Jody sitting beside him. He glanced at the boy, then reached across and squeezed his shoulder. "You okay?"

"You didn't have to drag me out of there like some kid." Jody gave him a hostile look. "She was just tryin' to help."

Jett blew his breath out, thinking about it. He'd gone all these years thinking she'd agreed to the adoption. That she'd sold his baby to the highest bidder like a calf at a stock auction. That she was back here now to lay claim to the son she'd abandoned fifteen years ago.

And all she'd been doing was trying to help some kid she'd befriended to get a passing grade or two.

"You could have come to me if you needed help," he muttered.

"And got a lecture on how I was just lazy and needed to *apply* myself more?"

In spite of himself, Jett had to smile. "I never said you were lazy. Bullheaded, maybe, but not lazy."

"That's what she said about *you*."

Again Jett surprised himself with an involuntary smile. "Yeah, she probably would."

"You know her pretty good, huh?"

"Knew." Jett took a deep breath, dispelling the past. "A long time ago." He looked at Jody and smiled again. "Before you were born, Slick. Back with the dinosaurs."

"Not that long ago." He looked at Jett for a long moment, eyes thoughtful. "You were pretty young when I was born."

"Nineteen," Jett lied casually.

"More like eighteen." Jody gave him a half smile. "I ain't so bad in math I can't figure that out."

Jett kept his eyes on the road, trying to keep his voice unconcerned. "Glad to hear it. Now, if we can work on your civics and chemistry, you'll have it made." When Jody didn't reply, he added, "So why all the questions?"

"Nothin'," Jody said absently. "I was just wondering when you knew her, that's all."

"Long before you were around, and long before I married your mother," Jett replied carelessly, praying Jody couldn't hear the tightness in his voice. All of a sudden, things were getting very complicated.

Because the question he didn't want to ask himself, didn't want to even *think* about, kept flickering through the darker reaches of his mind, demanding to be heard. And Jody's seemingly casual questions had only brought it closer to the light.

Was he going to tell Kathleen the truth?

Or just leave well enough alone and let her go back to Baltimore never knowing that the gangly dark-eyed kid she'd befriended in Burnt River was her son?

He didn't sleep well that night. Got up and wandered around at two in the morning, telling himself he was being eleven kinds of fool even worrying about it. It wasn't as though he'd been deliberately hiding the truth from her for all these years.

He'd *thought* she'd given Jody up for adoption fifteen years ago. Had abandoned the son as easily and with as little regret as she'd abandoned the father. So it wasn't as though she'd spent those fifteen years *thinking* about him. Perhaps waking at two in the morning to stare at the ceiling and wonder if he was all right, if he was happy, if she'd done the right thing.

She didn't know, period.

So if she went on not knowing, no harm would be done. It would be easier on all of them. She would go back to Baltimore, he would go back to ranching, and Jody would go back to dreaming of rodeos. And old man Patterson would still be dead and buried, the secret dead and buried right along with him.

Swearing gently at himself, Jett raked his fingers through his hair and wandered aimlessly around the big bedroom, stopping finally by the window. Moonlight poured through the glass and puddled around him, cold as ice. He set both hands on the frame and leaned on his braced arms, staring out at nothing.

He'd been nine weeks old when his mother had walked up the front steps of this same ranch house and handed him over to his grandmother like a bundle of old clothing.

"Here," she'd said. "This belongs to your son." Then she'd turned and walked away without even looking back, and had gotten into a beat-up old pickup truck with North Dakota plates to disappear from his life in a plume of dust and blue exhaust.

His grandmother had talked about it for years. "Just like that," she used to say with a grim shake of her head. "Just dropped the boy off as if he weren't nothin' at all, just some old thing she'd picked up by the side of the road."

Her fierce blue eyes would blaze, and she would touch Jett's head and smile down at him. "Don't know how a mother could do that, just walk away from her boy like that, as though he didn't count for nothing. Even half white, he's her son. And blood's blood, no matter the color of the skin."

He'd never even known her name, Jett thought dispassionately.

He'd sworn that would never happen to a son of his.

And now...hell, it didn't make any difference, he told himself almost angrily. Jody thought Pam was his mother, and that was all that mattered. He knew he'd been loved. Thought he'd been wanted. To tell him otherwise now would just stir up a whole lot of trouble for everyone concerned and wouldn't accomplish a damned thing but a lot of anger and heartache and confusion.

Swearing again, he shoved himself away from the window and rubbed his face with his hands, feeling tired and suddenly very old. Let it be, he advised himself as he turned back toward the bed. Just let it be....

For some reason, nothing went right the next morning. He and Jody argued about some damn silly thing he couldn't even remember later, and the boy wound up storming out of the house to catch the school bus, doors slamming like artillery in his wake. Then Mrs. Wells had gotten on his case about something else, and after he'd gotten that sorted out, he and Angel went head-to-head over the best way to repair a damaged gate on one of the stock corrals.

Finally, about noon, he just gave up. Saddling his buckskin mare, he headed for the hills, wondering why he didn't just sell the Kicking Horse and move to Helena and become a...hell, a ranching consultant or something! He could sit at a desk in a nice office with a view and get paid to tell people what to do. Same job he had now, except the pay would be better and people wouldn't be arguing with him every time he turned around.

He was still thinking about that when Dixie gave a sharp whicker and tossed her head, pulling at the bit. Jett shook off his fantasies about the good life—hell, what did he know about city living, anyway?—and gave his surroundings a startled look.

Cougar Ridge. He hadn't even remembered turning Dixie onto the trail. Below him lay the Kicking Horse, the ranch house and outbuildings the size of dollhouses, and ahead, rising up against the sky in a wild tangle of wolf-toothed rock, the Rocky Mountains in their full splendor. They stood along the edge of the world like a fortress of stone, snow and glacial ice glittering like treasure, the melting ice pack tinseling the walls of rock with waterfalls that looked from here like threads of silver.

Jett shoved his hat onto the back of his head and drew a deep breath of crisp air so heavily perfumed with pine that he could taste the pitch. There was a little valley tucked in behind the ridge, dotted with tamarack and pine, and he urged Dixie down the trail toward Beaver Creek.

She gave a snort, then whickered again, ears pricked forward, and a moment later there was an answering whicker from a clump of trees to his left. A tall bay with a white blaze and stockings came out of the trees, favoring its left foreleg. Dried mud caked its shoulder and side, and clumps of grass and dirt clung to the small stock saddle and stirrup leathers.

Jett dismounted and walked over to it, speaking gently as it gave a snort and tossed its head, spooked and nervous. It wasn't one of the Kicking Horse herd, but it wasn't until he could get close enough to see the brand on its left flank that he realized where it had come from. Two overlapping circles.

The Oaks.

He managed to grab one of the horse's dangling reins before it could move away, then ran his hand down its shoulder and leg. Nothing broken.

And the rider? Jett straightened and looked around. He might have been thrown clear, in which case he was probably already halfway back to The Oaks, on foot and madder than hell. Or he was still out here somewhere, busted up, unconscious, dead...there were a lot of possibilities, few of them pretty.

It didn't take him long to find where it had happened. The trail down to Beaver Creek was steep here, and the ground was all torn up just at the water's edge, the deep hoof marks where the horse had lunged back onto its feet still filling with water. But there was no sign of the rider. Then he found

boot prints on the other side of the creek where the bank was
low and wide and sandy, and followed them south.

When he finally found her at the deep pond just above the
beaver dam, he wasn't even surprised. Nothing else had
gone right this morning. It seemed only fitting that the
footprints he'd been following belonged to the last woman
in the entire world he wanted to see just now.

And here, of all places. Where else but here, where it had
all started?

She was unhurt, from what he could see. Which wasn't
much, considering she was neck-deep in creek water. A fact
that in itself was a mixed blessing, Jett decided virtuously.
Because from the quantity of clothing draped haphazardly
on the bushes along the bank, it was pretty obvious that she
was buck naked.

And suddenly, in spite of everything, he found himself
grinning like some kind of fool. Shoving his hat onto the
back of his head, he just stood there and watched her. If she
spotted him, he was a dead man, but for the life of him, he
couldn't take his eyes off her. She'd set her boots and hat
beside a nearby log, and he could see a small heap of pink
silk beside them. Bra and panties, no doubt.

Just like old times.

Unaware of him, she swam lazily across the pond, then
twisted and dove hard, giving him a tantalizing glimpse of
pale wet skin before she vanished.

Jett swallowed, a sudden rush of memory tightening his
chest. It had been hot that summer. The hottest summer in
fifty-seven years, the old-timers had said. But he barely remembered that. Another heat had consumed him that long,
dry summer, the kind that started low in the belly and
burned bone deep.

Kathleen reached up to smooth her hair back, the water
barely covering her breasts, her wet shoulders and throat
gleaming like satin in the sunlight. Jett's gut knotted,
memories tumbling over each other. A hot Saturday afternoon. Unsaddled horses grazing nearby, tails swishing. The
occasional thump of a shod hoof on grass, the rattle of a bit.

A blanket spread on the grass. Kathleen naked for him for the first time, slender and lithe and as supple as a sun-warmed cat.

The first touch of him against her, man to woman. The look of surprise in her eyes as he pressed her thighs apart and eased himself against her, into her. The first snubbing pressure, not quite pain, but not what she'd expected, either. The tiny frown marring her forehead.

Then he was through and it was over and she made a tiny sound in her throat and arched slightly against him, lips half parted as the not-quite-pain gave way to something else altogether. He'd felt her melt around him, hot silken flesh eager for every touch, every sensation, and they'd damn near set the valley ablaze that afternoon.

Jett wet his lips, realizing that his body had responded to the all-too-vivid memories with a vigor that surprised the hell out of him.

He had to get out of here. Now. He would leave her horse tethered to a tree and hotfoot it home before he did something he would wind up regretting. Because if there was one thing he knew for damn sure, it was that this woman and trouble just sort of went hand in hand.

Then that damn fool horse of hers gave him a nudge between the shoulder blades that nearly sent him sprawling, and by the time he'd caught his balance, grabbing at tree branches and swearing, it was too late.

It took Kathleen a startled moment to even realize someone was there. And even then she couldn't tell who it was. He'd stepped out of the deep shadows under the trees and was standing with his back to the sun, not saying anything, and she felt a jolt of automatic fear. And then, very abruptly, she realized it was Jett.

It sent another jolt through her, not quite fear this time, but something near enough to it to make her stomach tighten. She gave a strong kick that sent her to the far side of the pond, putting as much distance between them as possible.

"If you came up here to harass me again, just forget it!"
Glaring at him, she gave her head a flip to get her hair out
of her eyes, feeling naked and vulnerable and not liking the
sensation one little bit. "I don't know what your problem
is, Kendrick, but I'm tired of you taking it out on me."

"Are you all right?"

"Of course I'm all right. Why shouldn't I be all right?"

"I found your horse. I thought you might be hurt."

It wasn't at all what she'd expected. More anger, more
accusations she didn't understand—*those* she was prepared
for. But not this. It left her with nothing to say. "Oh."
Treading water, she eyed him suspiciously. "Is he all right?"

"A little lame, but nothing a day or two of rest and a pail
of oats won't fix. What happened?"

Kathleen's eyes narrowed slightly. That had to be—what?
Two dozen words? And not a hostile one in the bunch.
"Something spooked him. He shied and lost his footing,
and I landed flat on my back in the mud. Then he bolted
before I could catch him."

Jett hooked his thumbs into the front pockets of his jeans
and wandered down to the edge of the pond, his expression
slightly troubled. There was none of last night's anger there,
none of the suspicion and hostility she was expecting. Just
a quiet thoughtfulness she had no idea how to react to.

"That water must be damn cold."

"It's fine," she lied.

He hunkered down on his heels at the water's edge and
picked a blade of grass, twirling it in his fingers. "I, uh..."
He frowned, not meeting her eyes. "I'm sorry about yesterday. I had no right coming over to your place like that.
Causing a scene."

Kathleen stared at him for a long, mistrustful moment.
"Why are you being almost pleasant, Jett? What's the
catch?"

"No catch. I've been acting like a jerk, that's all."

She wasn't going to argue with *that,* Kathleen decided,
but she wasn't gullible enough to believe this sudden change

in attitude was for real, either. She swam leisurely to the far side of the pond, then halfway back, trying to ignore him.

"I'm apologizing here, in case you hadn't noticed," he rumbled.

"You've got a long way to go yet, mister."

"You're turning blue, Kath." A hint of laughter warmed his mouth. "If I take much more time with all this apologizing, you're going to catch a godawful cold."

"Let me worry about that."

"I said I was sorry, and I meant it. I said a lot of things I shouldn't have said." The smile widened. "Come on, Kath, cut me a little slack here. How many times do you want to hear me say I'm sorry?"

"You can't count that high."

But even as she said it, she felt the anger slipping away. Part of her wanted to stay furious with him, to hold him at a distance so he couldn't hurt her again. But another part didn't want to hold him away at all.

"Come on, Kathy, you're not going to freeze to death just to make a point, are you? Don't you think it's time you got out of there and dried off?"

"And you're offering to help, no doubt."

He looked up at her from under the wide brim of his hat, his gaze filled with unexpected humor. And then he grinned slowly, not saying a word.

Not having to.

But then, he'd never had to. Sixteen years, and that grin was still as lethal as ever. It was about a case of beer and a pickup truck and some time on your hands. It was about parking on a side road on a cold night with the radio turned down low, and steamed-up windows, and deep kisses that turned you inside out. But mostly it was about young love and wildfire sex, and even today, a lifetime later, she could feel that old familiar heat blossom low in her belly.

To her surprise, it made her laugh. "God, you're still bad news! I thought you'd be too old for that sort of thing by now."

"A man's never too old for that sort of thing," he said, the grin widening. It did something to his eyes, something warm and teasing and just a little dangerous.

"Is that so?" She grinned, laughter bubbling up through her. She couldn't believe he was flirting with her! And that she was flirting back. Old times.

His eyes held hers for a heartbeat, glinting with deep mischief; then he just laughed and got to his feet. And slowly, deliberately, started popping open the pearl snaps on his Western-cut flannel shirt.

Chapter 6

"Kendrick, what are you doing?" Still laughing, Kathleen gave her feet a kick and took a couple of backward strokes.

He just grinned and pulled the shirt off, then waded into the shallows and held it up like a bath towel.

Kathleen considered it for a moment. "Close your eyes."

"You never used to be this shy."

"Yeah, well, with age comes wisdom. And the inroads of gravity." She grinned. "Things have moved a little south since those days. So close your eyes or risk going blind."

He gave a snort of laughter and wisely kept his mouth shut. But he did close his eyes. And finally, deciding it was take him up on his offer or risk freezing to death, she waded into the shallows and scampered into the welcoming depths of the shirt.

Jett wrapped it around her like a blanket, laughing again as she started to shiver, teeth clattering like castanets. "Remember now why we never used to go skinny-dippin' in May?"

"Oh, shut up," she managed to get out between chattering teeth. "It was either go s-skinny-dipping or walk home caked head to f-foot with mud."

Jett's big, warm hands were rubbing her back briskly, and Kathleen closed her eyes, trying to ignore the broad, naked chest not four inches from her nose and the warm scent of him, still so familiar after all these years that it made her breathless.

"Come on." He wrapped one muscled arm around her and started wading back to shore. "You could probably use a cup of coffee."

"C-coffee? You've g-got coffee?"

And he did, to Kathleen's delight. A thermosful of a dark, strong brew cut with real cream, still hot enough to burn her tongue. Bundled up in the plaid picnic blanket she'd tied behind her saddle that morning, she cupped the plastic mug between her hands and sipped at the coffee greedily, feeling it start to fight off the chills as she watched Jett light a small fire.

"Warming up?"

Kathleen nodded and handed him the cup. He downed a swallow, then handed it back to her and rummaged through one of his saddlebags until he found the paper bag containing his lunch. "You're in luck, Slick." He took out two stacks of sandwiches wrapped in waxed paper. "Turkey or ham?"

"What is this, Kendrick's Catering?" Kathleen unwrapped one of the bundles and helped herself to a sandwich. Then she pulled her own set of saddlebags nearer. "What'll it be? Brandy pâté with French bread, quiche with tarragon, or—oh, hell!"

Nose wrinkling, Kathleen pulled out a rumpled brown paper bag and looked at it in dismay. "This isn't the lunch I packed! This belongs to one of the kids...oh, man...peanut butter and jelly!" She looked up at Jett and broke into peals of laughter. "I don't believe this! Right now my niece is at play-school trying to choke down quiche, and we're stuck with peanut butter!"

"Quiche?" Jett lifted his eyebrow. "I don't think so."

"Philistine."

"City slicker." He cut off a slice of beef jerky with his pocket knife and tossed it into her lap. "Pâté, cowboy-style."

It was hard to believe they were here like this, bantering over peanut butter and jelly sandwiches as though the intervening sixteen years had never happened. It gave him an odd feeling, looking across and seeing her there.

She looked about sixteen again, wet hair slicked back and not a speck of makeup on. Wrapped in a plaid blanket, she was leaning against a weathered old log, bare legs stretched out in front of her to get the fire's heat, slender ankles crossed.

It was hard keeping his eyes off her. Hard not to think of the fact she was as naked as the day she was born under that blanket and flannel shirt, its tails demurely covering her thighs. Hard not to recall the way she'd felt under the cradling warmth of his hands when she'd first come out of the water. Or the things he'd suddenly found himself thinking. Things he hadn't thought in years...

He tried not to think of them now as he poured the last of the coffee into the cup and handed it to her wordlessly, forcing himself to ignore the little shock he got when his fingers brushed hers. He still didn't know what the hell he was doing here. He should have tethered her horse to a tree and gone the hell home instead of—

"Ready yet to tell me what you're up to?"

He looked at her sharply, realizing uneasily that she'd been watching him all this time. Trying to read his expression, maybe. See something in his eyes. "Meaning?"

Kathleen smiled around the rim of the red plastic cup. "You were ready to take on the whole Patterson clan with your bare hands yesterday. Today you're plying me with hot coffee and that not inconsiderable Kendrick charm." Her smile widened. "It makes me wonder about your motives."

A jolt of guilt went through him, sharp and hot. It was an opening, tailor-made for the truth. All he had to do was tell her. A few words, a handful of truths, and she would know. About her father. About him. Pam. Jody. The whole damn can of worms.

But he just shrugged and leaned forward to toss a handful of wood onto the fire. "Seeing you again brought up a lot of feelings I figured I'd put to rest a long time ago, that's all."

"I guess we both had some stuff to sort through," Kathleen said quietly. "I lay awake half the night thinking about what you said. About how you came looking for me." She smiled at him, feeling suddenly shy. "That meant a lot. Knowing you cared, I mean. Knowing that I *had* meant something to you and hadn't been just a . . . a trophy."

Jett whispered something short and profane and rubbed his forehead with his hand. Then he looked at her finally, his eyes glowing with a deep, healthy anger. "You were never a trophy, Kath. I liked the attention we got, I admit that. Every guy in town had the hots for you, and I got off on knowing you were mine. But it went a hell of a lot deeper. I think we could have had something real if we'd had the chance."

His words sent something warm through her, like a hug on a cold day. "Yesterday you asked me why—if I'd really loved you—I'd gotten *rid* of the baby. Is that what you thought? That I'd had an abortion?"

"Adoption." The skin tightened around his eyes slightly as he stared into the flames. "I thought you'd given him away."

"They wanted me to." Kathleen heard the crisp bite of anger in her own voice and took a deep breath. "Mom and Dad tried to talk me into agreeing to an abortion, and when that didn't work, Dad started talking adoption."

She took another deep breath and looked up to discover that Jett had turned his head to look at her, his dark eyes unreadable. "Just before the baby was due, he came to Baltimore to talk me into signing an adoption agreement. He kept saying how much better it would be for the baby, although I knew he meant how much better it would be for *him.* My uncle is a doctor, and Dad said how he had all these contacts, how easy it would be to find a good adoptive family.''

Jett was listening intently, his expression fierce, as she went on.

''I told him I wasn't agreeing to that, either. That I'd take the baby and run away if I had to, but they weren't taking him away from me.''

''Run where?'' His voice was raspy. ''You were a kid. Where would you have gone? How would you have lived?''

Kathleen shrugged and tossed the rest of the coffee into the flames. ''I have no idea. I had no idea back then, either, I just knew I was keeping my baby—*your* baby.'' She sighed. ''But it doesn't matter now, does it?''

Jett nodded very slowly, looking as though he was thinking about something else all together. ''Do you think about him?''

It surprised her slightly. ''Of course. I'll hear a baby cry, or see a woman pushing a stroller, or I'll be watching TV and a diaper commercial will come on…it never really goes away. But it's not so much grief anymore. It's just a sadness now. For him. For the life he missed. Like when I saw Jody for the first time.''

Jett's face went suddenly blank. Careful, almost. ''Jody?''

She gave him a rough smile. ''I'll admit it was a shock, actually seeing him. I knew you and Pam had a son, but I hadn't realized he was only a few months younger than *our* son would have been if he'd lived. It…'' She had to laugh quietly. ''I don't know why I was so surprised. You never did have any restraint—that was part of your charm, if I remember.''

Jett flushed and looked away, jaw going hard and stubborn.

''Sorry,'' she murmured. ''That was a cheap shot.'' He didn't indicate he'd even heard her, and Kathleen reached out with one bare foot and nudged his knee. ''Hey. I just said I was sorry.''

"I never touched her while I was with you," he said finally, looking at a twig he was twirling between his fingers instead of at her. "Even if you don't believe anything else, I want you to believe that."

She wanted to say something to him, Kathleen thought. About how much it meant to hear him say that. About so many things. But he'd put a wall up suddenly, as though unsettled by the unexpected closeness between them.

He draped his forearm across his knee, the twig between his teeth. Staring now into the fire. Anywhere but at her.

"My father played us against each other sixteen years ago," she said quietly. "He lied to both of us and got exactly what he wanted. He was good at that."

Jett didn't say anything, still toying with that damned twig like it was something important. She could read the anger in the tautness of his wide shoulders, the tension in his jaw as he bit down across the end of the twig and spat it into the fire.

"He gave you money, didn't he? To leave Burnt River. To leave . . . me."

He gave her a startled glance, then looked away again, telling Kathleen all she needed to know. It had been a wild guess, right off the top of her head, with no reason to think it might be true beyond a chilling awareness of how her father's mind worked. "That's why you married Pam and moved to Arizona. Because my father gave you the money for a new start."

"Something like that," he muttered finally. Then he swore dully and sat up, raking his fingers through his hair. Still not meeting her eyes. "I'd just turned nineteen, I had a baby, a wife . . . hell, yes, I took his money. Burnt River meant nothing but grief to me back then. I got a job in Arizona with a stock contractor and put a down payment on a small spread of my own and—" He swore again and gave his head a weary shake. "Hell, Kathy, it's all old news now."

Kathleen nodded slowly, wondering why she felt so little anger at his admission of yet another betrayal. She found herself thinking instead of what it must have been like for him back then. He'd been cocky and self-assured, but in many ways—in crucial ways—still no more than a boy. He would have been no match for her father.

"Did you love her?" The question, never far from her thoughts, slipped out before she could catch it.

Again Jett gave her a startled look. And again she saw a flicker of guilt in his eyes before he looked away again.

"Of course you did," she said quickly. "I'm sorry. That was a stupid—"

"I tried." The words sounded torn from him. "I swear to God, I did that much. It was the least I could do."

"Jett, this isn't any of my business. You don't have to—"

"I thought you'd used me and walked away. I just wanted to get away from Burnt River and you and your old man and start over. Love was the last thing on my mind."

"I'm glad you did," she said softly. "Start over, I mean. I hope you and Pam were happy. And I meant what I said the other day about being sorry for your loss. And . . . the other thing I said." She flushed, unable to meet his eyes. "About how she deserved better. If Jody's anything to go by, you two had a good, solid marriage. She was very lucky."

Jett lifted his head slowly to look at her, his expression oddly bleak. "She was a good mother."

"It shows." She smiled. "He's a great kid."

Jett just nodded, thoughts in turmoil, only half listening. Thinking, instead, about Pam. About what she'd been like, once. Before the anger, the resentment. The drinking. She'd been eighteen and in love, and it had taken no effort at all to talk her into marrying him.

Oh, he'd been honest with her. Up to a point, anyway. He'd told her right up front about Jody. About how he needed a wife to make getting custody easier. She'd loved the idea at first, helping him beat old man Patterson and Kathleen at their own game. But he hadn't told her all of it. He'd never told her that he didn't love her. . . .

"I'd give you a penny for them," a quiet voice said beside him, "but I have an idea I might wish I hadn't."

Jett glanced up and discovered that Kathleen was on her feet, the blanket draped loosely around her, her expression pensive as she looked down at him.

Shaking off the past, he just grinned lazily and reached up to tug on the shirttail dangling to just above her knee. "I've got a thought or two you can have free."

She tried not to laugh—he could see her fighting it. But finally she gave up and laughed softly. "You always did make every word you said sound like an invitation to bed."

This time it was Jett who laughed. He got to his feet, rising above her so she had to tip her head to look up at him, and he found himself thinking she was still one of the most gorgeous things he'd ever set eyes on. More so now. Sixteen years ago, she'd been a girl—pretty and sexy as hell, but still a girl. But the beauty looking back at him now had a woman's eyes and a woman's smile, and the body under that flannel shirt was a woman's body.

And again it made him think things he hadn't thought for a long, long while.

"Depends who I'm talkin' to," he told her with a grin.

"You're a liar. Flirting's like breathing with you."

Jett shrugged, letting his smile fade. "Once, maybe."

Kathleen didn't say anything. She looked up at him thoughtfully, her gaze taking in his features one by one. "We had some good times back then, Jett. Those few months with you that summer were some of the happiest of my life. I'm glad I've had the chance to tell you that."

He should be saying something, Jett thought distractedly. But for the life of him, he couldn't think of what. Except how he suddenly wanted to touch her again. How easy it would be to take a half step forward and lower his mouth to hers and—

He caught the thought right there, but not before Kathleen had seen at least some of it in his eyes. A hint of pink washed across her cheeks—so faint he never would have noticed it if he didn't know her so well—and she moved away, letting her gaze slide from his, a troubled little frown wedged between her eyes.

"If you'll do the gentlemanly thing and turn your back for a minute, I'll get dressed," she said all in a rush. "I imagine you want your shirt back."

Not half as badly as he wanted what was *in* it, Jett found himself thinking with unexpected savagery. But he kept his mouth firmly shut and turned his back on her, trying to get his unruly thoughts corralled. Damn it, what did he think he was doing? She wasn't his to touch anymore. Wasn't his to kiss. Or even *think* about kissing.

Teeth gritted, he tried to remember what he'd been doing before finding her horse this afternoon. Calves, that was it. He'd been looking for a couple of stray calves. Behind him, the blanket fell to the ground. He could hear the click of the snaps on his shirt part under her fingers and tried, desperately, to ignore it.

Ranching, that was what he was supposed to be thinking about. Cattle. They had to get the last of the herd moved up to the summer range, for one thing. There was the whisper of silk on skin behind him, and he closed his eyes, telling himself flatly that it was his imagination.

Except imagination was worse than reality. In his mind he could see her sliding those pink silky briefs up one long slender leg, then the other. Could see her smooth them over her hips, settling lace around a waist he'd once been able to span with both hands.

He opened his eyes and took a deep breath. This was crazy. Sure, it had been a long time since he'd been with a woman. But that didn't explain why he was standing here thinking these kinds of things. Thinking of her sliding her bra straps up over her arms and those smooth white shoulders... remembering what it had been like taking it *off* her.

She used to smile at him and arch her back, offering herself to him, and he remembered what it had been like to cup her firm little breasts in his hands and hear her breath catch. Her nipples were a rich rose color and they would be slightly swollen by then, and he used to lower his mouth and cap-

...ween his lips like something sweet, sucking it ...ile it hardened in his mouth. And then she would ...er fingers into his long hair and press his mouth against ...r, and he would hear her heart fluttering in her chest like a bird's wing and that breathy catch in her throat as she whispered his name.

But that would be only a prelude to what he'd really wanted. The true treasure lay farther south, and he used to tip her gently back and peel her jeans down and nuzzle the downy skin on her belly. And then lower, finding that wonderful pouty little softness at the juncture of her thighs, tantalizingly sweet under the thin, silky fabric of her briefs. He used to kiss her there and tease her with his tongue, running the tip of it along the elastic legs of her briefs, down the moist cleft in the middle, half drunk on the tastes and scents and sounds of her.

He would tease her like that for as long as either of them could take it, then he'd reach up and slide her briefs right off and finish what he'd started, having discovered that it was better for her like that.

Better for him, too, to be honest. Because once he'd pleasured her, he didn't have to try so damn hard to hold on. He would keep at it until she cried out in startled satisfaction and arched fiercely against him, fingers tangling in his hair. And then he would ease himself up and between her thighs and sink down into the honied heat of her with a groan of raw pleasure, and the whole world would just come to a shuddering stop while he—

"Here. And thanks."

Silken blond hair swirled near enough to brush his shoulder, and the scent of her filled his nostrils, and then she was right *there,* right in front of him, smiling up into his eyes. She held up his shirt, and Jett took it automatically, feeling dazed and stupefied, as though he'd been in the sun too long.

He pulled on the shirt without even thinking, wishing he hadn't the instant the flannel hit his skin. It was warm with the heat of her, and it wrapped around his ribs as intimately as the woman herself. The air was suddenly scented with her, so familiar it left him feeling hollowed out and aching with a wanting he hadn't felt in years. Had thought he'd put behind him so long ago that it didn't even count anymore.

"Come on," Kathleen said beside him suddenly, her arms full of blankets and gear. "I'll help you saddle the horses."

Jett didn't say a word the entire time they saddled the two horses and collected their things. Kathleen glanced at him now and again, but he wouldn't look at her, his expression like a thundercloud, although she couldn't for the life of her figure out what she'd done.

He moved with smooth economy, hat pulled low so she couldn't see his face clearly, shirt still unbuttoned and hanging loose over his jeans. It left his chest and muscle-corded belly bare, and she was annoyed at how badly that glimpse of smooth, golden flesh distracted her.

Sex, that was all it was, she told herself ferociously. They hadn't been able to keep their hands off each other sixteen years ago, so it made sense that her mind would keep drifting in that direction when he was around.

"Don't bother making that cinch too tight." A sun-browned arm reached past her, and Jett checked the saddle. "You can't ride him when he's lame like this. I'll take you back."

"I can walk." She said it more impatiently than she'd intended, unnerved by how close he was standing. The heat from his skin pressed against her back like a caress, and she was finding it suddenly difficult to breathe properly, which didn't make a *bit* of sense.

"It's ten miles, Kathy," he said, and laughter ran through the words. "You scared of me after all this time or something?"

"I can't think of any reason I should be." Annoyed by her own silly reactions, wanting to prove to herself that she wasn't lying, she turned to face him almost defiantly. Trapped between man and horse, she gave her tangled damp hair a toss to get it off her face and looked up into his dark eyes. "Can you?"

He didn't say anything, just standing there so close to her that she could see the rise and fall of his chest, the faint line of a healing cut across his cheekbone, the full swell of his lower lip. She swore she could hear the thump of his heart, but maybe it was her own, the sound as loud as the beating of ancient drums.

"Oh, yeah," he said then, so softly it was little more than a whisper. "Oh, yeah, I can think of a reason or two...."

He'd no more intended to touch her than fly, but Jett found himself reaching for her without conscious thought. Found himself slipping his arms loosely around her and pulling her closer and looking down into those summer-sky eyes and wondering where in the hell the past sixteen years had gone.

She stared up at him, full red lips parted slightly, and he could feel the unsteady beat of his heart. And against his chest, the beat of another, faster, wilder, as familiar as his own.

Under the surprise in those blue eyes was something else now: an awareness that something was happening, *had* happened, *could* happen. That awareness was filled with memories and warmth and a kind of breath-held anticipation, as though she had no idea what was going to happen next and wasn't sure whether she should wait to find out or not.

He didn't know, either. So he did the first thing that came to mind and dropped his mouth gently over hers.

It surprised him nearly as badly as it surprised her. But after a moment he forgot all his good intentions and his doubts and even his guilt, and started to enjoy the process. And Kathleen must have, too, because after the first little indrawn squeak of surprise, she sort of melted against him and parted her lips and kissed him back with the same enthusiasm.

Jett pulled his mouth from hers after a leisurely while and smiled down at her. "Welcome home."

Looking a little dazed, she stepped back unsteadily. "Thank you." She drew a deep breath, as though testing her own reactions. "I think."

"You didn't like it."

"Oh, I didn't say that." Laughter warmed her mouth, but she refused to give in to it, looking up at him very seriously instead. "I'm not sure you should have done that."

"It seemed like the right thing to do."

"Did it?" Another deep breath.

She ran the tip of her tongue across her upper lip, and he watched the gesture avidly, gut tightening. "Mmm." Grinning, he pulled her against him again. "Seems like the right thing to do again, in fact."

The thought occurred to Kathleen in that instant before Jett's lips met hers again that it might be a good idea to push him away and tell him to go straight to hell if he thought he could treat her like a leper for days on end and then, with no warning at all, start kissing her as though it was going out of style.

But somehow the words got all muddled up between thinking them and actually saying them and then he was kissing her again and by then it was too late, anyway.

Besides, it wasn't all that unpleasant, being kissed by Jett Kendrick again.

One thing was certain: he hadn't forgotten how.

His tongue moved against hers lazily, and she just relaxed into the experience, telling herself that they were adults now, for heaven's sake, and one little kiss couldn't hurt. Trying to ignore the distinctly disturbing thoughts that kept pushing into her mind. Thoughts about what it would be like to make love with him again. Of what his skin would feel like against hers after all this time. Of what they would be like now, all grown up, with time and experience on their side....

Jett groaned softly into her throat, and she murmured something in reply as he caressed her back with one strong hand, pressing her against him. She could feel the play in his thigh muscles as he shifted his weight in the loose sand, and she moved slightly to keep her own balance. She felt his belly tighten as she moved against him. Felt the subtle yet unmistakable stirring of his body in response to her. Felt her own stomach quiver in anticipation...

Pulling her mouth from his, she clung to him and tried to catch her breath so she could tell him that this was all very nice, but that they had to stop now. He was nuzzling the side of her throat, his mouth warm on her skin, and she had the sudden insane realization that if she didn't stop it now, she wasn't going to stop it at all.

"I—I have a feeling..." She closed her eyes and fought to make sense of what was happening, thoughts still scattered to the four winds.

"I've got one or two of those myself," he murmured against her ear. "Funny how that happens, isn't it?"

In spite of herself, Kathleen had to laugh. "I'm serious!"

"So am I. C'mere and I'll show you *how* serious."

But to her relief, he lifted his warmly questing mouth from her ear and loosened his embrace, grinning down at her. "Like old times, huh?"

"Too much like old times," she said unsteadily. "This is crazy. We haven't seen each other in sixteen years and—"

"It doesn't feel like sixteen years," he said softly, his eyes holding her with electric intensity. "Feels like only hours ago that I made love to you for the first time right over there under those trees."

"I don't think we should talk about that," she said a trifle desperately.

"Like I said before, you never used to be this shy."

"I was too young to know better."

"Fifteen." He gave his head a wondering shake. "Just a kid."

"We were both just kids."

"But we're not kids now," he heard himself say softly. And then, not allowing himself time to think about it, he lowered his head and settled his mouth over hers with lazy enjoyment.

It didn't seem to surprise her. Her lips parted with no hesitation at all, and she kissed him back as though she meant it.

It wasn't a kiss for old times, or stray sparks from years ago, or even a kiss given out of curiosity just to see what it would be like. This was a grown-up, enjoying-every-minute-of-it, done-because-it-feels-good kind of kiss, slow and lazy and full of enough sexual energy to light up a small city.

And when he finally pulled his mouth from hers and looked down into her eyes, she just looked back at him, not saying a word.

"There's a barn dance over in Indian Springs night after next. I'll pick you up about seven."

"Jett..." Frowning, she ran her fingers lightly through his hair. "This has been nice, being here with you today. But..." The frown deepened.

"It's just a dance."

"Like that movie and hamburger sixteen years ago was just a movie and hamburger." But she was laughing as she said it, her eyes alight with mischief.

He had to smile. "I'd be a liar if I said there haven't been a couple of times today when I've wondered what it would be like to get you into bed again. But that's not why I'm asking you to the dance."

She was insane if she even *thought* about it, Kathleen told herself very deliberately. Absolutely, certifiably insane. So she formed the word *no* very clearly in her mind, opened her mouth, and promptly heard herself say, "I'd love to."

They headed back to The Oaks a few minutes later, riding double on Jett's big, loose-gaited buckskin and leading Kathleen's horse. They talked quietly, of old times mainly, laughing over this memory or that one, trying to remember details gone fuzzy with time.

He hadn't bothered buttoning his shirt, and the heat from his bare chest and belly soaked into her, and she could feel the slow, steady thump of his heart against her back, the warmth of his breath against her ear, her throat. His hand had settled warmly on her ribs, fingers splayed, a possessive touch she doubted he was even fully aware of, the angle of his thumb and finger almost but not quite cupping her breast.

She thought of moving it at one point and even put her hand on his to slide it down a little, but then he said something, and she laughed, and a few minutes later she realized she didn't mind the intimacy of his touch at all.

She was still contemplating this—what it meant, what she *wanted* it to mean—an hour or so later as she brushed the bay thoroughly, then put him into a box stall with fresh water and a pail of oats.

Today was going to complicate things. If she decided to stay in Burnt River, would she be doing it for the right reasons—or because some small part of her was in love with Jett?

Or thought it was in love with him. In spite of herself, Kathleen had to grin. There was a very good possibility that what she was feeling was nothing more complicated than lust. Hormones and curiosity: a deadly combination, even at her age.

She was still grinning as she pulled open the door and stepped into the big mudroom. Dropping onto the built-in bench along one wall, she started pulling her boots off, vaguely aware of voices drifting through the half-open kitchen door.

It was only when one of them rose in anger that she realized Gord and Sherry were arguing. Wincing, she sat there for a moment, boot in hand, torn between going back outside and pretending she'd never come in, or dropping the boot to let them know she was there.

And then she heard her own name and realized they were arguing about her. Cheeks burning—not knowing what they were saying and not *wanting* to know—she set the boot down gingerly.

"I am telling you, Gordon, I stood right here in this kitchen and saw him with my own two eyes," Sherry was saying furiously. "I'm not imagining things! If you don't ask his father about it, I will!"

"I don't want you going anywhere near Jett Kendrick," Gordon replied just as angrily. "The man's insane! He came into my office yesterday looking for Jody, and started ranting and raving some crazy stuff that didn't even make sense. If someone hadn't come in just then, I don't know what he might have done."

"Gordon, I know what I saw!"

"What you're saying is flat-out impossible, but I'll look into it," Gordon muttered, sounding none too happy about it.

"Nothing is impossible where your father was concerned. If I'm right, it's going to devastate Kathy. And Kendrick should go to jail for... for something!"

Kathleen winced again. So Sherry had figured it out. When she'd seen Jody yesterday, she'd been clearly startled at how old he was and had obviously concluded that Pam must have gotten pregnant at almost the same time as Kathleen. For Jett's sake, she should explain the whole thing to Sherry—how her father had bought Jett off, how Jett had taken up with Pam out of hurt and anger only days after Kathleen had left.

But there was no way to do that without also admitting she'd been standing out there eavesdropping.

Tiptoeing across to the outside door—trying desperately to wade through the clutter of toys and coats and boots without tripping—Kathleen stepped through onto the back porch. Then she came back inside, making plenty of noise this time.

The voices in the kitchen stopped abruptly. Kathleen picked up the boot she'd already pulled off and dropped it loudly, then started pulling the other one off.

"Kathleen?" Sherry's voice, still tight with anger.

"Yeah," Kathleen called carelessly. "Sorry I was gone so long. I ran into a little problem." Planting a smile on her mouth, she walked through into the kitchen, pretending not to see the guilty glance that passed between Sherry and her brother.

Sherry's eyes widened as she took in Kathleen's wrinkled clothes and damp, tangled hair. "Good golly! Are you all right?"

"That tangle-footed bay of Dad's dumped me in Beaver Creek, but I'm okay."

"Are you sure? I could run you in to Doc Jones just to—"

"I'm fine," Kathleen assured her with a laugh. "I'll be as good as new once I shower and get into some clean clothes. Then I think I'll, uh, go into town. Is there a... Uh, anywhere in town I can buy something suitable for a barn dance?"

"A *barn* dance?" Sherry blinked in surprise. "Who are you—that is...yes. Brenton's Ladies' Wear has some nice things."

Kathleen had to smile. "Jett. I'm going to a dance in Indian Springs with Jett the day after tomorrow."

Sherry's expression of astonishment was almost comical.

"It surprised the hell out of me, too," Kathleen admitted ruefully.

"He didn't seem to be in any mood to take you dancing when I saw him yesterday," Gordon said quietly.

"We, uh, talked." That wasn't all she and Jett had been doing, but Gord didn't need to know everything.

"Kathy...."

He looked so worried that Kathleen had to laugh. "Gord, I know what I'm doing. Trust me." And she prayed, as she turned to go upstairs, that she was telling the truth.

Chapter 7

"Kathleen Patterson?" Jody sounded stunned. "You're going out with Kathleen *Patterson?*"

Jett eyed his own reflection in the small bathroom mirror, wondering why the hell he felt so nervous. "So?"

"You mean, like a *date?*"

The word held such astonishment that Jett looked at his son impatiently. "You got a problem with that?"

Jody shrugged and shoved his good hand into the pocket of his jeans, trying not to grin. He'd been hovering around the bathroom door like a maiden aunt for the past five minutes and showed no sign of leaving anytime soon. "Well, no, I guess not." The grin widened. "But ain't you kinda old for that sorta thing?"

"Old?" Jett's voice made the mirror vibrate.

"Well, you know. I mean…I can't remember the last time you had a date."

Jett just gave a noncommittal grunt and straightened his shirt collar for the third or fourth time.

"So, where are you takin' her? A movie or something?"

Jett glared at the recalcitrant collar, wondering if he should change shirts. "A dance. Over in Indian Springs." He glanced at Jody, then back at his own reflection, wishing he'd thought to get a haircut while he'd been in town. "Guess you'll be thinking about dances yourself one of these days," he said casually.

Jody shrugged, as though the thought didn't appeal one way or another.

"You, uh, got a special girl or anything yet?"

Jody gave another spectacularly offhand shrug, kicking at the floor. "Nah. Not really."

Oh, boy. Jett took a deep breath. "You, uh, remember that talk we had last year?"

"Oh, jeez," Jody groaned, flushing with embarrassment. "Not the sex thing again! Dad, I know all that stuff, okay?"

"Yeah, I know you *know* it," Jett growled. "Just *knowing* isn't enough. You think you're cool and in control, and then one day you're with a girl you like a whole lot and you start feeling things, and pretty soon you're kissin', and before you know it, that's all she wrote."

"Jeez," Jody groaned softly, shoulders hunched, head tucked down so low that all Jett could see were the tops of his ears, glowing bright red.

Jett took a deep breath. Fifteen. Hard to believe Jody was fifteen already, standing as tall as a man. Last year, the only things on his mind had been horses and rodeo. And now, suddenly, he was thinking about going to dances. Next would come his first pickup truck. Then his first steady girl. Then . . .

"Stay right here." Stepping by Jody, Jett headed down the corridor to the big master bedroom at the back of the house. He pulled open the top drawer of his dresser and took out the small box of condoms he'd put there a few months ago for another reason entirely, then walked back to the bathroom.

Jody took one horrified look at the box and started to back away, ears crimson. "Oh, man!"

"I'm going to put them here." Jett opened the medicine cabinet door and set the box on the middle shelf. "I'm not going to count them or keep track. But I want you to *use* them, understand?"

"But I'm not even—" Jody flushed again, looking as though he wished the floor would swallow him whole. "I mean, I ain't—"

"You will," Jett said flatly.

Jody looked so miserable that Jett nearly smiled. "Look," he said more gently, "I'd as soon you waited a few years. Hell, I'd as soon you waited until you're *married*. But things happen, Jody. I want you to be careful, is all."

"Yeah, yeah," Jody muttered, starting to turn away. "I gotta go before—"

"This isn't a joke, damn it." Jett reached out and caught Jody's arm, pulling him around. "Life's tough enough without havin' a kid before you've even grown up properly yourself."

"Like you did, you mean?" Jody's face was dark with sudden resentment. "That's what you're gettin' at, ain't it? That you don't want me making the same mistake *you* made."

Jett went very still. Then, not loosening his grip on Jody's arm, he said with quiet steel, "You were never a mistake, Jody."

"No?" Jody pulled his arm free. "That's why you quit rodeo, ain't it? Everybody keeps sayin' how good you were, how nothing was going to stop you. And then you just up and quit and never rode again. It was because of me, wasn't it? Because you had a kid to take care of."

Very carefully, Jett drew a deep breath. "Partly."

Something bleak crossed Jody's face. Jett swore under his breath and scrubbed his fingers through his hair. "Look, Jody," he said quietly, "I'm not saying things weren't hard. It would have been easier on all of us—you included—if your mother and I hadn't . . . if we'd waited. I was eighteen and green as grass and never had a thought in my head that wasn't about horses or girls. Then one day I had a son, and things got real in a hurry. I just want you to have some options, that's all.''

"Grandpa was only seventeen when you were born." Jody's eyes were filled with defiance. "*He* didn't quit rodeo."

"And he was never any damn good as a father, either," Jett said bitterly. "I lived here with his mom and dad while he went off ridin' rodeo, and I used to see him maybe twice a year, if he was in the neighborhood. Now and again I'd get a birthday card, but mostly I got nothing. You're damn right I quit rodeo when you were born—no kid of mine was going to grow up with no real home or family."

Jett bit the words off, breathing quickly. Remembering standing in a book-filled room up at The Oaks with Cliff Albright at his side, telling Cliff and Patterson and God Himself that nothing short of a bullet was going to stop him from getting custody of his son. And it hadn't. Not threats from Patterson, not pleas for common sense from Albright, not even the siren lure of the rodeo.

He realized that Jody was looking at him and forced himself to relax, managing a rough laugh. "Hey, I'm just saying that life's a lot easier when *you're* making the choices."

Jody nodded, not saying anything, but looking subdued and thoughtful. He turned to leave, then paused and gave Jett a sly look. "Maybe you should hang on to a couple of those things yourself. That Kathleen Patterson's a mighty pretty lady, and you're lookin' pretty irresistible yourself tonight, with that new shirt and all that cologne you're wearin' and all."

He turned and headed down the corridor, chuckling to himself, and Jett eyed the box on the medicine cabinet shelf thoughtfully.

"Kinda like old times, huh?" Jett paid for the beer and took the can the bartender handed him with a nod of thanks. He tore the tab off, then tipped it up and took two long swallows, throat muscles rippling, his coppery skin sheened lightly with sweat. Grinning, he wiped his mouth with the back of his hand and handed the can to Kathleen. "Having a good time?"

Kathleen nodded and took a grateful sip of the icy beer, still out of breath from a fast Texas two-step. The band had gone straight into a hard-driving boogie that was rattling dust from the rafters, and she grinned, gazing around the huge community hall.

It had been an old barn once, and little had been done to change its character. The decor was unabashedly Western, from the bales of straw piled around to the saddles and ropes hanging from the walls and peeled pine posts, and there was even a mechanical bull set up in one corner. It was surrounded by a mob of boisterous young men in jeans and denim shirts, all shouting encouragement to the unfortunate kid being flung around like a rag doll to howls of laughter from his compatriots.

"Going to give it a try?" Kathleen grinned up at Jett.

"You crazy?" He took another deep swallow of beer. "This tired old body ain't up to that kind of abuse anymore."

Kathleen pinched his ribs lightly, feeling nothing but muscle and bone, honed lean with hard work. "This tired old body looks pretty good to me."

Jett gave her a look of mock surprise. "You flirtin' with me, Miss Patterson?"

Kathleen had to laugh. "Habit. I always did have a hard time keeping my hands off you."

"Talk like that could get a girl into all sorts of trouble."

"Oh, I think I can handle it."

Jett gave a gust of laughter and draped his arm loosely across her shoulders, tugging her closer. "Honey, feel free to handle whatever catches your fancy."

"That goes past flirting into outright solicitation."

"I love it when you talk dirty."

Laughing quietly, Kathleen relaxed into the curve of his arm and watched the crowd ebb and flow around them, happier than she'd been in too long to remember. The place was packed, the dance floor a mass of dizzying colors that swirled and shifted in time to the music blasting out of the big speakers on either side of the raised stage. The band was good, a local group that had a little something to please everyone, from rockabilly to soft rock to hard-core country, with a little old-fashioned fiddle and banjo picking tossed in for good measure.

Those people not dancing were sitting on straw bales or at tables, shouting themselves hoarse over the music. Kathleen recognized a few people and smiled a greeting now and again when someone caught her eye. It seemed strange, being here. Stranger still being here with Jett. Out of time, almost. Like a dream that was half now and half then, not quite real.

She glanced up at him to reassure herself that it *was* real.

He grinned easily, as though reading her mind. "Get to many barn dances in Baltimore?"

"Oh, sure." She grinned back. "If we were in Baltimore right now, you'd be in black tie and we'd be drinking expensive wine and making small talk with eight-hundred-dollar-an-hour attorneys and their mistresses."

"Sounds boring as hell."

"It was." *Was.* Interesting choice of tense, Kathleen thought. Did that mean she'd made up her mind but just hadn't admitted it to herself yet?

"Kathleen? Kathleen *Patterson?*"

The voice came from somewhere out of the music and laughter surrounding them, and Kathleen looked around. A tall, good-looking man with nice shoulders and a mop of sandy-brown hair was weaving his way through the crowd toward them, grinning with delight.

"Who the hell is *this* guy?" Jett muttered, his expression thunderous.

"I have no idea, but he's awful cute."

All she got in reply was a low growl, and she had to bite her lip to keep from laughing out loud as the newcomer got close enough to see who she was with. He paused in midstride, smile faltering as his gaze flickered to Jett, then back to Kathleen.

"Be gentle with him," she murmured to Jett. Then she let her smile widen welcomingly. "Hi! It's nice to see you again."

The man's grin clicked confidently back into place, and he shoved his hand toward her. "I heard you were back in town, but I didn't believe it! What's it been? Fifteen years?"

"About that." Kathleen shook his hand, frantically rummaging through her memories for a name. Glasses. He wore heavy glasses back then. And acne. Ken Mitchell? Kathleen blinked in surprise. "How are you, Ken? You're looking great!"

He gave an aw-shucks grin and shoved his hands into his pockets, doing everything but scuffing at the dirt with his toe. "Yeah, well, I started working out and got contacts and—" He blushed suddenly, as though aware he was babbling. "If, um . . . if you're going to be in town for a while, maybe we—"

"She's going to be busy," Jett interrupted impatiently. "Nice talkin' to you." He slipped a proprietorial arm around Kathleen's waist and swung her out onto the dance floor.

"For heaven's sake," Kathleen protested with a sputter of laughter. "The poor man was only trying to—"

"I know what he was tryin' to do," Jett growled, spinning her into his arms expertly. "He was tryin' to steal my woman."

My woman. There was something about the words, or maybe just the possessive little growl in his voice as he said them, that sent a tiny shiver down Kathleen's spine. She laughed softly, trying to ignore it. "Competition got you jumpy, Sundance?"

"Hell, no." He laughed close to her ear, the warmth of his breath making her giddy. "None of 'em has a chance while I'm in the picture."

"Oh?" She arched one eyebrow and looked up at him, still laughing. "You sure about that?"

Jett's smile was slow and lazy, and his gaze held hers for a long heartbeat. "Dead sure," he murmured, his breath caressing her mouth.

And then he tightened his arm around her and spun them out among the dancers, and it was too late to tell him he was wrong.

The music was something fast and hard-driving, and Kathleen caught the beat instinctively, the hem of her flounced denim skirt swirling at mid-thigh as Jett spun her around expertly. Then he pulled her close against him again, teeth glinting in an easy grin as they moved with the surge and flow of the other dancers.

It was exhilarating and magical, like being caught up in a kaleidoscope, the beat of the music coming up through the plank floor and reverberating through her entire body. Laughing faces swirled around them in a mélange of denim and fringe and Navaho prints, and Kathleen laughed again, joy bubbling up through her like fine champagne.

"Jett, you old hound dog," some man shouted at them, swinging his redheaded partner in close. "It's been a long time, old buddy!" He looked at Kathleen and winked. "Glad to see he's still got some life in him."

The redhead glared at the man as they swung away again. Kathleen could see her say something to him, and he gave Kathleen a startled look, obviously not having recognized her.

It made her smile. People had been giving her curious glances all evening, some looking mildly amused at seeing her with Jett, others registering outright surprise as word spread that Judge Nelson Patterson's daughter was back.

"People are going to start talking about us," she said, breathless with laughter.

"People started talking about us the minute I walked through that door with you on my arm." He pulled her tight against him and grinned down at her. "Just like old times."

"Except this time you don't have to worry that someone's called Dad and you're going to take me home and find him waiting for us with a deputy and a twelve-gauge pump action."

"Who said I was planning on taking you home?"

There was something in his eyes—something hot and male and more than a little dangerous—that made Kathleen's heart do a somersault. "Aren't you moving a little fast, Sundance?"

Jett's dark gaze held hers, glittering slightly. "If I was moving fast," he said in a husky undertone that made her toes curl, "I'd already have you in the truck on some back road, so deep inside you it'd take us a week just to catch our breath."

Kathleen's knees went weak, and she closed her eyes, having trouble catching her breath right there. "Jett, this is . . . crazy. What are we doing?"

"What I've wanted to do every day for the past sixteen years," Jett growled, not even knowing he was thinking it until he heard the words tumble out of his own mouth.

In truth, he didn't have the damnedest idea what he was doing. But it had been like that with her the first time, too. No time for thought, for reason, for playing it safe. He'd taken one look at her and known he wanted her. And it was no different this time.

He could feel her moist breath curling under his collar and around his throat, and he could imagine her mouth against him, kissing, teasing, the delicate touch of her tongue. Could feel the soft pressure of her breasts against his chest and knew exactly and vividly what it would be like to have them spill into his hands, soft and velvet-tipped. Could remember every detail of what it had been like making love with her, every whisper and sigh and indrawn breath. Could almost feel the silken heat of her and taste the perfumed nectar of her skin. . . .

Not unexpectedly, his body responded as enthusiastically as it always had, and Jett groaned, having to laugh. "Things are getting a little out of hand, darlin'."

She was laughing, too, thank heaven, her eyes sparkling with mischief. "What were you saying about it being like old times?"

Jett tugged her a little closer. Or tried to. She pulled back slightly, holding him firmly at bay, and he grinned. "Shy?"

"Just not the pushover I used to be."

"Sixteen years ago I'd have taken that as a challenge."

"Sixteen years ago, it was."

"And now?" Jett let his hand slide down Kathleen's back so his fingers rested lightly on the upper swell of her bottom. Gently, ever so gently, he pressed her closer to him. And slowly, ever so slowly, she responded.

She looked up at him from under her lashes. "I'll take it under deliberation."

"You're givin' me some seriously bad thoughts here, lady."

"So what else is new?"

The music changed into something slow and romantic without so much as missing a beat, and Kathleen smiled, letting herself relax into the familiar warmth of Jett's embrace. He'd always been a good dancer, moving with a natural grace and rhythm she'd found irresistible, and it was no different tonight. Someone had dimmed the lights, and Jett smiled down at her, saying nothing, then dropped both arms around her and pulled her close, moving slowly to the music, his cheek against her hair.

Kathleen slipped both arms around his neck, breathing in the faint, spicy scent of his after-shave and loving the silken feel of his cleanly shaven cheek, the warmth of his body moving against hers, the undemanding intimacy of his hands on her lower back. It had been a long time, she thought drowsily. A long time indeed . . .

"You're still one of the best dancers around," she murmured.

"Rusty as hell." He nuzzled her ear. "Couldn't tell you the last time I've gone dancin'."

"Me, neither. For fun, anyway. There was a charity ball last year, but it was work. Half the people there were clients, or people we were wooing as clients. I smiled so much my face hurt."

"You need a different line of work."

"You need to get out more." She smiled against his throat, wondering if she should tell him about Gordie's job offer. About how tempting it was. Especially now. Maybe too tempting . . .

"When you were out here for your old man's funeral, people said you were with someone," he said very casually. "Slick city lawyer with expensive threads, a hundred dollar haircut and plenty of attitude. He, uh, anyone important?"

"In what way?" she asked, just as casually.

"In the usual way," he replied dryly.

"Do you mean, are we romantically involved?"

"I guess that's one way of putting it."

"Would it matter if we were?"

"Considering I'm dancing with his woman, it might." He tightened his arms slightly, and his breath warmed her ear. "Considering the only thing I've been able to think about for the past hour is getting her naked and making love to her until we're both beggin' for mercy—yeah, I'd say it matters."

Kathleen gave a gasp of laughter, trying to ignore the erotic tingle that his words sent through her. Trying not to think of what it would be like to let him peel her delicately out of her clothes and set about finding all those magical places he'd once found with such ease, his hands and fingers and tongue driving her insane until— "You need to put a lid on that imagination of yours, Sundance. But no, we're not involved."

"But you were."

Kathleen hesitated. Then she just nodded.

"And you never got married? In all those years?"

Again she hesitated. "The opportunity never seemed to present itself." She listened to the lie dispassionately, then found herself wondering if it *was* a lie. There had been Brice, of course. And a couple of others over the years, nice, steady, serious men with impeccable backgrounds and good prospects. And all of them as appealing as week-old mashed potatoes.

"I figured you'd have found yourself a rich, smooth-talking city boy by now and be livin' in a mansion with twin Porsches in the garage and a couple of kids in private school."

Kathleen stiffened. "Is that the kind of man you think I'm looking for? The kind of *life* I'm looking for? A smooth-talking, rich, city lawyer with a Porsche and a—" She bit the sentence off cleanly, flushing. "Buttons," she muttered. "You just pushed a couple of buttons. Sorry."

The smile lifted a corner of Jett's mouth. "So what was his name? This slick city lawyer with the Porsche?"

"Brice Thornton. And it was a Lamborghini Testarossa."

"Red."

"Of course."

"And you loved him?"

"No." The word popped out all of its own accord, surprising her a little.

"But you were going to marry him."

"I told myself I was." She stepped closer to him again, tucking her face into the hollow of his neck, taking refuge in the music. In him. "I don't think I would have gone through with it, but it was a comfortable game to play for a while."

"Game?"

"Convincing myself that I'm something I'm not. That I could actually be happy living in a mansion with a man named Brice."

Jett chuckled, a warm, comfortable sound that wrapped itself around her like a hug. "Tough for old Brice."

She didn't say anything, simply letting the slow, rhythmic beat of the music flow over her. She thought of Brice... or tried to. But his image kept eluding her, slipping away when she tried to pin it down. It had been like this for almost a week, ever since she'd come back to Burnt River. It was as though Brice and Baltimore and her job at Adams, Caldwell, and even the expensive, beautifully furnished town house she'd once thought important, were fading from memory, part of a life that had been becoming steadily less real with every day that passed.

It scared her a little. That life had been her reality not long ago, and Burnt River the dream-gone-bad. If she lost it, what did she have? She still wasn't entirely at ease in Burnt River, hadn't made up her mind about Gord's offer of a job, wasn't sure she would *ever* fit in here again. It was like hanging suspended between two worlds, neither quite real.

She didn't realize she'd sighed out loud until Jett's arms tightened slightly. She could feel the steady thump of his heart against her, the warmth of his body, the undemanding pressure of his hands on her back, and she smiled. *This* was real. This was here and now. For the moment, anyway, she was safe.

The music stopped finally, to Kathleen's regret, and then the band went right into a fast-paced, hard-driving, rockabilly two-step that soon had the entire place rocking.

But finally, too soon, the dance was over. They wandered out to the truck hand in hand, still laughing over something, and Kathleen took a deep breath of icy mountain air as she waited for Jett to open the door for her. The air tickled her throat like fine champagne, and she grinned up at the night sky, feeling half drunk on nothing more than laughter and good times. The sky was filled with stars, brilliant shards of light so clear and bright she swore she could reach out and touch them, and she just stood there for another moment gazing up at them in wonder.

"I'd forgotten how beautiful the sky is out here." She leaned into the welcoming curve of Jett's arm as he put it around her shoulders. "Remember how we used to put a blanket in the back of the truck and lie there counting stars?"

"I remember the blanket part just fine," he murmured, nuzzling the side of her throat. "I saw plenty of stars back then, all right, but not the kind you're talking about."

Kathleen had to laugh as his breath tickled her ear. She moved her face into the curve of his throat, loving the warm scent of his skin, and found herself running her lips along the angle of his jaw without even planning to.

Jett's arm tightened; then he kissed her on the cheek and stepped away from her, his eyes filled with memories as he pulled the truck door open. Not saying anything—not having to—Kathleen just laughed again and stepped up into the cab of the truck.

Jett walked around and got in the driver's side, then started the engine, letting it idle for a moment or two to warm up. "So." He draped his arm across the wheel and turned to look at her, eyes shadowed under the brim of his hat, a hint of lazy laughter warming his mouth. "Home, or . . . ?"

To her astonishment, Kathleen actually found herself hesitating. Then she laughed quietly and shook her head, scattering the memories. The sudden, unexpected temptations.

Sixteen years ago, the question would have made her heart leap. She would have gone all hot and dizzy and wouldn't have said anything at all. And he would just have grinned and taken off in a spray of gravel. Minutes later they would have been on an isolated side road somewhere, the radio playing softly as they spent the next half hour lost in the hot, syrupy urgencies of sex.

"Home," she said firmly, fending off the too vivid memories.

Jett grinned lazily and took her hand to tug her across the seat toward him. "Sure about that?"

"Pretty sure." She laughed again and let herself be coaxed nearer. The truck radio had come on with the engine, and a woman was singing about a man with slow hands, in a husky, sensuous voice that sent a little quiver through every cell in Kathleen's body. Time seemed to stand still suddenly, the air filled with promise as she gazed into Jett's dark, dangerous eyes.

Those eyes dipped nearer, and she turned her face toward him instinctively, arms going around his neck as his slid around her, enfolding her against him and pulling her into the captive heat of his body. And then his mouth was on hers and she turned her head to capture it fully, letting her lips part and suppressing a shiver of delight as his tongue slipped easily and naturally against hers. And then he was kissing her with that deep, slow intensity that had once set every inch of her afire.

It had much the same effect now, she thought dizzily as tendrils of sudden desire shivered through her. As though sensing it, Jett's kiss deepened, and she could feel his breathing quicken, the tension in his body as he pressed her against him.

"Jett!" Giddy with just the taste of him, Kathleen pulled her mouth away and rested her forehead on his shoulder, trying to catch her breath, heart hammering like a drum.

"Remember what it used to be like, Kathy?" he whispered, his breath tickling her ear. "Remember what it used to feel like when I made love to you? Remember what we used to do?"

"I've got to get home...." It was just a moan of denial.

"Remember this?" Jett whispered, pressing his palm gently, so gently, against her breast. Even through the thin stuff of her blouse and the silk and lace of her bra, he could feel the nipple tighten. Driving himself crazy, he rubbed it slowly, hearing the catch in her breathing, relishing the near pain of his own body as it responded with a vigor that made him groan.

He couldn't remember ever wanting a woman this badly this quickly before, every cell of his body on fire for her, unable to think of a single thing but getting her out of her clothes and astride him, open for him, sinking himself so deep inside her that he would never be free. Sixteen years…it had been sixteen years since he'd felt this heat, this urgency, this *need,* and God help him, he wanted her right here, right now. Wanted to be inside her, wanted her all over him and around him, wanted to touch her and tease her and hear her cry out for him, her voice no more than a sob of desire and satisfaction. Wanted to lose himself in her, to—

A car maneuvering its way out of the parking lot swung in front of them suddenly, catching them in the full glare of its headlights, and a horn blared raucously, followed by shouts and catcalls and loud laughter.

Jett swore and moved to shield Kathleen from the glare; then the car was gone, the occupants' laughter still hanging in the cold air. Starlit darkness enfolded the truck again, and Jett let his hand drop from Kathleen's breast, breathing heavily as he leaned back against the door.

She sat back, too, lifting her hand to brush a spill of golden hair from her face, looking shaken.

He should be taking her home, Jett told himself resolutely. Right now. He should just put the truck in gear and head up Deer Jump Road without another word. And then he should kiss her good-night—a quick kiss, on the cheek— and turn around and get the hell out of there and consider it finished.

That would be the smart thing to do, all right.

Instead, he found himself taking her hand and setting it on his thigh. Then he put the truck in gear and and headed toward the exit. ''Let's find someplace a little less public.''

Chapter 8

Kathleen drew a shaky breath, feeling as though she'd just been hit by a train.

But it hadn't been a train, of course. Just Jett Kendrick. Old times.

"Maybe we should just call it a night," she half whispered, not sure if she meant it or not. Not sure of anything other than the fact that things were on the verge of getting seriously out of hand.

She'd spent most of the past two days telling herself that this dance—she'd refused to call it a date—was simply a chance for the two of them to get to know one another again. That it had nothing to do with the past, nothing to do with all those little sparks and sizzles up at Beaver Creek, nothing to do with *anything*. It was just two people who had known each other a long time ago getting reacquainted.

Kathleen nearly smiled. If that kiss had gone on much longer, Jett Kendrick would have reacquainted himself with a lot more than either of them had anticipated.

She did smile then, not taking her hand from his denimed thigh. "I'm half afraid to even ask what you've got in mind."

He grinned, catching her gaze in the rearview mirror. "You can stay out as late as you want, Kath. Your old man's not waiting up for you."

"No, but my big brother might be. And he's got the key to Daddy's gun cabinet."

"Your daddy's gun cabinet didn't keep me away from you sixteen years ago."

Kathleen had to laugh. "And now?"

He paused, his eyes capturing hers in the mirror again for a taut moment. "Guess that depends on you, Kathy," he said softly.

Kathleen's heart gave an odd little backflip. "This is all happening kind of fast, Sundance."

"It always happened fast between us." Jett took her hand and gently pressed it against himself. He was aroused and hard, and he heard her draw another unsteady breath. But she didn't pull her hand away.

Sixteen years ago he would have had the truck pulled into a quiet, sheltered spot on a side road by now, with them on a rough, wool blanket in the back, surrounded by saddles and a hay bale or two. He would have been lying between her thighs, so deeply embedded in the honied warmth of her body that he was unable to tell her heartbeat from his own.

He looked at her in the mirror again. "There's a motel not far from here."

"No motel." Her voice sounded tight and breathless, and Jett heard her swallow.

He could still take her home. There was still time.

And yet, even as he thought it, he knew it was a lie. That it was already too late for that. He'd known this was going to happen from the moment he'd knocked on the big front door of The Oaks. It had swung open, and there she'd been, standing there with that torrent of golden hair tumbling around her shoulders and those sky-blue eyes filled with laughter.

She was wearing a denim dress that pressed itself across the full swell of her breasts and then down and over her slender hips before flaring out gracefully, and he'd just stared at her, the blood thundering in his temples. She'd said something to him, but Jett had no idea what it was, hearing nothing but the drum sound of his own heartbeat. And then she'd stepped through the door, and her perfume had swirled around him, and he'd nearly lost it then and there.

It had taken all his willpower not to scoop her up in his arms and walk into the trees by the side of the house and skin her out of that pretty blue dress and make love to her then and there. Up against a tree or in a pile of leaves or any old place at all—just as long as he could ease himself all the way into the heat of her and hear her moan his name the way she used to and feel those long, silken legs tighten around him.

"I'm going to make love to you," he said very quietly, not even looking at her. "I just want to get that out of the way, because I don't think I'm going to be able to hang on long enough for a lot of sweet talkin'."

To his surprise, she gave a low laugh. "Been a long while, has it, cowboy?"

"Not so long I can't remember how."

"Somehow," she murmured, "I don't doubt that for a minute."

It wasn't until Stumpy Jones's old barn loomed into sight that Jett knew where he was going to take her. The Oaks was out on principle alone—hell, if Gordon didn't get him, her old man's ghost would. And the Kicking Horse wasn't much better. Jody would still be up, wanting to know all about his father's first date in almost a year. And Jett was in no mood to wait until the coast was clear to smuggle Kathy into his bed and then have to worry about every creak of the springs. He wanted to paw the dirt and beat his chest and throw his head back and bay at the moon.

But then, suddenly, he spotted the old barn rising lop-sided against the moonlit sky, and a flicker of memory made him smile.

She'd snuck away from The Oaks to meet him on horseback that day. They'd gotten caught in a rainstorm and had tumbled into the dim silence of the barn, soaked to the skin and giddy with laughter. The dust-spangled air had been sweet with the scent of rain and clover, and in no time at all they'd been tucked into a nest of hay in the loft, pretending they had nothing on their minds but getting dry and warm.

He remembered that they were suddenly naked without being able to remember how they'd gotten that way. Remembered running his hand down the long, smooth sweep of her body and feeling his blood pound. Remembered easing himself between her slender thighs and the throaty little purr she'd made when he'd pressed himself into the taut, silken heat of her.

She'd sighed against his mouth, her hands clutching at his shoulders, and then he'd started to move, and she'd moaned something and clasped her long legs around his. They'd caught fire like lightning-struck prairie grass at the end of a hot, dry summer.

Near the end he'd looked down and had seen their bodies braided together, hers as soft and pale as satin, his dark and savage and wild, and he remembered thinking how right they were, how perfect....

"I wonder what ever happened to Cindy Braedon," she said out of the blue. "Remember when she and Darryl and you and I used to park out here in his car and neck up a storm?"

"Yesterday, wasn't it?"

She laughed quietly. "Sure seems like it."

"She married some guy from Billings. And Darryl's doing five-to-ten for armed robbery, last I heard."

"I never could figure out what Cindy saw in that guy."

"A lot of people couldn't figure out what you saw in me."

"You were cute and dangerous and looked real good in jeans, mainly."

"That was it?"

"That was enough. I was fifteen, remember."

"You *told* me you were sixteen."

"Of course I told you I was sixteen. If I'd told you the truth, you wouldn't have looked at me twice, let alone...do what you did."

"And what exactly *did* I do?" he asked lazily.

"What you *did*," she whispered, "was take me to heaven and back."

The old road was just ahead, twin tracks that meandered through the hay field. Jett turned onto it without saying anything, aware of Kathy's amused glance as they bounced and rattled along the rough trail, headlights swinging wildly through the darkness.

Jett pulled the truck in behind the barn where it was out of sight, then cut the engine and lights. The night was like sapphire, all hard edges and blackness, and it closed around them, the silence dropping down like a cloak. Jett reached over and turned the radio up a bit, then turned and draped his arm along the back of the seat, looking at her. "Well. Here we are. Again."

Kathy put her head on her hand and smiled at him through the shadowed starlight. "It's been a long time, Sundance."

"I never thought I'd see you again." The words surprised him. They weren't what he'd planned to say. But then, the night seemed full of surprises.

"You must have hated me."

"I guess that's what your father counted on."

"Did you think about me after I was gone?"

"All the time."

"Pam must have been delighted with that." She smiled.

"Pam was convenient."

Kathy looked startled, and Jett felt himself flush. "You were gone, and your old man made it clear I was never going to see you again. I'd gone out with Pam a few times before I met you, and when you were out of the picture, she wanted to pick up where we'd left off. I—hell, I didn't put up much of a fight."

"She was very pretty."

"Yeah." Jett frowned and looked away, draping his other arm across the top of the steering wheel. He hadn't planned on talking about this. Hadn't planned on talking at all, in fact. Had just planned to drive in here and make love to her as though nothing had changed.

And yet, sitting here in the star-bedazzled night with her, Stumpy Jones's old barn and all the erotic memories it held only a few steps away, he realized he'd just been playing some sort of game with himself. It wasn't that easy. Could never be that easy again. Not with all that had happened.

"How did she die?" Kathy asked suddenly, her voice soft. "I heard it was a traffic accident."

"She'd been drinking. She . . . was doing a lot of that by then. We'd had a fight, and she took off, saying she was going to file for divorce and I'd be hearing from her lawyer."

He thought about it, as he had a thousand times over the past six years. "Maybe she meant it that time. She was in no shape to drive, and I tried to get the keys away from her. But when she got like that . . ." He shook his head. "She took off before I could stop her. About an hour later, I got a call from the sheriff. She'd missed a curve in the road and hit a telephone pole. They figured she'd been doing close to a hundred when it happened."

"I'm so sorry." Kathy's fingertips brushed his cheek.

Jett eased out a deep breath, not even realizing he'd been holding it. "It was pretty rough on Jody. He tried his best to be real grown up about it, but—" He shrugged. "He still doesn't talk about it much."

He stared out the windshield, seeing nothing but a million stars. He never talked about it much, either. Couldn't remember the last time he'd told anyone what had happened that day. But it was different with Kathy. *She* was different.

"This is a good time to tell you I'm sorry." Even as he said them, he thought how ineffectual the words were. How powerless to erase the past. She was looking at him curiously, eyes filled with moonlight and memories, and he had to take a deep breath.

"I was eighteen when I started making love to you. Old enough to know you didn't make love to someone without some kind of protection. I told you that first time that I'd take care of it, and most times I did. But there were plenty of times when we went too far too fast, and I didn't want to stop long enough to—" He bit off the thought, feeling suddenly ashamed. "It was wrong, not taking care of you. You were important to me, Kathy. I should have been more careful."

"Oh, Jett." Laughter caressed the words, his name like honey in her mouth. "I was old enough to know better, too. We were kids, and we figured nothing could hurt us. But it happened a long time ago. Let's just let it go, all right?"

Let it go? How, when he was reminded of it every time he looked at her? At Jody? He should be telling her, he thought dimly. It wasn't right, not telling her....

She reached out and lifted off his hat, setting it on the dash. She didn't say anything for a moment, simply looking at him; then she smiled and put her hand on his shoulder. "You can kiss me now, if you want to."

Again she managed to surprise him. But, of course, she always had. Maybe he'd been counting on that. Maybe he'd wanted to be surprised. Had wanted her to make it easy so he didn't have to think too hard about the right or wrong of it. He fought it for a heartbeat longer, telling himself he wouldn't do it. Couldn't do it. Not with such secrets between them . . .

And then he simply slipped his hand around the back of her neck, pulled her toward him and dropped his mouth over hers, and that was pretty much the end of it.

Her lips were already parted, and she kissed him back, tongue sliding against his, slippery and seductive and as tantalizing as sin itself. Her mouth was berry-sweet, and he felt his senses slip-slide away as her fingers caressed the back of his neck and she leaned into him, back arched a little so he could feel the tender pressure of her breasts against his chest.

He caressed her back with his hands, slowly, enjoying the friction of cotton against skin, teasing himself. Knowing if he wanted to she would probably let him slip a few buttons free and fill his hands with warm flesh, but suddenly in no hurry. Leisurely, he drew one hand down and around the firm curve of her bottom and thigh; then he pulled her denim-clad leg over his.

Past, present, future...all ran together like ink on wet paper, the edges blurring until they were indistinguishable. And with them, right from wrong. He thought fleetingly of her father, of the lies, the betrayals. Thought of the papers hidden away in the safe-deposit box in the bank, which even now, even as he prepared to make love to her, prepared to trespass beyond the trusting boundaries of her body, revealed the greatest betrayal of all.

But then she opened her eyes and whispered his name, her gaze blurry with desire, and he forgot it all—her father, the papers, the betrayal, all of it. Forgot everything except the need reflected in her eyes and the demanding urgency of his own body, and the inarguable reality that *this* was all that mattered for the moment, that *this* was the one thing he could give her freely and without artifice or lies.

And it was then that Kathleen realized this was what she'd wanted all along. The dance had been just a prelude to what they'd both known was going to happen, just as it would have been sixteen years ago. They'd wanted nothing back then but each other, unable to get their fill, to satisfy the wildfire consuming them.

And that fire was as urgent as ever. His hands moved over her, following memories of their own, and her body responded just as it had all those years ago, sudden desire sizzling through her. Her breasts ached for his touch, and she arched her back again so he could fill his hands with them, teasing the nipples through denim and lace until she felt dizzy with need.

He knew her by heart and played her from memory, every touch and erotic whisper taking her back through time. Laughing, she slipped the buttons of his shirt free so she could kiss his chest and shoulders. His skin burned against her lips, and she settled her mouth over his nipple and sucked on it, teasing it with her tongue. She could feel his heart hammering and knew by the way he flinched and groaned her name in a thick, agonized whisper that he was close to the edge already.

She lifted her head and found his mouth and claimed it, kissing him with a slow, drugging intensity that made him groan again, one arm tightening around her to support her as he fumbled with the buttons on the front of her dress. Impatiently, she pulled his shirt out of his jeans and struggled with the heavy buckle of his leather belt, suddenly half wild to touch him, to caress him, tease him.

She had trouble with the zipper on his jeans, and he laughed breathlessly and slipped his hand between them and pulled it down himself. And a moment later he let his head fall onto the seat back with a gratified groan as she wrapped her fingers around him. He lifted his hips involuntarily to press himself into her hand, then groaned again.

"Kathy, Kathy... for the love of God, wait! Stop!" Managing a bark of laughter, he caught her hand and pulled it away from him. "Not yet. I don't want it to end yet. Not this way."

He got the last button free and pulled the front of her dress open, then started kissing her throat, moving south, laying a burning trail of biting kisses down to the lacy rim of her bra.

Kathleen had to catch her breath, and she leaned back against his supporting arm, eyes closed, and cradled his head against her. He kissed her breast through silk and lace, then settled his mouth wetly over the nipple and nursed it rhythmically.

It sent spirals of fire through her, and Kathleen flexed her hips, pressing herself against his thigh, wanting, needing, the pressure of his body against her. She ached there, urgently aroused and half wild for his touch.

He slipped one hand under her skirt and slowly ran it up her thigh, almost but not quite touching her. Then he did touch her, just a fleeting brush of fingertip against silk, a delicate stroke of such tantalizing promise that it made her sob his name.

"More?" His voice was a seductive whisper against her ear.

"Jett..." It was hard to even speak, and Kathleen had to concentrate on each word, every atom of her being focused entirely on that one, tiny molten core where her whole being seemed to be centered. "Please... please..."

"More?" He laughed against her mouth.

"More. Definitely more... now. Please, now..."

"I want to set you on fire," he whispered. "Tell me what you want, Kath. Tell me what you need."

"You know." She shivered. "You know what I want...."

"Yes."

His large warm hand cupped her belly, and he caressed it slowly. Kathleen let her eyes slide closed, barely even breathing, his touch so wondrous she thought she might go out of her mind before he finished. Slowly, delicately, he ran his fingers along the lacy waistband of her briefs, sliding them under it in a long, slow stroke of flesh on warmed flesh, then out, under again, fingers moving lower this time, still slow, still leisurely, as though he had all the time in the world.

Kathleen gave an impatient wriggle, and he just laughed; then gently, with the most exquisite slowness imaginable, he stopped teasing her and eased his hand lower, fingers touching her, parting her, stroking the molten silk of her. Kathleen tried to say something but couldn't catch her breath, and then he slipped his fingers into her heat to sweetly impale her.

She gave a gasp as he started massaging the tiny, vibrant nub with the pad of his thumb. And finally she gave up any pretense of holding herself back, not caring that she'd sworn this wasn't going to happen, that it *shouldn't* be happening, that she was crazy to even consider letting it happen. It was a little late now for maidenly embarrassment or shy protests, so she simply gave herself over to the sheer physical pleasure of her own body, hips moving as though of their own volition, the silken sensation of each knowledgeable stroke of his fingers like heaven itself. She shivered and moaned his name, trusting him absolutely, knowing he knew her better than she knew herself.

Everything vanished but the deftness of his touch and the growing responses of her own body. She could hear the radio in the distance and Jett's rapid breathing against her ear and soft moans she thought could be her own. Was aware of the feel of his hot skin against hers, the familiar scent of him. And the tension within her, growing, growing, until she thought she was going to scream.

And then Jett was saying something to her, his voice raw with desire... and then, suddenly, wondrously, impossibly, sensation exploded through her in an uprush of pleasure so crystalline pure it made her cry out in gratified delight.

It faded finally, like the heat of a blush, leaving her limp with release as Jett eased her out of it so gently that she wasn't even aware when he'd taken his hand from her and was just holding her.

And finally it was over, and she turned her head to kiss the side of his throat. "To heaven," she whispered. "And back."

"Nice to know I haven't lost the knack."

"The question is, have I lost mine?" Kathleen smiled and pushed him gently back against the seat. "Let's see, shall we?"

"Not without this." He pulled down the sun visor, and a small avalanche of plastic-wrapped contraceptives tumbled into his lap.

"Good grief!" Kathleen gave a whoop of laughter. "What in heaven's name were you planning?"

Jett grinned and started tossing them onto the dash-board like tiny flying saucers. "Everything I could get away with. Do you think I brought enough?"

"I think you brought enough for the entire Pacific Fleet!"

"Don't underestimate your sex appeal, darlin'. This may only get us started."

Grinning, she picked one up and tore open the wrapper, her eyes never leaving his. "Do you mind if I . . ."

"No," he managed to whisper, wetting his lips. "Honey, I don't mind at all."

He draped both arms along the back of the seat, legs widespread, eyes narrowed, and made no move other than a perceptible ripple of his belly muscles as she gently and playfully sheathed him, taking her time.

"This *would* be easier if we got out of the truck." She slid away from him and just as playfully finished unbuttoning her dress. "I think I'll just slip out of this first, though."

Taking her time, she eased it off one shoulder, then the other. Then she slid out of it completely and shook it out, folding it tidily before setting it on the dash. Jett's breathing was getting labored, and she slid him an amused look.

"More?" She paused with one fingertip under the strap of her bra and looked at him questioningly.

He nodded with an effort, fingers flexing, although he still made no move to touch her.

She slid the strap off her shoulder, then peeled the lacy cup away from her breast with her fingertip, watching him as he watched her, loving the desire in his eyes. She slid the other strap down in the same way, then eased the bra down one lazy inch at a time until both breasts were free.

Jett groaned and started to reach for her, then relaxed against the seat again. "You're killin' me," he groaned through clenched teeth. "I'm dying here, darlin'."

"You'll live," she assured him with a throaty laugh, eas-ing herself up onto her knees. Slowly, deliberately, she slid her briefs down over her hips, the raw hunger in his nar-rowed eyes making her all shivery and hot inside.

And then, naked, she looked at him. Lifted her arms to run her fingers through her hair, back arched.

"Kathy..." His voice held dire warning.

"More?" she whispered.

"All of it," he growled. "Now."

And then, suddenly, she was tired of all the teasing. That aching little tautness was back, urging her to hurry, and she started to tug his jeans down and over his hips. He raised himself up helpfully, and they came off with one good pull, and she smiled as she realized he wasn't wearing briefs.

"You must have had trouble on your mind tonight, cowboy."

"I had high hopes."

"Well, then," she murmured as she knelt on the seat again and rested her hands on his broad shoulders for balance, "I guess it's only fair to give you what you wanted."

He settled his arms around her loosely, and Kathleen lowered her mouth to his and kissed him slowly and sweetly, feeling that spark of desire deep within her blossom into something hot and urgent. She eased one leg across his bare thighs, laughing. "This is a lot more dangerous than I remember, between the steering wheel and the gearshift and that gun rack behind your head...."

"Having second thoughts?"

"What do you think?" She kissed him again, then very slowly lowered herself over him, flesh cleaving flesh.

Jett groaned and let his head fall back against the seat as he thrust his hips fiercely upward, hands clamped on her hips. They stayed like that for a long, breathless moment of time, then he lifted his head, narrowed eyes blazing, and started moving.

There was no need to say anything. Jett was watching her, his eyes burning into hers, and she shivered at what she saw there reflected in moonlight. His breathing was just a rasp, and she held his gaze, letting him set the pace, listening to the silken whisper of flesh against flesh, the hot scent of naked skin and night air and sex like musky perfume.

And then, when it was almost time, he just smiled and slid his hands down to her thighs. He spread his legs so she was forced to spread hers, never breaking the strong, surging rhythm of his hips, and when he touched her and massaged the tiny sensitive heart of her, she gasped and nearly collapsed against him. And then it took no time at all, and within a moment or two she gave a soft cry as that now familiar uprush burst through her.

She clung to it, to his hand, to the bright urgency unraveling within her, for as long as she could. But then Jett groaned and dropped his head against the seat back and thrust upward once, then once again, straining against her, teeth bared, and Kathleen let herself fall down, down, into that delicious place within herself, trembling slightly from the force of it.

He lifted his head finally, and Kathleen cradled it against her as he panted for breath, tremors running through him like tiny aftershocks. And still she moved, but very, very gently now, letting him come down with her, caressing him with her body.

"You're dangerous," he finally groaned a long while later, well after they had both stopped moving and were just wrapped in each other's embrace. "I swear to God my heart stopped cold a few minutes back."

She sat up, his body still sheathed in hers, and smiled down at him, brushing a loop of sweat-tangled hair off his forehead. "That was twice, Sundance. I don't think I managed it twice even on your very best night sixteen years ago."

"I was young." He relaxed back against the seat and ran his hands up and down her back. "Selfish. In too much of a hurry. Didn't know what I was doing half the time."

"Oh, you knew what you were doing." She smiled. "I think maybe I've just improved with age."

"Now that's something I'd figured out on my own." He kissed her breast. "This was pretty spectacular, Slick. Reckon we were on to something all those years ago?"

"I'd definitely say that, cowboy."

"Cold?"

"Not yet."

"Here." He wriggled out of his shirt and draped it around her. "Unless you were thinking of getting dressed right away."

Kathleen kissed him lightly on the mouth, then eased herself off him. "And what were you thinking?"

"I was thinking of just sitting here listening to the music for a while, then making love to you again. Slow, this time." He pulled an old blanket from behind the seat, then motioned for her to stand up so he could spread it across the seat. Then he sprawled back, buck naked, and grinned at her. "Real slow."

Feeling deliciously wicked, Kathleen just grinned back, then curled up in the curve of his arm. "Do you realize we could stay out here all night if we wanted to? I don't have a curfew or school tomorrow or anything." She laughed delightedly and turned in his arms, sliding one leg between his so they were all tangled up and warm, head on his shoulder, happier than she could ever remember being. "God, I love being grown up!"

They stayed like that for a deliciously long while, all wrapped up in each other's arms as they talked quietly, catching up on old times and new between long, comfortable silences when they simply listened to the radio. Jett started the truck to run the heater a couple of times, but mostly they just lay curled up together, sleepy and warm, exchanging the occasional kiss.

And then the kisses got longer and deeper, and the caresses went from playful to skillfully erotic, and after a long while Jett sat up and pulled her into his lap, then eased her over him, and they made love again, but so slowly and leisurely this time that it seemed to just go on forever.

In his wildest dreams, Jett had never imagined it could be this good. This perfect. The girl he'd made love to sixteen years ago had been enthusiastic but uncertain, too inexperienced to know what she needed or how to ask for it. And God knows, he'd been no help, so quick off the mark most times he hardly had time to enjoy it before it was over.

But that girl was gone. And in her place was a woman who knew exactly what she wanted and was poised enough and self-confident enough to take it. And in taking, she gave—gave more than any woman had ever given him before, taking him places he'd never thought existed. She moved like silken witch fire, using her body and hands and sly, sweet mouth to coax sensations from him he'd never dreamed possible, and just when he thought he couldn't take any more, she would take him somewhere even higher.

Although it finally got away from her in the end, and she lost touch with him for a while, caught in the delights of her own body. And Jett, grinning, made it as good for her as their awkward surroundings allowed, driving her right to the edge time and again and then holding her back from it, letting it build to an almost unbearable heat until, finally, he took her that last fire-bright distance.

She gave a low, hoarse cry and arched away from him, her body as taut as a bowstring, the muscles in her belly rippling as she sought to capture those last elusive threads of sensation.

It nearly swept him over the edge then and there, watching her in those last moments of it, hearing her quick, sharp cries. But he held on by a thread and stayed with it, with her, as long as he could, relishing the near pain of it, never wanting it to end.

But finally there was no way he could ignore the fire storm within himself, and he groaned and just let himself go, moving strongly and urgently until it swept him up and away and everything vanished in a burst of white-hot sensation.

They collapsed against each other, too breathless to do more than whisper wordless things, bodies slick with sweat, hearts pounding. Jett finally collected his wits enough to pull the blanket up and around them, cocooning Kathy in its sheltering folds, and he buried his face in her hair and just sat there for an eternity, breathing in the warm scent of her skin and thinking dazedly that if it had been like this sixteen years ago, she never would have gotten away from him. Never.

He would have been content to stay there in the truck in Stumpy Jones's hay field until the end of time itself, but Kathy got practical after a while and eased herself off him, groaning a little. She collapsed on the seat, looking damp and tousled and well-loved, and scooped a handful of hair off her face, looking around the truck as though just becoming aware of where she was.

"My God," she finally whispered. "I had no idea it could be like that. No idea..."

Jett kissed her, cradling her head in his hand. "That's only a taste of what it's going to be like," he whispered. "I've spent sixteen long, cold years away from you, Kathleen. I've got a lot of catching up to do."

She laughed shakily, resting her forehead on his. "It scares me a little. This whole thing is just so wild and out of control."

"It was always wild and out of control with us, Kath. Don't you remember that day I picked you up after school, and we stopped just below the ridge this side of The Oaks and made love up against that big rock? I had your skirt up and your panties down and was inside you in about thirty seconds flat, and the whole thing took maybe a minute and a half. Or that night we drove out to Cougar Ridge and put a blanket down and I taught you how to—"

Laughing, Kathleen stopped him with a kiss. "Keep talking like that and you're going to get me all hot and bothered again before you're in any kind of shape to do something about it."

"I'll find a way to do something about it," he said with a chuckle. And, whispering against her ear, he proceeded to tell her exactly how, in minute and exquisite detail.

She gave a little moan of protest, and Jett laughed and nuzzled her ear, thinking that it wouldn't take a whole lot more to set them both off again.

Kathleen sighed finally and pulled away, raking her hair back with both hands. "You'd better get me home before Gord calls the cops. If he hasn't already."

"No." Jett held her gaze stubbornly. "No, damn it, I'm not taking you home. It's always been this way between us, quick and dirty, in the truck or a hayloft or in the grass somewhere, and—"

"Quick and dirty has its moments," she said with a grin.

But he shook his head impatiently. "I want to make love to you in a proper bed just *once*. More than once, in fact. Tonight's the first time we ever took the time to catch our breath and start all over again. We were always in a hurry, scared of getting caught, scared of keeping you out too late."

"We never needed long," she reminded him with a chuckle.

"Yeah, well . . ." He did have to grin then. But he let it fade and looked at her seriously. "Come home with me, Kathy. Come to bed with me and stay the night. I want to make love to you and fall asleep with my arms around you and then wake up in the morning and make love to you again."

She didn't say anything, a frown tugging her brows together. "Jett, this was wonderful, but I'm not sure we should—"

"I want you in my bed, damn it," Jett told her impatiently. "I've wasted sixteen years I could have had with you. I don't want to waste another five minutes."

It made her laugh. "Remember up at Beaver Creek when you said tonight was going to be just a dance and that it wouldn't get complicated?" She leaned forward to kiss his chin. "It *wasn't* just a dance, and it *is* getting complicated."

She had no idea *how* complicated, Jett thought. But instead of telling her everything he should be telling her, he simply smiled coaxingly. "No more complicated than you want it to be."

She thought about it for a moment longer, still uncertain. Then she smiled and shook her head, as though amused by her own folly. "If you could bottle that cowboy charm of yours, Sundance, you'd be a wealthy man." She lifted his hand and kissed his fingertips, eyes locked with his. "I'll call Gord from your place and tell him not to wait up."

Jett's belly muscles tightened as she ran the tip of her tongue along the length of his thumb. "I'll make it worth your while."

"I'll see that you do." Then, laughing, she retrieved her bra and panties from the dashboard and proceeded to get dressed. "What about Jody? I realize that he's old enough to understand you have a life, but if he runs into me as I'm coming out of his dad's bedroom the morning after, it might embarrass him half to death." She slipped him a sly look. "Unless he's used to seeing women wander out of his dad's bedroom the morning after, of course."

Jett finished pulling on his jeans, then shrugged into his shirt, still warm with her heat. "There's been no woman in my bed since Pam died," he said quietly. "I won't lie to you and say I haven't been with anyone in those six years, but I never took them home. It was just a rule I had. I didn't want Jody thinking—" He shrugged. "Well, what he'd think."

"I'll stay out of sight until he's left for school."

"No." Jett looked up at her, tempted in that moment to tell her everything. But the time wasn't right, and he just shook it off. "I'm not going to make a big deal out of this, but I'm not going to lie to him, either. He has a right to know there's something between us. He, uh, seems to like you."

"Yeah, we seemed to hit it off. He's a great kid. How's he doing with that civics project?"

Jett bit back a wince. "Not too good. I tried to give him a hand with it, but..." He gave his head a weary shake. "I'd be mightily obliged, actually, for any help you can give him. I know I acted like a prize jerk the other night, but if you were serious about wanting to help out..."

Kathleen gave him a slow smile. "It'll cost you, cowboy."

"Name your price."

"I'll have to give it some thought." She started buttoning the dress, not taking her gaze from his. "But I'm sure I'll be able to come up with something that will make us both happy.''

"Funny, I was going to say the same thing.''

She laughed. ''Are you trying to tell me something?''

Jett settled his hat over his hair, then reached down to start the truck. ''Just that I want you stretched out across my big old bed without a stitch on, so ready for me you're half out of your mind with it. Just that I'm going to take my time, lady. I'm going to play you like a concert violin, and by the time I'm finished with you, you'll figure you've died and gone straight through those pearly gates.''

Chapter 9

He was true to his word.

And much, much later, lying in his arms in the wide, soft bed, Kathleen smiled into the darkness, stroking his sweat-dewed back with her fingertips and listening to his heartbeat slowly return to normal.

"You were right," she murmured. "Bed *is* best. That was...pretty intense."

She felt him smile. Then he rolled gently off her and onto his side, carrying her with him, so she was cradled against him full-length.

"It's not that I didn't enjoy making love with you in the truck tonight," he said with a husky laugh, "but I do my best work in familiar territory. With plenty of room to maneuver."

"I noticed." Sighing in utter contentment, she nestled against him sleepily. He'd used this big, old bed to spectacular advantage for the past hour or so, and there wasn't a square inch of her that he hadn't deliciously explored with hands and mouth and tongue, not a tiny spot of her that he didn't know by heart.

She could get used to this, she thought as she drifted toward sleep. Montana. Burnt River. Jett. It was as though all the scattered parts of her life were coming together finally, creating something whole and satisfying. Maybe Gord was right. Maybe it was time she moved back.

That thought never strayed far from her mind over the next three weeks. Every time she watched Gord playing with the kids, or took a moment to draw a deep breath of pine-scented mountain air, or simply walked along the streets of the town where she'd grown up, the temptation grew stronger.

But she had to be sure. It wouldn't be fair to Gord to tell him that she was staying, then turn around in a month or two and admit she'd made a mistake and wanted to move back to Baltimore. But most of all, she had to be sure for *herself*. Sure that she wanted to stay for the right reasons.

And not just because she was falling head over heels in love with Jett Kendrick all over again.

She hadn't believed it at first. Sizzle and sparks, that was all she'd figured it was. Curiosity and old times and a heady, reckless awareness that, this time, no one could stop them.

They'd spent every spare moment together after that first night. Jett wanted her with him all the time, riding with him when he went looking for a missing cow and calf, attending a stock show with him, going to the church picnic hand-in-hand and setting tongues wagging from Burnt River clear down to Butte.

And making love, of course. All it would take was a glance, a slow smile, the touch of his hand on her back, and she was lost. They made love every chance they got, up at Beaver Creek on a bed of soft grass, on a blanket in Stumpy Jones's hay barn, in a meadow up on Cougar Ridge with nothing but wildflowers and sky around them. And, best of all, in Jett's big, old, wide bed, with all the time in the world to make it just perfect.

It made Kathleen laugh out loud every time she thought of it. The man should come with a warning stamped across his taut, denim-upholstered backside: Handle With Care. Contents Hazardous To Your Peace Of Mind. And heart. Jett Kendrick was *definitely* hazardous to the heart.

Not that she'd put up much of a fight. A couple of kisses, a cuddle or two and some spectacular sex, and she was as good as done for.

Smiling, Kathleen glanced over her shoulder. Jett was still asleep, sprawled on his back with one arm thrown out as though seeking her in his dreams. The pale morning light gentled his strong features, and a half smile curved his mouth to one side as though he was remembering something sweet.

Her smile widened, and she pulled the light quilt she'd wrapped around herself a bit tighter, then turned again to look out the window. The sun's light had just reached the highest mountain peaks across the valley. They were glowing like polished gold, and she watched as they seemed to catch fire.

Last night had been magical. They'd gone to a dance just outside Helena and come back late, then tumbled into bed still flushed with laughter and good times. They'd lain there for an hour or more, just talking quietly, and then Jett had made love to her for a long, long while, more gently and sweetly than he ever had before. And it had been then, lying in his arms, that she'd finally admitted to herself that she was in love with him.

"See something that catches your fancy?" Jett materialized behind her, as silent as a shadow. He slipped his arms around her and kissed the back of her neck.

Kathleen looked at their reflection in the window, smiling as she met his gaze in the glass. "Yeah. As a matter of fact I do."

"Good."

He kissed her again, his parted lips moving around to the soft indentation under her ear, and Kathleen laughed softly, toes curling. "You're asking for trouble, cowboy."

"Countin' on it." He tightened his arms around her, then rested his chin on the top of her head to look out the window. "So, what's out there that's so interesting?"

"Mountains. Trees. And sky. Lots of sky. Something I don't see a lot of in Baltimore."

Jett nodded slowly, his eyes holding hers in the reflection. "So. You're thinking about Baltimore."

"Yeah." Kathleen sighed quietly.

"I've had a feeling something's been on your mind." He kissed her hair. "I guess this was coming sooner or later. When are you leaving?"

He asked it so matter-of-factly that Kathleen had to smile. "Would it upset your plans too much if I said I wasn't?"

He stared at her, as though not quite understanding what she'd said, and she smiled again. "So. Not quite what you expected after all."

He didn't say anything. Not a single word. Just stood there with his arms still around her, although she could tell he'd all but forgotten they were there, his eyes locked on hers in the cold reflection of the darkened window.

"Well." She took a deep breath and forced herself to smile. "By the look of raw panic on your face, I guess I can safely assume that this is something you were *not* counting on."

"You never said you were thinking of staying." Looking distracted, he let his arms fall from around her.

It shouldn't have hurt, she knew that. He'd never once asked her about Baltimore. Had never talked about tomorrow or the day after that. It had just been day by day, and she'd been willing to take it like that, not allowing herself to take too much for granted or expect it to last.

So she took a deep breath and fought a sudden prickle of tears, reminding herself that he'd never promised her a thing. She stepped away from him and started walking around the room, collecting bits of discarded clothing. "No, I guess I didn't. Gord wants me to go into partnership with him, and I agreed to come out for a couple of weeks to talk with him and look things over. I like what I've seen. I told him yesterday that I was staying.''

Again he said nothing, and she looked around impatiently. He was still standing by the window, tall and wide-shouldered in the pale light, seemingly unaware of the fact that he was naked, his face etched stone, so immobile he could have been painted there.

A wisp of annoyance flirted through her, and she gave her head a toss to get the hair off her face. ''For heaven's sake, Jett, stop looking so damned worried! I'm not moving back to Burnt River because of you. We had three weeks of great sex, and that's all it was. No strings, no commitments, no expectations.''

His mouth went hard and stubborn, like it did whenever he heard something he didn't want to hear. ''You never said a damn thing about a partnership. That you were thinking of moving back.''

''I didn't say anything because at first I had no intention of accepting his offer. Then, after I'd been here awhile, I—'' *I fell in love with you,* she thought angrily, tempted to say the words aloud just to see his reaction. Except the only person who would get hurt was her, so there didn't seem to be much point. ''I didn't want to tell you about it until I'd decided one way or the other.''

She turned away again, looking for her jeans. She found them finally, lying in a heap in the corner where she'd kicked them last night, in too much of a hurry to get out of them to care where they fell. ''Look, I have to get home. Can I borrow your truck, or should I call Gord and have him pick me up?''

Jett gave himself a shake, as though releasing himself from some spell. Raking his fingers through his hair, he wheeled away and grabbed his blue jeans from the back of a chair and started pulling them on, his actions abrupt and angry. ''You should have told me about this, Kathleen. It makes a difference.''

She started getting dressed, yanking her panties and bra on, then pulling on her jeans. ''It doesn't make a damned bit of difference. Just because I'm going to be living in Burnt River again doesn't mean that you're obligated to keep me entertained. We never even have to *see* each other again, let alone—''

"If you're going to be in town," he said with a low, intense voice, "I'm going to be seeing you. Count on that."

"We're adults, Jett. We can handle it." She gave her head another toss and pulled on her white cotton shirt, not looking at him as she started buttoning it.

"I deserved to know, damn it." He caught her by the arm and pulled her around, forcing her to face him. His eyes were dark with anger, mouth hard. "You've been sleepin' in my bed for almost three weeks, lady. It might have been nice if you'd at least given me a *hint* you were thinkin' of staying."

"It had nothing to do with us!" She wrenched her arm free. "I came back to Burnt River to discuss a business deal with my brother, not get involved with you. You just... happened!"

It made him blink, and he backed off after a moment, looking sullen and edgy, dark eyes glittering with a dozen emotions she didn't even want to try to name.

She finished buttoning her shirt and rammed it into the waistband of her jeans, then looked around for her socks and boots. Jett was on the other side of the room now, with his back turned solidly toward her, as unapproachable as a granite cliff.

She watched as he pulled a down-filled vest over his work shirt. Then she sighed. "Look, I didn't expect what we had to last forever, but I didn't want it to end like this, Jett. I'm sorry. For some silly reason, I thought you might be glad I'm staying."

When he didn't indicate he'd even heard her, she bit back a hostile comment and stalked out of his bedroom, slamming the door behind her. Her boots were in the kitchen, kicked off just inside the back door, and she pulled them on over her bare feet, then stood there, realizing she still had no way to get home.

"Damn it, how do I get myself into these messes!" Close to tears of frustration, she wheeled around and headed for the phone just as Jody walked into the kitchen, looking bleary-eyed and half asleep, shirt undone, feet bare, hair standing on end.

He stopped dead when he saw her, then grinned sheepishly and wandered across to the fridge. "You and Dad had a fight, huh?"

"A disagreement," Kathleen said grimly.

"Mom used to slam the bedroom door like that when she and Dad had a fight." He hauled out a jug of milk and took it across to the table, dropping into a chair.

"Oh." It always bemused her slightly, the way Jody accepted finding her wandering around his house at all hours of the night or day. She and Jett hadn't kept their relationship a secret, but she was sure Jett had never talked to Jody about it. And yet Jody seemed to take it for granted that she spent most nights here, and he didn't seem to mind in the least.

She was going to miss him, she thought suddenly. Maybe as much as Jett himself, she was going to miss this lanky kid with the loopy grin and his father's eyes.

Smiling, she got the box of his favorite cereal out of the cupboard and took it and a bowl over to him. "So? How long are you going to keep me in suspense? You told me your teacher promised to grade your civics paper yesterday."

"I passed." He said it with an offhand shrug, dumping cereal into the bowl. Then he dug a wad of folded paper out of his shirt pocket and handed it to her. "I done okay, I guess."

Kathleen unfolded the paper, then gave a whoop of delight. "Ninety-four? Now that is more *like* it."

"Passed that snap algebra quiz on Monday, too," he said with a grin. "I guess all that homework you made me—" He stopped, spoon poised halfway to his mouth.

Kathleen glanced around just as Jett stepped into the kitchen. He paused, looking at the two of them; then his face went all shuttered and grim, and he strode by them to take the truck keys down from the hook by the door. "I'll drive you home."

She nearly told him to forget it, not relishing having to sit in the truck with him for the half hour it would take to get to The Oaks. Then she realized she was being silly and nodded, dredging up a smile for Jody. "You take care of yourself."

She stepped by Jett as he pushed the door open for her. He followed her to the truck without saying a word, their feet crunching through the light frost on the grass. He opened the truck door for her, and she got in, ignoring his helping hand, and he slammed the door shut on her heels, mouth tight, hat brim pulled low as he went around to the driver's side and got in beside her.

The truck was ice-cold, and Kathleen turned her jacket collar up and shoved her hands into her pockets, trying to get warm until the heater kicked in. "I could have called Gord."

"We have to talk."

"I think we've said all there is to say."

He slammed the truck into gear and accelerated out of the yard too fast, fishtailing on wet grass and gravel. "We haven't even scratched the surface."

"Which is just the way you *like* it, isn't it." He didn't reply or even look at her, and she gave a snort of laughter. "This is exactly what happened sixteen years ago! We had a great time together back then, too, as long as it was just sex. But the minute I got pregnant and it looked serious, you were out of the chute and down the road."

His profile was like jagged steel, and she could see a muscle ripple along his jaw.

"I'd love to know how Pam ever got a saddle on you. She must have come up on your blind side."

"That's not the way it was." His voice was low. Almost quiet. "Nothing back then was what it seemed."

"You've sure got that right. Believe it or not, I *had* figured that out by myself."

"You haven't figured out a damned thing," he said gratingly, eyes narrowed on the road. "Maybe that's what I was hoping for. Maybe that's why I kept throwing you and Jody together, hoping you'd finally sort it out yourself and I wouldn't *have* to tell you. I'd sit there and watch the two of you and tell myself it would all work out. That one day you'd look at him and all the pieces would fall into place and you'd just... know. Instinct or something."

"Jody?" Kathleen looked at him, thoroughly confused. "What's this got to do with Jody?"

"Everything." The one word fell between them, crisp and quiet, like the first flakes of snow. "He—" Jett clenched his jaw. "I should have told you right off, I know that. But the longer I waited, the harder it got, and—"

"Just *say* it! What's Jody got to do with us? With me?"

He shook his head disbelievingly. "You really don't have a clue, do you? Your sister-in-law figured it out in about thirty seconds flat, though I'm damn sure that bullheaded brother of yours hasn't, or I'd be history."

"Figured *what* out!"

"Don't you ever look in a mirror?"

It was making no sense, Kathleen thought dizzily. Now he was talking about mirrors, and it made no sense at all.

"He's your son, Kathy," Jett said in a soft voice. "Jody is your son."

She heard the words, but they could have been in some alien language for all the sense they made. She stared at Jett, then made a rough attempt at laughter. "What on earth are you talking about?"

"Your baby didn't die, Kathy. *Our* baby. He didn't die like they told you."

It was impossible, of course. Some bizarre joke, although she'd never known him to be deliberately cruel before. "Why... why are you saying that?" Her voice was almost childlike in its hurt bewilderment. "Why would you say a thing like that, Jett?"

He slammed his hands against the steering wheel. "Damn it, I didn't want to tell you like this. I wanted—"

"He . . . didn't die?"

She turned in the seat to face him, the words still making no sense. He was talking about something else, obviously. About some*one* else. Not about her. Not about her baby . . .

"No." She wet her lips and took a deep breath, straightening her shoulders. "No, that's not true. My baby died. You—you're wrong. Mistaken." She wanted him to stop frightening her. She didn't want to be hurt again. Not like this.

"Damn it, Kathy," he said roughly. "He didn't die. It was all a lie your old man concocted. They adopted him out— your dad and your uncle. Except the adoption fell through and—"

But Kathleen wasn't listening. Had stopped listening deliberately, not knowing why he was doing this to her, but knowing for certain that she wasn't going to put up with it.

Memories flew through her mind. The sound of a baby's high-pitched cry, then her own voice, an echoing cry of pain and grief. Waking in the night, drunk on tranquilizers, her breasts full of milk and aching. Crying out for the child no one ever brought.

"Kathy, we have to talk about—"

"No." She reached for the door handle, feeling suddenly smothered and frantic to get out, knowing if she stayed even another minute she was going to start screaming or crying or hammering at the windows like a frenzied moth. "I don't know why you're doing this to me, but I want out." The tears caught her so unexpectedly that she nearly choked on them, and she pulled blindly on the handle. "Stop the truck!"

"What the hell are you doing!" Jett caught her by the upper arm and pulled her back against him roughly. She started to fight him, but he managed to hang on to her somehow, swearing as he swerved the truck onto the shoulder of the road, dust flying, and managed to bring it to a gear-grinding stop. "Are you crazy?"

"Let go of me!" Kathy wrenched free of his grasp and was out the door in the next instant.

Swearing ferociously, Jett threw his door open and went after her, catching her in a few long strides. He caught her by the arm and swung her around to face him. "Kathy, this isn't—"

"Don't touch me!"

Her fist hit his cheekbone, and he gave a grunt of pain and grabbed both her arms. Then he more or less force-marched her back to the truck, ignoring her enraged threats of what was going to happen to him if he didn't let go of her, plus some profane suggestions of what he could do after he *did* let go of her.

And that was when he saw the police car. It had eased in behind the pickup like a cruising shark, and he swore almost as colorfully as Kathy was doing as the driver's door opened and Sheriff Carmody got out, looking like he meant business.

Then he recognized Jett and broke into a lazy grin. "Got yourself a little woman trouble, Jett?" Kathy was still swearing a blue streak and trying to pry her arm out of Jett's grip, and Carmody watched her, looking amused. "Didn't your daddy ever tell you never to promise 'em anything you might not want to deliver on, son?"

"I want him arrested!" Kathy wrenched free finally, eyes flashing. "I want you to lock him up and—"

Carmody scratched the back of his neck. "Well, ma'am, it ain't as easy as that. I need something to arrest him *for.*"

"I'll give you something to arrest him for," she all but shouted. "Kidnapping and lying and fraud and—"

Jett took his hat off and wiped his forehead with his arm. "Do me a favor, Buck, and take Miss Patterson home, would you?"

"Patterson?" Carmody looked at her with renewed interest.

"That's right," Jett said. "Old man Patterson's daughter."

Carmody gave a low whistle. "She drunk?"

"Just mad as hell. She...she's had some unsettling news."

"I want you to arrest this man," Kathy said heatedly. "Now!"

Carmody didn't look amused, and Jett dredged up a grim smile. "Get her home, Buck. Give her a couple of hours to cool off, and if she still wants you to arrest me—well, you know where I live. I'm not goin' anywhere."

Carmody nodded thoughtfully. "No, I don't suppose you are. You go on home and don't worry about it. I'll take care of her. Miz Patterson?" He turned to Kathy. "Why don't I take you home, and you can tell me what's on your mind?"

She was still crying hours later. It didn't seem possible that she could hold so many tears. But maybe no more impossible than any of it.

Jody. Jody was her son.

As she had a thousand times, Kathleen tried to grasp the words in her mind, to force them to make sense. But they kept refusing to take shape, slipping away from her even as she tried to comprehend them. It wasn't possible, she kept thinking over and over, wanting to believe, not daring to.

And yet . . .

And yet. Nothing was impossible when it came to her father. Not even a lie this monstrous.

And in the end, it was that—knowing her father, knowing what he was capable of—that made it all seem possible after all.

Jody. What was it Jett had said? *Don't you ever look in a mirror?* Yet Jody didn't look anything like her. He was his father's son, that wild Kendrick blood unmistakable.

She thought of that first time she'd seen him, handsome and tall, and had felt her heart break a little. Thought of how endearing he was, how shy and awkward.

She drew a sob, trying to absorb the immensity of what was happening. Of the incredible gift she'd just been handed, wrapped in lies and deception. She had a child. A tall, good-looking boy of fifteen with a loopy grin and his father's eyes. A half-grown son who loved horses and rodeos and hated algebra and blushed when you teased him and even had a girlfriend worth learning to dance for.

Tears welled up, and she sobbed again, scrubbing at her cheeks with a wadded-up tissue. Until a few hours ago her life had been just ordinary. Yesterday she'd told Gord she was going to stay in Burnt River and had made an appointment with a Realtor to look at houses, then helped Sherry plan a birthday party for Chelsea. She'd bought shampoo at the drugstore and stopped by Vic's Café for lunch, and had made love with Jett half the night.

And now, in the span of a mere handful of hours, she'd become the mother of a fifteen-year-old boy.

She drew a shaky breath and wiped her eyes with the tissue again, then sat on the floor beside her bed. She had to stop crying. She couldn't think when she was crying like this. It was just shock, she knew that. Her mind's way of handling something too big to comprehend. But she felt drunk on tears, and now she just wanted them to stop.

There was a soft tap at the door, and she lifted her head, too exhausted to even tell whoever was out there to go away. The door opened, and she turned her face away from the shaft of light that speared the comforting darkness.

"Kathy?" It was Sherry's voice, soft with caution. "Honey, I brought you some hot tea and a bran muffin. You've got to eat something. You've been up here all day, and you've got to—oh, hell, what am I talking about?" Despair ran through her words, and she set a tray on the bed, then squatted beside Kathleen, looking forlorn. "Mother instinct—got a crisis, reach for the muffins."

Kathleen surprised herself by smiling. "Thanks." Her voice caught on just that one word, and she gave another sob.

"Oh, Kathy." Sherry slipped her arm around her shoulders and hugged her. "I should have told you. I should have *made* Gord believe me. I should have—"

"W-when did you find out?"

"I think I knew that first time you brought Jody out to the house. I'd seen him around town and had noticed how much he looks like Jett, but when I saw the two of you standing there side by side, I knew." She sat on the floor beside Kathleen, then grabbed a tissue from the box on the bed and blew her nose. "Gord thought I was imagining things. But it drove me crazy, and finally I just went out to the Kicking Horse and asked Jett straight out. He denied it, but I knew he was lying. But without proof, there was nothing I could do. I couldn't tell you my suspicions in case I was wrong, and—oh, brother! What a mess!"

Kathleen wiped tears from her cheeks. "How's Gord taking it?"

"He's pretty shaken up. He's talked to Jett. And—" Sherry paused. "And he called your uncle. Mac wants to come out here. To talk with you."

"MacKenzie Patterson is the last person I *ever* want to talk to." Kathleen felt a surge of anger at just the mention of her uncle's name, and she hung on to it, preferring it to the other things she was feeling. "He's the one who arranged the adoption in the first place. He helped my father give my baby away."

"You have to hear his side of it, Kathy," Sherry said softly. "You know what your dad was like—when he wanted something, he got it. And in the end, it was Mac who called Jett and told him about the baby. Without him, Jett would never have known."

"And me?" A sob ran through her angry words. "Why didn't he tell *me?*"

"You were fifteen, Kathy," Sherry said gently.

"Sixteen. By the time the baby was born, I was sixteen."

"Look, I'm not saying Mac made the right decision, not telling you, but I can see why he thought it was for the best."

Kathleen gave a short, angry laugh. "If there's one thing we've never had a shortage of in this family, it's people doing what's *best*. Best for my father. Best for the almighty Patterson name." She gave her cheeks an angry wipe with her hand. "Well, I'm through with it. I'm getting on a plane tomorrow, and I'm not getting off until I find a place where they've never even *heard* of Nelson Patterson. Then I'm changing my name to Smith, and I never want to hear of or from anyone in this family as long as I live!''

Sherry started laughing. ''I wanted to do that right after I married Gord and your father took me aside to advise me what was expected of me, now that I was a Patterson. Gord thinks there might be a village somewhere in Mongolia where no one's heard of your father, but he won't guarantee it.''

In spite of herself, Kathleen had to laugh. She pulled her knees up and braced her elbows on them, holding her aching head in her hands. ''God, I hate him. How could he do that, Sherry? How could he give his own grandson away?''

''I don't know,'' Sherry said quietly. ''I asked Gord the same thing, and he didn't know, either. I doubt we'll ever know.''

''And Mom. I can't believe my own mother would—''

''I doubt she knew. According to Mac, the only people outside the hospital who knew the truth were him and your father.''

''And Jett,'' Kathleen said coldly. ''You forgot that Jett knew.''

''And Jett.'' Sherry sighed. ''Kathy—'' She bit off whatever she'd been about to say, then got to her feet. ''Try to get some of that tea and muffin down, okay? And Gord's really upset, Kathy. He needs to talk to you when you're up to it.''

Kathleen nodded, a sudden wave of exhaustion washing through her. ''I said some pretty awful things to him a while ago. Tell him I'm sorry, will you? I know he didn't have anything to do with it.'' She smiled wearily. ''And thanks, Sherry. You must get awfully tired of holding this family together when we go into meltdown.''

''You're all worth it.'' Sherry started to turn away, then saw something on the tray that made her smile. ''Oh, Shaun asked me to give this to you.'' She squatted beside Kathleen again and tucked something into her lap. ''He says he'd like it back sometime, but figures you need it more than he does right now. It's really good for crying on, he says.''

Kathleen stared at the ragged little stuffed rabbit and felt her eyes fill. She sobbed and clutched the small soft thing against her chest, then started crying again, not even bothering to stop the tears this time.

It was almost an hour later that someone rapped lightly on the door. Kathleen lifted her head from her arms and combed her tangled hair back with her fingers. "It's open, Gord."

The door opened, and someone came into the room. Then the door closed again, and the darkness dropped back around her like a blanket. It was his scent she recognized first, that familiar blend of hay and leather and horses, and she lifted her head slowly to look disbelievingly across the room.

She couldn't see him clearly in the shadows, but she knew it was him, though she could see only the outline of wide shoulders and a Stetson hat. He stood there like something carved, then reached up and pulled his hat off and ran his fingers through his hair, shifting his weight uneasily, like a stag scenting danger.

She knew he was looking at her, could sense his wariness, his caution. Then he swore in a soft, tired voice and squatted on his heels, hat dangling from his fingers, not looking at her.

Oddly, she discovered she wasn't half as angry as she would have expected. She didn't feel much of anything, in fact. "It's true, isn't it," she finally said, her voice as ragged as old cloth.

"Yeah." He took a deep breath and lifted his head. "Yeah, it's true." Wearily, he sat on the floor and leaned back against the closed door. "What have they told you?"

"Everything I need to know."

"Not everything." His voice was low and rough. "They gave him away, Kathy. Your old man and your uncle. Problem was, when the people who adopted him got a good look at him, they knew right off he had some buckskin in him somewhere. They'd *paid* for a white baby and sure a hell weren't going to settle for some half-breed, so they sent him back.''

Kathleen didn't say anything. Couldn't imagine what she had left to say.

''When your uncle phoned to tell me he had a baby boy there with my name on the birth certificate, and did I want him, I thought it was some kind of joke.''

''Your name wouldn't have been on the birth certificate,'' Kathleen said, wondering how many other lies she would catch him in. ''I know my father. He would never have left a trail like that.''

''Your old man wouldn't have, but your uncle didn't seem to mind. He made sure my name got put on the thing, as legal as hell. He said if I wanted Jody, he'd help me with the paperwork.'' He smiled grimly. ''I don't think it had much to do with me. I think he just wanted to tick your old man off.''

Which was the only thing he'd said so far that made sense. Mac had been her father's younger brother and had put up with Nelson's tyranny for most of his life. But now and again he would have enough. Defying her father on something this big would have appealed to him.

''And you're saying my father just backed off without a fight and let Mac have his way?'' She gave a snort. ''I don't believe that for a minute!''

''Oh, there was a fight, all right. Your old man swore he'd have me charged with statutory rape if I even *thought* about bringing Jody back here. He said he'd make sure I got hard time, and plenty of it.'' Jett could still hear the cold anger in her father's voice, the memories as vivid as yesterday. ''Your uncle called Cliff Albright and told him I needed help. Cliff hated your old man almost as much as he loved a good fight. He was all set to take it to court, but your old man didn't want the publicity. So we came to an... agreement.''

''And you got my baby.''

''*My* baby,'' Jett reminded her with an edge in his voice. ''As far as I knew, you didn't want him.''

"And the *agreement* you had with my father?"

Jett didn't say anything for a long moment. Then he realized all he had left to give her was the truth. "I got thirty thousand dollars, a job with a stock contractor in Arizona and the guarantee you were giving up all rights to Jody. In return, I agreed to stay out of Burnt River and never contact you or anyone in your family. No one was to know Jody was your son. Not even Jody." He smiled humorlessly. "Your old man didn't want Jody turning up on his doorstep in a few years, looking for his grandpa and maybe some of that precious Patterson money."

She didn't say anything, sitting there on the floor looking lost. Her hair was all tangled, and he could tell she'd been crying by the roughness in her voice and the way she kept her face averted. Pam hadn't liked to cry in front of him, either.

It must be a special knack he had, he thought dully, making his women cry.

He thought of telling her that he was sorry, but wondered what good it would do. Found himself thinking he had to go home pretty soon and tell Jody, and that wasn't something he was looking forward to. The lies had wound themselves into the fabric of their lives like strands of wire, and he wondered what was going to be left when it finished unraveling.

Jody. If he lost Jody, he had nothing left at all.

"But you didn't stay out of Burnt River."

"When my granddad died and left me the Kicking Horse, I decided I'd had enough of your old man's threats. I knew he didn't want you finding out that the adoption had fallen through and that I had Jody, so I figured he couldn't afford to cause trouble if I moved back. I just made damn sure Jody never went near him."

"That's what you were talking about that first day I was back. That's why you were so angry, so...scared."

"When I saw you with him that day, I thought you knew. I thought that was why you'd come back. That now your old man was dead, you were going to try to get Jody away from me.''

"And Pam?" She took a deep breath. "How did she fit in?"

"I was eighteen. A rodeo bum. I didn't know anything about babies. Marrying Pam seemed like a...good idea. And Albright told me that if the people who'd originally wanted to adopt Jody changed their minds and came after him, my chances of keeping him were better if I had a wife."

"How in God's name did you talk her into marrying you to raise *my* baby?"

"She loved me," he said simply.

Kathy nodded slowly, her eyes meeting his through the shadows. They were still stunned with shock and hurt, but there was something else in them now. Something cool and thoughtful that reminded him very suddenly of her father.

Something prickled the back of his neck, and he wondered what she was thinking. But before he could ask her, she got to her feet and walked across to the window. She pulled the drapes open, and he was surprised to see it was already dark.

"You weren't going to tell me, were you?" Her voice was controlled and remote. "You thought I was going back to Baltimore. That if you didn't tell me, that would be the end of it. You knew that if Mac hadn't told me by now, he never would." She turned to look at him, her eyes like ice. "You never intended to tell me at all."

Jett gritted his teeth and considered trying to lie his way through it. But he was sick of the lies. Sick of looking into his own eyes in the bathroom mirror every morning and despising what he saw. "Not at first," he finally admitted roughly.

"You bastard." She said it coldly and turned her back on him.

There didn't seem much point in arguing with her, so he said nothing. Wondered where they went from here. Then, finally, he swore and got stiffly to his feet. "Look, it was wrong, I admit that. But I was scared you'd...do something. Try to get him away from me or something. But later, I knew I had to tell you. That—''

"You knew you had to tell me because Sherry suspected the truth. You knew you wouldn't be able to keep her quiet for long."

"I was planning on telling you long before I talked to her."

"But not before you slept with me."

Jett tried not to wince. "I...hell, Kath, what do you want me to say? That I'm sorry? That I should have told you that day up at Beaver Creek? I was all set to, but—'' He shook his head wearily, not even knowing how to explain it.

"You should have told me fifteen years ago." She turned her head to give him a long, cold stare.

"They told me you didn't want him," he said in a tight voice.

"And you believed them?" Her eyes were chilly with disbelief. "I loved you! Did you really think I'd give your baby away?"

"As far as I knew, you didn't want me *or* my baby. How the hell was I supposed to know they'd lied to you?"

She held his gaze for a long while, her eyes hostile and angry; then she turned away from him again. He stood there and looked at her, wanting to walk across and pull her into his arms and have things back the way they were. Wanting it all to be over.

Knowing there was no way it was going to be that easy.

"That's what these past three weeks were all about, wasn't it?" She didn't even look at him as she said it, her shoulders rigid. "I was stupid enough to think it meant something, but it didn't have anything to do with me—it was all about Jody. All about making sure I wouldn't try to take him away from you."

"No, Kath, it wasn't like that. I never even intended to—''

"Oh, you *intended,* all right." She turned on her heel to look at him, eyes sultry with anger. "You damn well *in-*

tended to get me into bed again, because you knew if you did, I'd do anything for you, just like last time. You knew all you had to do was make me fall in love with you again. That I'd never fight you for Jody if I loved you." She blinked and turned away abruptly.

Jett took a step toward her, one hand out to touch her shoulder. He caught himself just in time and lowered his arm. *Loved you.* "Kath, that's crazy. It wasn't like—"

"You planned the whole thing. It must have scared you half to death, coming up here to The Oaks that afternoon and finding Jody here. You knew you had to do something. So you followed me up to Beaver Creek the next day, all sweet and nice." She gave a ragged laugh. "I *knew* you were up to something that day. But I never could resist that Kendrick charm. And you knew that. You knew all it would take was a little sweet talkin', a little kissin'…push all those old buttons and I'd be head over heels in love with you again in no time at all."

"There was never any plan," Jett said harshly. *Love.* She kept talking about love, talking as though…

"The problem, Jett, is that in all your scheming and plotting, you forgot one salient fact. The one thing you should *never* have forgotten." She crossed her arms in front of her, looking every inch the attorney she was, and leveled a look at him that was so hostile, so cold, that Jett felt a jolt of raw fear. "You forgot I'm my father's daughter."

Jett just stared at her. Dread clotted in his belly, and he swallowed, knowing what came next.

"I suggest you spend the next few days finding yourself a good lawyer, Jett. Because the next time I see you, it's going to be across a courtroom."

Jett could hear the blood pounding in his temples. "What…what the hell do you mean by that?" he finally managed to whisper.

"I want my son back." She enunciated each word clearly and slowly, letting them hang in the air like ice crystals. "And if you thought my father was one mean son of a bitch in a fight, you haven't seen anything yet."

Chapter 10

He had to hand it to her, Jett thought with admiration. She sure as hell knew how to hit where it hurt. Just like her old man. She'd been right about that. He should *never* have forgotten who she was. Never.

He lifted the glass and took another deep swallow of bourbon, teeth gritted as it burned its way down. Then he picked up the bottle and filled the glass again, ignoring the little whisper of warning in the back reaches of his mind. To hell with it. He was half drunk already, and with any luck he would make it the rest of the way before the bourbon gave out.

He leaned back in the big easy chair and closed his eyes, head swimming slightly. The house was dark and quiet, and it seemed to echo every sound, oddly empty without her. Funny how he'd gotten used to having her in his life so easily.

Or had he just made that up, too? He gave a snort of bitter laughter and took another swallow of liquor. He'd been lying to Jody and to her and even to himself for so long that it was hard to tell where truth ended and fabrication began.

Maybe she was right. Maybe he *had* taken her to bed with ulterior motives. Maybe the things he thought he felt for her were just part of a desperate lie he'd spun to protect the life he'd built here with Jody. But one damn thing was certain: he wasn't giving Jody up without a fight that would make the Little Big Horn look like a church social.

If he could find an attorney who would take the job on. He smiled grimly and took another drink. Question: how many lawyers does it take to change a light bulb? Answer: how many can you afford?

Not enough, probably. And where was he going to find even one willing to go head-to-head with her and Gordon? They had it all on their side: the name, the money, the contacts. They were going to roll over him like Crazy Horse over Custer. And they wouldn't be taking prisoners.

"Hey, Dad?"

Jett looked up a little drunkenly as Jody walked into the room. The boy frowned. "What are you sittin' in the dark for?"

"I like it that way." Jett leaned forward and braced his elbows on his knees, rubbing the back of his neck and staring at the rag rug between his feet. "You finish welding that stock gate like I told you?"

"Yeah." Jody circled him cautiously, eyeing the glass in Jett's hand, the half-empty bottle on the floor, his young face tight with concern.

He was thinking of Pam, Jett knew. Of all those afternoons when he came home from school and found her wrapped around a bottle of bourbon.

"You, uh, want something to eat? I can make spaghetti."

Jett's stomach roiled unpleasantly. "No. Got any homework?"

"It's done. And my chores. They're all done, too."

Jett nodded, scrubbing his fingers through his hair. *Just say it,* something whispered at him. *Sit him down right now and tell him you've been lying to him all his life. Tell him* about Kathy, about her old man, about Pam, about all of it.

"You, uh, you and Miz Patterson had a fight, huh."

"A difference of opinion."

"So she's . . . not comin' over tonight?"

Jett swirled the bourbon in the glass, then downed it in one swallow. "No."

"Then maybe . . . I, uh, she said she'd help me with this experiment I'm supposed to be doin' for chemistry. Maybe I could go over to her place and—"

"No!" Jett's voice cut through the room like a whip crack. "I don't want you going over there, you hear? You stay *away* from Kathleen Patterson and that whole clan of hers."

Jody's mouth went hard and stubborn. "So just 'cause you and her had a fight, I can't even talk to her?"

"That's what I'm saying." Jett got to his feet, grabbing the bourbon bottle by the neck and heading for the kitchen. He wasn't making any sense, he knew that, but he had to keep Jody away from her. Had to figure out some way to get through this without hurting the boy. "You just do as I say. And if you're hard up for something to do, the truck could use a good hosing down."

Jody looked sullen and angry and ready to argue; then he just turned on one boot heel and strode out of the room without a word.

And Jett, listening to the back door slam almost off its hinges, eyed the bourbon bottle for a speculative moment, then capped it tightly and put it out of temptation's way.

"Kathleen, I think you'll be making the biggest mistake of your life if you go through with this." Gordon handed her a glass. "Drink this. You look like you could use it."

"I hate bourbon."

"Then pretend it's something else." He shoved it into her hand. "I can't recommend strongly enough that you give up this idea of taking Jett to court. For one thing, it's entirely possible you'll lose. And for another, even if you win, I'm not sure the victory will be worth it.''

"He has my son!"

"His son," Gord barked. "You seem to keep forgetting that fact, Kathleen." He walked around to the other side of the desk, looking angry and out of sorts, and gestured at the papers scattered across it. "It's all here. The agreement Dad made him sign, the deal they cut—thirty grand for Jett's silence. He *kept* his side of the bargain."

"That agreement was signed without my knowledge or consent. I never agreed to give Jody up, so how can Jett claim he got sole custody? The whole thing was a fraud!"

"Look, I'm no fan of Jett Kendrick's—I'd still like to beat the hell out of him for what he did to you sixteen years ago. But the man was as much a victim of our old man as you were."

"Victim?" Kathleen stared at her brother in disbelief. "*Victim?* Gordon, that man *stole* my son!"

"He thought you gave the boy up for adoption." Gord's voice rose. "He was eighteen, for crying out loud! Little more than a kid himself. As far as he knew, you'd rejected not only him, but the baby, as well." He took a swallow of bourbon. "As far as I'm concerned, Kendrick deserves a medal, not a court battle. He fought tooth-and-nail fifteen years ago to get his son, and he's been a good father to the boy. Give him credit for that, at least, before you go off half-cocked with some idea of—"

"Jody Kendrick is my son," Kathleen said coldly. "*My* son." She set the glass down with a bang, and bourbon slopped onto the desk. Once she would have been horrified at the defacement; today she relished it. She wanted to smash the glass. To throw something. Break something. "I can't believe you won't support me in this."

"I didn't say I wouldn't support you," he said, making an effort to lower his voice. "But I *am* saying I won't help you drag Kendrick through the courts." He paused, looking at Kathleen steadily. "Have you given any thought to what's best for Jody in this? How he's going to react to a long, bloody custody battle? And it *will* be long and bloody, Kathleen. Kendrick will fight like a cougar to keep the boy, you can count on that."

Kathleen drew a deep breath, preparing to launch into an angry rebuttal, then let it out again with a weary sigh, holding the cool glass to her temple. Gord was at least half right, but she was damned if she was going to admit it. Not in this room, with her father's smug portrait looking down on them.

"Have you talked with the boy? With Jody?" Gord said the name almost awkwardly, as though still having trouble believing.

"No." Kathleen's voice was hoarse, and she took a sip of the bourbon without thinking. She made a face and set the glass down again, paced to the window, then back to the desk. "I don't even know what to say to him, Gord. I..." She lifted her arms helplessly, then let them drop to her sides. "I'm not even sure I really believe it yet. It's just so...impossible."

"Sometimes when I look in on Chelsea and Shaun at night, I have to pinch myself to prove it's real. That they're real." Gord smiled. "You've been handed a miracle, Kathy. You're never going to look at things the same way again. You'll see through different eyes. And feel through a different heart."

Kathleen looked at him in surprise. "Have you turned into a poet while I wasn't looking, Gord?"

"No. Just a father. And that," he added very quietly, "is why I can't help you take Jett's son away from him."

The next afternoon she was standing on the veranda of Jett's big ranch house, looking at the front door and wondering what in God's name she was doing there. Swallowing, she raised her hand and knocked on the door, praying he wasn't home. It would be easier if he wasn't home.

To her relief, no one answered. Taking a deep breath, she was starting to turn away just as the door opened. And she found herself standing face-to-face with her son.

"I...oh." It took her so by surprise that she simply stared at him, her mind going utterly blank. "It's ... you."

He grinned engagingly. "Some kind of teacher convention goin' on, so there ain't no school this week. I'm supposed to be out back helpin' the vet inoculate calves, but I got kicked in the ribs, and Dad said to take a couple of hours off."

She felt suddenly breathless with concern. Wanted to reach out and touch him, but felt suddenly too shy to do more than just look at him wonderingly. "Are you ... are you all right?"

"Hurts a little, but I'm okay." His grin widened. "Come on in, Miz Patterson. I'll tell Dad you're here."

Miz Patterson. She blinked. "I—what did you call me?"

He frowned, as though wondering what he'd done wrong. "I, uh..." He shrugged, obviously nonplussed. "I called you Miz Patterson, ma'am." His young face went all worried.

He didn't know. Numb with shock, Kathleen fought to drag in a deep breath. She was going to kill Jett. Right here, in this house, this afternoon, as God was her witness, she was going to kill him.

She forced herself to laugh. "Jody, I think we know each other well enough by now that you can call me Kathleen without the roof caving in. Miz Patterson makes me feel kind of ... old."

He blushed and grinned sheepishly. "Okay."

Kathleen followed him through to the kitchen, trying to form the words in her mind that would tell him he was her son. But they sounded all wrong. He would never believe her. He would think she was here trying to cause trouble because she was angry with Jett. Or that she'd simply lost her mind.

No. It had to come from Jett. Except Jett obviously wasn't in any kind of rush.

"How's school?" Keep it simple, she told herself. She found herself wanting just to look at him, trying to take in the miracle of who he was. It didn't seem possible that this was the same child she'd carried inside her. The child whose cries she still heard in her dreams.

She scanned his face for some sign of herself and thought she saw it finally in the curve of his mouth, in the way he smiled. Her heart gave a thump, and she felt tears burn her eyes suddenly and had to look away, pretending to leaf through a school book lying on the kitchen table.

"Pretty good. Chemistry's still giving me some trouble, though." He said it hopefully.

Kathleen smiled. "Well, maybe I can give you a hand with—"

"What the hell are you doing here?"

Jett's voice cracked through the room, startling Kathleen so badly she nearly dropped the book. She wheeled around as Jett strode toward her, his face like a thundercloud.

"What have you been telling him about—"

"Nothing." She said the word quickly, giving him a look of cold warning. "I haven't been telling him a thing. We were just talking about school."

Jett gave her a suspicious look, glancing at Jody, then back to her. His eyes narrowed. "What do you want?"

"We need to talk."

He thought about it, then nodded. "Jody, the vet needs a hand with those calves. You feel up to it?"

Jody looked from one to the other of them. "Yeah. Sure."

He walked to the door, and Kathleen waited until she heard it close behind him. "You haven't told him yet."

To her surprise, Jett flushed. "No." His voice was hoarse. "Not yet. I...will." He breathed an oath and walked across to the stove, grabbing up a cup and filling it with coffee. "I'm trying to figure out what to tell him, that's all. He's gone fifteen years thinking Pam was his mother. It's...not that easy."

It surprised Kathleen even more to discover she wasn't as angry as she should have been. "How are you?"

He looked at her quizzically. "I'm...okay. Hung over." A smile shadowed his mouth, gone in an instant. "You?"

"Well, I'm not hung over." She surprised herself a third time by actually smiling. "Still in shock. Confused. Scared silly."

"Scared?"

She shrugged. "I don't know anything about being a mother."

He didn't say anything, just watched her over the rim of the cup as he took a swallow of coffee. She cradled her handbag against her chest, thinking of the papers inside. And she found herself wondering if maybe Gord wasn't right after all. If maybe there wasn't some other way.

"I'm not giving him up, Kathy."

Kathleen looked up, realizing he'd been watching her all this time. "Jett—"

"No." The word echoed between them, and he simply looked at her, his eyes hard. "No negotiations, no deals. You're not coming back after fifteen years and turning his life upside down. I'm not going to let you do that."

Impatience flirted through her, but she ignored it, reminding herself that he had every right to be suspicious. After all, she'd set the battle lines yesterday. If he felt under siege, it was her fault. "It was never my intention to turn his life upside down," she said through clenched teeth. "You keep talking as though this is all my fault. Remember, I didn't know he *was* my son until a day ago. Remember that you were the one keeping the secrets."

"So you keep sayin'."

She gave him a sharp look. "What do you mean by that?"

"Just that I'm finding it hard to swallow all this coincidence stuff—your old man dyin', your brother starting to work for Albright, then you back in town, makin' friends with Jody, all over me like a—"

"All *over* you? You came on to me like a stag in rut that day up at Beaver Creek. I never had a chance."

"You didn't put up much of a fight, Slick. You must have been laughin' behind my back the whole time at how easy I was makin' it for you. Hell, I practically handed Jody to you."

"Handed him to me? You slept with me for three weeks before you even told me he was my son!" Anger shot through her. "Damn you, Jett Kendrick, you're not going to get away with this!"

"You're not getting my son away from me, lady. Get that straight right now. Patterson or no Patterson, this is one fight you are *not* going to win."

"I spent fifteen years believing my baby was dead, and suddenly I find out that not only is he still alive, but he's been living right here in Burnt River with you!" She gestured angrily. "God knows how many times I saw him over the years without knowing who he was. I may have even *spoken* to him. And you... you just kept him all to yourself!"

Even as she was saying the words, she knew they didn't make a lot of sense. Knew that Gord was right and that Jett had been as much a victim of her father's manipulations as she had. But she didn't give a damn about that. Didn't give a damn about any of it, in fact, except the vastness of the betrayal. The immensity of the lie. "I could kill you for what you've put me through," she said in a harsh whisper.

"What *I've* put *you* through?" Jett's face darkened with anger. "Lady, while you were playin' debutante in the big city, I was back here fightin' for my life! Your old man battled me every inch of the way, and I paid with *blood*, you got that? I swallowed my pride, and I took his money and his job, and I kept my mouth shut, just like he wanted. And I did it because of the son you didn't want!"

"Don't you dare say that! Don't you dare make it sound as though—"

"*I* raised him! Me! Where were you when he cried for three nights straight with colic, or when he came down with measles and mumps and every other damn thing goin' around? Where were you when he fell out of that tree and knocked himself cold, or the day he went through the ice on Big Spring Lake and I was sure I'd lost him for good?"

"Crying my heart out in Baltimore because I thought my baby was dead!" she shouted at him. "Don't you tell me how hard it's been! You've had him for fifteen years! You were there when he took his first step and said his first word. You put him on his first horse, and took him to school on his first day, and held the back of the seat the first time he rode a bicycle. You were there for all his birthdays and all his Christmases and all his school plays and Easter egg hunts. You had all those firsts, damn you, and I had nothing at all."

"And if it had been up to you and that old man of yours," Jett said, his voice so low and tight it sounded cut from steel, "I wouldn't even have known I had a son. So don't you come in here playing the betrayed mother, lady."

Kathleen sucked in an outraged breath. "That is a lie! I had no idea he was even alive!"

Jett gave a snort. "Yeah, or maybe you just figured you need a better story. Something to make you sound a little more sympathetic. Like a victim instead of just a woman who gave her baby away and then changed her mind." He leveled a hard look at her. "I figure the truth is that you gave him away, just like your old man said. And then you forgot all about him until you went through your old man's papers after the funeral and discovered *I* had him."

Something moved near the door, just a shadow on shadow, but it distracted Kathleen, and she glanced at it. She caught a glimpse of Jody's face, chalk-white. She sucked in her breath. "Jett!"

But Jett either didn't hear or simply didn't care about her gasp of warning. "Admit it, Kathy. The truth wouldn't look good in court, would it? That you gave Jody away like a stray pup no one wanted, handing him over to those people from Virginia five minutes after he was born. About the only thing in your story I do believe is that maybe you didn't know that they dropped him back on your uncle's doorstep like he had distemper when they figured out he had Indian blood in him. If your uncle hadn't called me, God knows what your old man would have done with him."

There was a strangled sob behind him, and Jett wheeled around. Jody was standing there, looking sick and disbelieving, and Jett felt his heart thud to a stop. "Damn," he breathed, taking a step toward his son. "Jody!"

"Jody, please...." Kathy stepped by him, her face the color of ice. "Jody, that's not what happened!"

Too late. Jody just stared at her for a stunned moment, then spun on one heel and was gone, the door slamming emptily behind him. Jett swore ferociously and took a couple of strides after him; then he stopped, swearing again, realizing it was no use.

"My God," Kathy whispered. She turned to look at him, still white, her eyes filled with accusation. She stared up at him for a long while, her gaze searching his. "I don't even know you anymore, Jett. You were never this cruel. Never this hard. What happened to make you this way?"

"You happened," he said brutally.

"Is hurting me this important?"

"Hurting you is about all I have left."

Too far. Jett knew it the instant the words were out of his mouth.

She made some sound, a tiny release of breath, and he saw something in her eyes crumble, saw the glaze of tears, and knew he'd struck right to the quick this time.

"I see." Her voice was just a breath of sound, so fragile he barely heard it at all. "If it's any consolation, you have."

Jett swore under his breath, wanting...hell, he didn't know *what* he wanted. But it wasn't this. "Kath..."

"No more." She turned away, her back ramrod straight, every inch of her held taut and tall. "I can't do this anymore, Jett. Go and find your son. He needs you."

Your son. Jett stared at her, feeling a prickle along his arms. Suddenly Jody was *your son.*

He drew a deep, careful breath, wondering why he felt so empty. It was what he wanted. He'd come at her with everything he had, going for the jugular, wanting her to back off, to get out of Jody's life, to stop pretending she was somehow still involved with the child she'd given away.

If she'd given him away. He'd tried to convince himself that she had. That she'd been lying through her teeth when she'd said she didn't know. It was easier that way, for damn sure. Easier to hate her. To fight her. To drive her off.

Well, he'd done that. Except now it didn't feel like anything he wanted at all. "For the record," he growled suddenly, "I believe you."

She made no indication she'd even heard him, and he realized it didn't make any difference now. It was way too late for that.

He knew he should be saying something to her, but he didn't know what. Or even how. So he just gave her a long, thoughtful look, then turned and went to look for his son.

Jody was in the corral behind the barn, trying to throw a saddle on the brown and white colt they'd bought at a stock show the previous week. Even with two good arms, he would have had his hands full. But hampered by the cast on his left arm, he wasn't managing to do much but spook the paint even more. It was rearing and fighting the bridle, ears flattened, and then it slammed into the fence, making the entire corral shudder.

Jody shouted an oath at it and threw the reins down, then wheeled away, his face distorted with anger and tears. He saw Jett and stopped dead, then wiped his eyes with his good arm and stalked by without a word.

"I'll give you a hand with him," Jett said quietly.

Jody stopped, chest heaving, not looking at Jett or anywhere near him. "I don't need your damn help."

"We've got to talk, Jody."

"Go to hell."

Jett didn't say anything. He watched the paint bang itself against the fence like a moth in a jar, thinking he should open the gate and let it out before it hurt itself.

Jody hadn't moved. Sighing noisily, Jett took the few steps separating them and put his hand gently on the boy's shoulder. "Look, Jody, I know I've—"

Jody knocked his hand away and spun away from him, his face twisted with grief and rage and a hundred other things. He stood there, fists clenching and unclenching, his chest heaving. "You lied to me! You're nothin' but a damn liar!"

There was a split second of time when Jett actually thought the boy was going to take a swing at him. He wanted to. Jett could see it written all over his face.

"Do it," he said softly. "If it'll make you feel better, if it'll make up for some of the things I've done, then go ahead and take a shot at me."

Jody lifted his fist, struggling not to cry, and Jett could see him fighting to do it, wanting it so badly he could taste it. But he wheeled away with a sob, slamming the corral gate open so violently it flew back against the fence with a crash.

Then he was gone, through the gate and into the barn, and Jett could only stand there and watch him go, feeling something break apart inside him. Swearing in a dull monotone, he picked up Jody's discarded saddle and tossed it onto the top rail of the fence, then just stood there, out-stretched arms braced on the fence, and stared at the ground.

He was losing it all. Kathy. Jody. Only a handful of days ago, his life had been darn near perfect. He would lie in bed in the first light of morning with Kathy in his arms and find himself smiling for no reason at all, filled up inside with a feeling of such completeness, such rightness, that it took his breath away.

And now...now it was all slipping away. He'd been ready to fight Kathy to keep Jody, but in the fighting he had lost the very thing he'd wanted to protect.

It had come full circle, somehow. All the lies and deceptions. He found himself wondering coldly if he'd ever intended to tell Kathy about Jody. Maybe he'd just been kidding himself about that, telling himself what he wanted to hear so he wouldn't feel so damned guilty when he took her to bed.

He was good at that. He'd once convinced himself it was justifiable to marry a girl he didn't love because he needed a wife for legal reasons and his baby boy needed a mother.

He'd told himself back then that it was all right because Pam loved him. That they were both getting what they wanted.

And he'd convinced himself for all these years that Jody didn't have to know the truth about his real mother, that knowing would do more harm than good.

Or maybe, Jett taunted himself grimly, he'd never told Jody because it was just easier that way. Easier than having to explain why he'd married Pam when he hadn't loved her, why she'd started drinking, why she'd died that day.

Was that why he'd put off telling Kathy the truth? Maybe he'd managed to convince himself that lie was justified, too. After all, he *had* believed she was going back to Baltimore. That she had a life back there, filled with cocktail parties and high-powered lawyers and men named Brice.

He'd told himself he'd been protecting Jody. But maybe he'd just been protecting himself.

"Are you an' Daddy mad at each other?" Chelsea gazed up at Kathleen with cherubic innocence, her small face dusted with cookie crumbs. She leaned against the table and waited for an answer with the patience of a small bureaucrat.

"Not really, honey." Kathleen smiled and stroked Chelsea's hair. "Sometimes grown-ups get into arguments and it sounds as though they're mad at each other, but really they're just... voicing opinions."

Sherry looked up from the sugar cookies she was icing. "How about a movie tonight? We can leave Gord and the kids at home and have girls' night out."

Kathleen tried to smile again, then just gave up. "I don't think so. It would be a waste of money. My head just keeps spinning in circles."

"In circles?" Shaun peered up at her curiously, a half-eaten cookie in one hand and his stuffed rabbit in the other.

"On the inside, sweetie," Kathleen assured him with a laugh. "Just on the inside."

"Oh." He lost interest and wandered off.

The front doorbell rang just then, resonating with impressive solemnity, and Sherry swore under her breath. "That'll be the guy who phoned about your dad's gun collection. Are you and Gord *really* sure you want to sell those things? They're all antiques."

"It's about the only thing we *do* agree on these days," Kathleen muttered. She started to get up to answer the door, but Sherry beat her to it, already through the kitchen door and heading toward the front of the house.

Kathleen walked over to where Shaun and Chelsea were playing with the puppy. It was a yellow labrador, as fat as butter, and it came dashing over to her, all tongue and wriggling excitement and shining eyes. Laughing, Kathleen squatted and rubbed its ears, and it whimpered in delight, trying to jump up to lick her face.

"Kathleen? It's...for you." Sherry stood in the kitchen door with an uncertain look on her face.

Kathleen's stomach dropped. "If it's Jett, tell him I don't want to talk to him. And if it's his lawyer, I don't want to talk to him, either. In fact, I don't want to talk to anyone."

"It's not Jett. It's...it's your son."

Just the very word made Kathleen's heart tumble to a stop. "Oh..." She held her breath. "Where?"

Sherry came into the room, and Kathleen saw that Jody was behind her, his face the picture of indecision, as though he was already starting to regret being here.

"Hey, it's Jody!" Shaun went hurtling over to him.

Chelsea's face lit up. "Is your arm okay now? Your face sure looks better! I'm gettin' a pony for my birthday, and I'll let you ride him, if you like. At least *he* won't buck you off!"

Jody glanced at Sherry desperately, and Sherry laughed. "Okay, you guys—into the living room." She started to hustle both kids through the door. "Let's go. Your aunt has company."

The door swung closed behind them, and a sudden silence tumbled through the room like falling snow, so thick it seemed to drift into the corners. Kathleen didn't have a clue what to say. Her mind had gone as blank as a freshly cleaned chalkboard and she just stood there stupidly, looking at him, her chest so tight with emotion she could barely breathe.

"Is it true?" He stared at her from across the room, his expression carefully guarded to give nothing away, eyes wary. "Are you my mother?"

Kathleen felt the earth slide to a stop and stood very, very still, afraid to move, to breathe. She could feel the beat of her own heart. Wondered if he could hear it. Heard the sound of cartoon voices from the living room, the laughter of children.

Slowly, slowly, she drew a deep breath. He was just standing there, chin lifted slightly in a gesture she recognized as her own, firm mouth a little hard, like his father's. He looked so vulnerable and yet so strong, a wild, young thing caught between adolescence and adulthood. Caught now in the complexities of something even she didn't fully understand.

He knew, she could tell it from his eyes. But he needed to hear it from her. Needed her to say the words to make it real.

"I..." Her voice caught, as dry as old parchment. She swallowed, the sound almost audible in the stillness. For one wild, insane moment she almost denied it. Heard the words forming in her mind, the words that would make his world right again, would make Jett happy, would set things back the way they'd been. It would almost be easy. There had been so many lies already that making him believe a few more wouldn't be difficult at all.

Except it was too late for that. Too late for easy.

"I—I guess I am." Even to her own ears, she sounded astonished and uncertain.

Jody's eyes never left hers. But then, suddenly, a hint of a shy smile brushed his mouth, and he looked, for one heartbreaking moment, like he was about five years old. "I, uh, guess this is pretty new for you, too."

To her relief, Kathleen found she could almost laugh, and she felt herself relax. "You could say that." And then she did laugh, tipping her head back to ease the knot across her shoulders. "Oh, Jody... I know I should be saying something to you right now. Something... motherly, I guess. Something right."

He was still watching her. Waiting. Looking a little more uncertain now than before, still holding himself away from her.

She eased out a long, quiet sigh, looking at him gently. "But I don't know what, or even how. Until two days ago, I didn't even know I had a child. Now, suddenly, I'm a mother. And I just don't know... how." The tears surged up so fast and unexpectedly that they caught her by surprise, and she had to gulp them back, turning away quickly before he saw them. Not ready yet, for some reason, to let him—this boy-child, this miracle that was her flesh and blood—see her cry. He didn't need her tears.

Holding them back by sheer willpower, she looked at him again and smiled a little ruefully. "Some reunion, huh? They make it look so easy in the movies."

"Yeah." Another of those quick, shy smiles. "Aren't we supposed to hug now or something?"

"Something like that, I guess."

But he made no move toward her. And Kathleen found the distance between them more daunting than she would have thought possible. To walk across and have him turn away...

Too soon, something whispered at her. *Don't push. Don't try too hard. It's as new for him as it is for you.*

And it had to be right, she realized with sudden clarity. No false moves, no false emotion, no lies. There had been too much of that already. They had nearly fifteen years of lies between them.

"What *did* you hear yesterday?" she quietly asked. "I mean, what do you know about... what happened?"

"Enough." Again the defiance was touchingly bold. But his gaze slid from hers, and he gave one of those ubiquitous adolescent who-gives-a-damn-anyway shrugs that told her more about his pain than words ever could. "That they told you I'd died when I was born. That you didn't know I was even alive." He turned his head and gave her a look so level and cool it could have been Jett standing there. "Is that true? Is that what really happened?"

And there it was, Kathleen found herself thinking a little numbly. There, in a handful of words, the sum of what he needed to know. Of what he *had* to know, before he would allow her closer. Or allow himself even to dare dream . . .

"Yes," she said quietly, eyes never leaving his. "I carried you inside me for nine months, Jody. Every time you moved, I felt you. Every breath I took was your breath, every beat of my heart was yours. I dreamed of you at night, talked to you during the day, made plans and even bought baby clothes."

She smiled, just thinking about it, surprising herself a bit. Remembering blue rompers. Even then, she'd known he was a boy. She gazed at him wonderingly, letting her eyes take in the magic of him. "I loved you from the moment I found out I was pregnant. All I wanted was to hold you. To protect you. And then..." She shrugged, letting the smile fade.

Shoving her hands into her pockets, she walked across to the window and stared out. "When you were born, they wouldn't let me see you. I should have guessed they were up to something, but I was..." Another shrug. "I was barely sixteen, and scared and exhausted, and I...I trusted them." The bitterness in her own voice surprised her. "I trusted them, and they came back and told me my baby had died."

Kathleen turned away from the window to look at him, suddenly weary and sad. "I can't even remember the next couple of months. After a while the worst of the pain faded. But not all of it. Never all of it." She met his gaze evenly. "There's been an empty place inside me since the day they told me you'd died. A place I thought I'd never be able to fill."

He blinked and looked away, scuffing at something on the floor, shoulders hunched slightly.

"I would never have given you away, Jody Kendrick," she said with soft fierceness. "Not in a million years. I loved you, and I would have died before letting anyone take you away from me. You have to believe that.''

He glanced at her sideways, his young face filled with a thousand emotions. And it was only then that she realized he was crying. ''How couldn't you know?'' he whispered raggedly. ''I was your *son*. How couldn't you know I was still alive?''

''They told me you'd died,'' she whispered, agonized. ''I was sixteen, Jody. I *believed* them, don't you understand that? I was this scared kid in a hospital full of doctors, and they told me you were dead. And my father...'' She swallowed the hot thickness in her throat. ''I had to believe him. Because if I didn't, then there was nothing at all I could believe in.''

''You should have known.'' His voice caught, rough as straw, and he didn't even bother trying to stop the tears. ''You were my *mother!* You were *supposed* to know!'' He gave a strangled sob and in the next instant bolted blindly for the door and was gone.

Kathleen took one step after him, then stopped, not even realizing until that instant that she was crying, too. Knowing she should go after him, should be saying something to him—but not knowing what or how. Knowing only that her heart felt ripped apart, and that if she moved she might shatter into a million pieces.

She'd lost him, she thought numbly. She'd just lost the son she'd never even known she had....

Chapter 11

About the last person Jett expected to see on the Kicking Horse the next morning was Kathleen Patterson. He'd just come out of the machine shed and was walking past the log corral at the back of the horse barn when he spotted her. She was standing with her back to him, hands shoved into the pockets of her sheepskin jacket, watching Jody's colt buck and play in the sun.

He stopped dead, then swore and walked over to her, in no mood for a replay of yesterday's confrontation. "Something I can do for you?"

His voice was gruffer than he'd intended, and she started badly, stumbling around to face him. She didn't seem overly glad to see him, letting her gaze slide from his as she turned to look at the colt again, shoulders hunched almost protectively. "N-no. I... was just leaving."

"If you've got something to say to me, say it," he growled. "I don't reckon I'm goin' to like it much, whatever it is, so let's just get it over with." He was tired, he thought. Worn down and worn out, like an old horse ridden too long and hard. He watched her watch the colt and wished he could bring himself to hate her. This would all be easier, somehow, if he hated her.

"I came out to see if... to see Jody. No one was at the house, so I came back here. I thought with there being no school..."

"He and my foreman went down to Butte to look at some cattle we're thinking of buying."

"Oh." She looked back at the colt. "This probably wasn't such a good idea, anyway. He came to see me last night...."

"I figured he might." Jett pulled his hat off and wiped the brim, then slapped it back on. "He's got a lot of stuff to sort out."

"I handled it badly. And I wanted..." She lifted her shoulders in a helpless shrug, still watching the colt. It bucked playfully, and he could see her smile.

Then she seemed to remember where she was, and she let the smile fade and turned away from the corral, not looking at him. "I—wrote him a letter." She pulled a folded envelope from her pocket. "I—would you give it to him? Please?" She held it out to him uncertainly. "I thought it might help him... understand."

Jett made no move to take the thing. It took all of Kathleen's willpower to stand there holding it, knowing what he must be thinking. How much he must hate her. "You can read it if you want," she whispered. "There's nothing...critical of you in it. Or of Pam. I just wanted to...to tell him some things."

An odd expression flickered across Jett's strong face. He frowned finally and took it between his fingers, not bothering to even glance at it before tucking it into his shirt pocket.

She stood there awkwardly, looking at the colt again. He didn't want her here, didn't want to talk to her or even see her again, but for some reason she couldn't bring herself to walk away just yet. There was so much unsaid between them, so many things still unresolved. And she hated it. Hated the anger and shouting. She thought of what it had been like here with him only a few days ago. Of how happy she'd been.

There was nothing more to say. Nothing he was interested in hearing, anyway. She turned away, not even knowing what she was expecting from him. He'd made it clear how he felt about her coming back into his life, into Jody's life. She took a deep breath and started to walk away. Then, abruptly, she stopped dead.

"Damn it, you're not the only one who's had his life turned inside out!" She wheeled around, tears springing into her eyes before she could stop them. "This isn't easy for me, either, you know! I'm thirty-one years old, and I just discovered I have a son I never knew about, and I don't know anything about being a mother, and he hates me and you hate me and—" The words got all tangled up in a sob, and she gulped, giving her cheeks a furious wipe with her arm, hating having him see her this vulnerable.

"Kathy—"

He caught her by the arm, and she wrenched away, angry and defiant, trying to keep her chin from wobbling. "I'm not handling it very well—so what! You've had fifteen years to get this parent thing down pat, and I've had two days, and if that isn't good enough for you, then sue me!"

To her surprise, Jett didn't look half as angry as she would have expected. In fact, he didn't look angry at all. He looked ... bemused. And then, even more surprising, he smiled. Granted, it wasn't much of a smile—a mere flicker of amusement that tipped that strong mouth aside for no more than a split second—but it *was* a smile. "You're right."

Kathleen drew a breath for an angry retort, then let it out in a surprised huff, taken unawares. "You—I ... what?"

"I said, you're right." He leaned one shoulder against the high corral fence, looking impossibly relaxed for someone who'd been bellowing like a bull in barbed wire for the past two days.

She blinked. "I am?"

Again a smile flickered across his mouth. "Yeah. You are."

"Well, I...that is, you're right! I mean, I am. Right." She took a breath, then let it out again in confusion.

The expression on Kathy's face made Jett smile, knowing how she felt. He was pretty confused, too. By rights, he should be tossing her off the ranch on her trim little backside and telling her not to come back without her lawyer. Instead, he found himself wanting to walk across and wipe the tears from her cheeks and tell her everything would be all right.

"Jody doesn't hate you, Kath. He's just confused. If he hates anybody, it's me." She stared at him mistrustfully, as though expecting a trap, and he managed a rough smile. "And I don't hate you, either. I should, God knows. But I don't."

She stood looking at him uncertainly, hands shoved down into her jacket pockets, shoulders hunched. "You...don't?"

He rested his elbow on the top rail of the corral, watching the colt frolic in the sun. "Would all this be easier if I did?"

It took her a long while to answer. She walked back to the corral thoughtfully and came over to stand beside him. "I don't think anything could make this easier."

He turned his head to look at her; then he just smiled and looped his arm around her shoulders and pulled her against him. "You got that right, darlin'." He rested his face against her hair for a moment, breathing in the warm, clean scent of her, then rubbed her shoulder idly. "How are you doin'?"

"Okay." She rested her head against his chest. "No," she whispered, her voice ragged. "I'm not okay. Anything but okay."

"I talked with him last night, Kathy," he said quietly. "Told him some things. About Pam and...me. About how it was back then. He's just going to need time to take it all in."

She nodded, saying nothing, cradled against him with her head tucked under his chin. He hadn't realized how badly he'd missed holding her. How much he'd just wanted to *touch* her. He'd gone fifteen years without her, but now even an hour or two apart was too much.

Which didn't make a lot of sense, all considered. But then, damn few things did these days.

"He's beautiful. You don't see many spotted horses."

Jett looked at the colt. "War pony. Jody took one look at him and had to have him. I figure they'll keep each other busy most of the summer."

Again she didn't say anything. Then she sighed and eased out of his embrace, giving him a tentative smile. "I have to go. I'm meeting Gord for lunch."

Strategy meeting, Jett thought dispassionately. They would probably spend the rest of the day working out the details of the best way to present her case in a court of law... the best way to get Jody away from him.

Reality came crashing down, and he nodded and shoved himself away from the corral. Not saying anything, he started walking back toward the house with her, not quite ready to let her go yet. It seemed impossible that they could be lovers one day and deadly adversaries the next. Given a choice, he sure as hell preferred the former. The thought made him smile, and he wondered what she'd say if he just came out and told her that.

But he didn't. In fact, neither of them said anything as they walked through the yard to where she'd parked her car. She pulled the keys out of her pocket and unlocked the car door, then gave him a sidelong glance through her lashes. "I was in Vic's Café this morning. Gretchen asked me to say hi next time I saw you." Her smile widened. "She looks like a serious handful of woman."

"About as serious as a chainsaw," Jett muttered, not quite meeting her eyes.

"Maybe I'll take Brice in to meet her. They sound as though they'd get along fine."

"Brice?" Jett's head lifted. "Mr. Lamborghini?"

"The same." She sighed, looking irritated. "He turned up out of the blue late last night."

Anger flickered through Jett for no reason he could figure. He wondered what a guy named *Brice* would look like. Clean-cut and suave as hell, no doubt. Expensive three-piece suits and gold watches to go with the flashy wheels. "So, you and old Brice are on again, are you?"

"Actually, Jett, that's none of your business."

"Damn right it's my business. If Mr. Lamborghini is in your life again, it means he's in Jody's life. And that means I want to know about it."

It took her by surprise, Jett saw. And he realized suddenly that she hadn't even thought it through that far. Hadn't considered the implications, the complications, of having a child in her life, of having a whole world of things to adjust to.

"I—" She closed her mouth and frowned. "You're right, I... guess." Her frown deepened, and she looked at him, her eyes clear and thoughtful. "Of course you're right. I'm sorry. I—I never even thought of that."

"I reckon there's a ton of things you haven't thought of," he muttered, trying hard to hang on to his righteous anger. Things were simple when you were angry.

"I'm sure there are." To Jett's surprise, she just smiled, looking unperturbed. "If it'll make you feel better, I told Brice to get lost. He's leaving this afternoon. And he won't be back."

Jett felt a surge of satisfaction that made as little sense as the anger had.

"I guess I'm going to have to start thinking about things a little differently now." She looked thoughtful. "This parenthood thing isn't as easy as you'd think it would be, is it?"

He felt a smile tug at his mouth, thinking of some of the surprises *he'd* faced over the past fifteen years. "Not by a damn sight."

"Does it get easier?"

He thought it over. "No. Every time you get one thing figured out, there's something new to trip you up. It's like starting over every time you get out of bed in the morning.''

"Great.'' She wrinkled her nose, then laughed quietly. "You seem to have come through it unscathed.''

"I've come through it,'' he corrected evenly.

She nodded slowly, her gaze holding his. "I have to admit you surprised me, Jett. Of all the guys I knew back then, you would have been my *last* bet as good father material.''

"I don't reckon I had much of a choice.''

"No.'' She sighed, shoulders slumping, and kicked at something in the grass. "No, I guess you didn't.''

Then she lifted her head and looked right at him, shaking her head fiercely. "No, that's not true. You *did* have a choice. You didn't have to take responsibility. You could have told my uncle you weren't interested and kept on riding your saddle broncs and winning your rodeo trophies and gone on as though nothing had changed.''

Jett didn't say anything. She was wrong, of course. More wrong than he would ever be able to tell her. There had been no choice back then at all.

"Most eighteen-year-old guys wouldn't have done what you did,'' she said softly. "A lot wouldn't have had the guts to go up against my father, but most just wouldn't have cared. They would have shrugged it off like it didn't have anything to do with them. But you gave up rodeo, and you married a woman you didn't love, and you made a home and raised our son.'' Tears suddenly filmed her eyes. "You're an honorable man, Jett Kendrick. And I've been a thorough-going bitch about the whole thing. I'm sorry.''

Sometimes talking with her was like steer wrestling, Jett thought, utterly confounded. You took out after a half-grown steer and figured out the angles and speed and all, and then you dove off your horse, and sometimes you grabbed that steer just right and over it went and you made some easy money. And other times the animal stopped or shied off, and you wound up on your face in the dirt with the wind knocked out of you, wondering what the hell had happened.

As he recalled, he'd never been much good at steer wrestling, either.

"But you're still planning on fighting me for custody," he said flatly, already knowing the answer.

She didn't answer right away, and Jett's gut wrapped itself into a knot. He'd already called three attorneys, one in Billings, one in Helena and the third in Bozeman, and all three had listened to his story with interest until he got to the name *Patterson*. Then each had suddenly remembered prior commitments and heavy workloads and declined to take the case, wishing him luck elsewhere. Although the guy in Bozeman had suggested someone else, a woman attorney over in Missoula who, rumor had it, would take on the devil himself if the price was right. Maybe he'd call her tonight. Maybe—

"No."

It took Jett a full half minute to realize what she'd said. And even then he just stared at her, not sure he'd heard her right.

But she just shook her head wearily. "No, I'm not going to fight you for custody, Jett. You've spent the past fifteen years raising Jody, and you've done a good job. He belongs out here, with his horses and his rodeo and you. Even if I managed to win the court case, he's going to be sixteen pretty soon and able to decide for himself where he wants to live. And I doubt it would be with me. So—" She bit off the words and pulled the car door open.

Still Jett didn't say anything, not feeling any of the jubilation he should have been feeling.

"He'd wind up hating me more than he already does."

It hit him finally, and relief surged up through him with the force of a river in flood, and he felt the knot in his belly dissolve. Felt like tipping his head back and giving a rebel yell.

And then he saw her face.

"Oh, hell, Kathy..."

Her expression just sort of crumpled, tears spilling, and then he was right there in front of her, taking the steps separating them without even realizing it, and the next thing he knew he was pulling her into his arms.

She shuddered, fighting it, fighting him, and then she sagged against his chest and started sobbing as though her heart was broken. Jett wrapped his arms all the way around her and tucked his face into her hair, his own throat pulling tight.

"It's all right," he murmured. "It's all right, Kath. It'll be all right."

It took what seemed like hours for her to stop shivering. Actually, it didn't take more than a few minutes in front of a blazing fire and a good swallow or two of bourbon, but it seemed a lot longer than that.

She'd scared the daylights out of him, coming apart like that. She'd always been one of the strongest people he'd known—one of the most stubborn, anyway—and seeing her break down and cry like that in front of him shook him up bad. Tears of anger, he could understand. He'd seen those before, plenty of times. But not this. Not heartbreak.

So he'd done the only thing he knew how to do: wrapped her in a blanket and got a shot of whiskey into her and kept talking to her, saying whatever popped into his mind in a soothing voice, like he would if she were a sick foal or a calf.

He never had been much good with women. Attracting them had never been a problem—in fact, it had always been a little too easy. But if lovin' them was easy, understanding them was near impossible.

They had layers of complexity to them he'd plain given up on years ago. For one thing, they never just came straight out and said what was on their minds. You had to dig it out of them, using guesswork most of the time, and if you guessed wrong, well, man, there was the devil to pay.

Like Kathy. She kept saying she was fine, that everything was all right, but you only had to look at her to know that was a lie. She was about as far from all right as he'd seen in a long while.

She was sitting on one end of the big sofa in the living room with the blanket he'd gotten off his bed still draped around her shoulders, a mug of coffee cupped between her hands, just staring into the fireplace with her mind someplace else altogether. He stood in the doorway from the kitchen and watched her, not knowing what he should be doing.

He'd called Gord, but although her brother had sounded almost friendly, he'd been no help. "Talk to her," he'd said. "What you have to do now is just talk."

Which was what they'd *been* doing when she'd started to cry, he thought irritably. The last thing they needed was more talk.

What he *wanted* to do was to take her into the bedroom and make love to her. He wanted to feel that feeling he always had when he was with her, to get drunk on the scents and tastes of her, to fill himself up with the joy he felt just by looking at her. And he wanted to make her laugh again. To bring that sparkle of mischief and delight back in her eyes. To have her look at him the way she once had . . .

But he shook the thought off impatiently, knowing it was too late for that. She would just think he was playing some game with her, trying to get her to feel something for him again so she wouldn't change her mind about taking Jody away.

Shoving himself away from the door frame, he walked back into the kitchen and poured himself a mug of coffee, then carried it into the living room. He sat on the sofa and leaned forward to brace his elbows on his knees, holding the coffee mug between his palms. He stared into it thoughtfully, seeing reflections on the surface and wondering if the answers were in there somewhere and he just couldn't see them.

"Look, Kath," he said carefully, trying to choose the right words for a change. "I . . . hell, I've screwed this whole thing up seven ways to Sunday. I've hurt you, and I've hurt Jody, and . . ." He shook his head slowly, swirling the coffee, waiting for it to reveal the mysteries he knew were there.

But it didn't, and after a while he just swore and shook his head again. "I guess what I'm trying to say is that I'm sorry. I never meant for all this to happen. I would have cut off my right arm before hurting you."

Kathleen didn't say anything at first. She traced the strong line of his profile with her eyes, following the thrust of his jawline and stubborn chin, the hard-hewn plane of his cheek. He looked drawn and tired and subdued, and she felt an uprush of love so pure and strong it took her breath away. It was hard to believe that a mere day ago she'd tried to convince herself that she hated this man. Had been fully prepared to go to court and rip out his heart.

"You haven't got anything to be sorry for," she said softly. "If it hadn't been for you, I wouldn't even know I had a son. He'd be living with strangers, and I never would have known."

"If it had been up to me," he said in a tight, even voice, "you wouldn't know now." He turned his head to look at her, eyes dark with shame. "You were right the other day— I wasn't going to tell you. I figured you had no right being here. Told myself it didn't matter if you didn't know. That you'd go back to Baltimore, and that would be the end of it."

"Maybe...it would have been better," she said raggedly. "Maybe I've been kidding myself all along. Maybe it would have been better if Jody had just gone on thinking that Pam was his mother." She swallowed. "In all the ways that mattered, she was."

"He has a right to know," he said with quiet certainty. "I know what it's like to grow up not knowing your mother. Always wondering what she was like. It wouldn't have been right, keeping you from him." He reached across and picked up her hand, then stroked the back of it with his thumb. "Or keeping *him* from *you*."

Even his touch made her heart leap. She took a deep breath, praying he couldn't tell. He would never believe it was real. Not now. He would just think she was playing

some elaborate game to get him to marry her or some other
silly thing to stay close to Jody.

"I didn't know you never knew your mother." She
straightened her fingers, running them between his. He had
square, competent hands, good for building fences and
breaking horses and making love. She thought of the
warmth of them on her skin, of the gentleness in them
whenever he touched her, and found herself near sudden
tears again.

Smiling, she pulled her hand carefully from his and took
a sip of coffee. "I thought you grew up on a reservation in
North Dakota until you came out here to Montana to live
with your grandparents. Wasn't your mother the daughter
of the tribal chief, Buffalo Walking Tall? I can't remember
her name...Running Deer?"

Jett gave an explosive laugh. "God Almighty, I'd forgotten all about that! Lynx, that was it. Running Lynx." Grinning, he looked at her. "You actually believed all that
stuff?"

"Well of course I believed it." Kathleen looked at him
indignantly. "You mean, it wasn't true?"

"Hell, no!" He tipped his head back and gave a belly
laugh. "I made the whole thing up. She was just some girl
my old man spent a night with. If she told him her name, he
was too drunk to remember it. Though she remembered his
well enough to dump me off with his parents when I was a
few weeks old."

"You fraud!" Laughing, Kathleen gave him a nudge in
the ribs with her bare foot. "So you're not the grandson of
a Sioux chieftain or anything romantic like that at all!"

"Well, he was Sioux, all right. That's what my mom told
my old man, anyway. But I wouldn't know about the chieftain part."

"So Jett Walking Tall was just plain old Jett Kendrick all
along."

He grinned. "I heard the name in a movie once and
thought it sounded cool."

"Was there a point, or was it just a great way to get laid?"

He shrugged. "I didn't like the truth much back then. So I invented one I liked better." He smiled, sliding her a lazy glance. "Though it didn't hurt when it came to gettin' laid, either."

"That's why you were so angry with me." Kathleen nodded slowly, the pieces falling together. "You thought I'd abandoned Jody like your mother had abandoned you."

Jett was swirling the coffee in the mug, gazing down into it as though seeing something reflected in its depths. "I know what it's like, growin' up without a real family. I just wanted to give him what I never had."

"You had your dad," Kathleen said quietly.

"My old man was seventeen when I was born, and he never had more than five minutes to spare for me." His voice was tight, and he glared into the coffee for a moment longer, then finished it in one swallow. "You want to know about my old man? He was one of the best saddle bronc riders in the country. Five times world champion. Enough other titles and championships and firsts to paper a wall. Inducted into the Pro Rodeo Hall of Fame when he was twenty-six. A damn hero."

Kathleen set her mug of cold coffee on the table, then put her hand on Jett's broad shoulder, feeling the tension in him. "You wanted to be like him, I know that."

"Hell, I worshiped him from the time I was old enough to walk. All I dreamed of was bein' just like my old man. And I figured when I got old enough and good enough, we'd tour the circuit together, father and son, both winnin' every trophy there was. Wild Bill Kendrick and his boy, champions of the world. Between us, there wouldn't be anything we couldn't ride."

Kathleen started rubbing his shoulder, working her fingers into the taut muscles at the base of his neck. He resisted her at first, holding himself away from her; then he relaxed slightly and let his head fall forward, giving her room to work.

"Then you quit rodeo to take care of Jody and that was the end of the dream."

"No." He leaned back against her hands. "The dream ended way before that." He didn't say anything for a while, and Kathleen didn't press him, knowing if he was going to tell her, it would be in his own way.

"Turn this way a little—that's good." She shrugged the blanket off and sat up to get a better angle, then started working the muscles along the tops of both shoulders.

"When I was thirteen, Grandpop and I had a hell of a fight about something. He always figured I should be spendin' more time working than rodeoin', and I felt otherwise. Anyway, this time I'd had enough. I decided to go live with my old man, wherever he was. I hadn't seen him in almost six months, but that wasn't unusual. I tracked him down through the pro rodeo association and found out that he was living just outside Bozeman. It didn't make any sense, why he'd be livin' down there when he could just as easily be living with his folks and saving some money, but I never saw that at the time. Ow!"

"Sorry." Kathleen frowned. "Quit tightening up on me. You've gone all tense and hard again."

He laughed and reached around to catch one of her hands, pulling it around and across his belly. "I'll show you all tense and hard, darlin'."

Kathleen pulled her hand free, laughing softly, and went back to unraveling the knots across his shoulders. "Start that kind of thing and I'm going home, cowboy."

Grinning, he rested his forearms on his thighs and let himself relax. "There was once a time when you couldn't get enough of that kind of thing."

Kathleen dug her fingers into his neck, making him gasp and swear. "So, you were thirteen and you went to live with your dad just outside Bozeman. Then what?"

He smiled. "You don't really want to hear this."

"Not if you don't want to talk about it."

"It's not that I—" He caught himself, then laughed wearily. "Hell, why not? I spent two days hitchhiking my way there, and when I finally found it, I figured I had the wrong place. It was a beat-up, old single-wide in a trailer park just off the freeway. There was a baby's playpen set up outside, and a clothesline full of diapers and I knew there had to be some mistake.''

Kathleen realized she'd stopped rubbing Jett's neck. She frowned and started working her fingers deep into the tight muscles again.

''But my old man's truck was parked at the side. I was standin' there trying to decide what to do when this blond, blue-eyed kid came out from around back somewhere. He was about a year younger than me, and when he asked me what I wanted, I told him I was looking for my dad. He told me I was lying. I couldn't be Bill Kendrick's kid, he said, because Bill Kendrick was *his* old man and in case I hadn't noticed, I sure as hell had more Indian in me than white man.''

''Am I going to want to hear the rest of this?'' She kissed his shoulder and slipped one arm around his chest.

But Jett was staring at the floor between his feet, almost as though he hadn't heard her. ''Then the door opened and this woman came out with a baby in her arms. She took one look at me and went back inside, and a minute or two later my old man came out. He hawed and hemmed and looked foolish, then admitted he and the woman weren't married, exactly, but that both kids were his.''

''Both?'' Kathleen rested her cheek on Jett's shoulder. ''Even the twelve-year-old?''

Jett gave a snort of laughter. ''Twelve and a half. There's about four months between us.''

''So much for what your dad got up to after he bade *your* mother a fond farewell. Had he and this other woman been together all that time?''

''Hell, no. She had a husband somewhere down in Texas and only saw my old man when he came through on the rodeo circuit. But then she got pregnant again and her husband tossed her out and she tracked my old man down. By the time I found them, they'd been living together for about six months. Tryin' it on for size, he said, before they told anyone.''

"So even your grandparents didn't know about it?"

Jett smiled. "Grandma Kendrick was a church-goin' lady. She loved her son, all right, but she made no bones about the fact that she didn't approve of his tomcat ways. I think Granddad may have known, but he wouldn't have said anything. To her *or* to me."

Kathleen nodded. She could feel the deep, steady thump of his heart and closed her eyes, almost able to feel the heat and dust of that trailer park on her own skin. "So how did your dad take having you turn up in his *other* life?"

"Better than the blonde did. He went back inside, and I could hear them arguin'. He was saying it couldn't hurt if I stayed a while, and she was saying she had enough to do raisin' his kids without takin' on some other woman's half-breed brat, and that if he wanted to take care of me so bad, maybe he should just leave."

"Oh, Jett." She tightened her arms.

"I didn't hang around to see how it worked out. I punched the blue-eyed kid and bloodied his nose, then I lit out." He was silent for a moment. "The cops picked me up as a runaway a couple of days later and brought me back here. I started calling myself Jett Walking Tall and copped an attitude and generally got on everyone's nerves, trying to see how much trouble I could get into. Then I got caught on a break-and-enter and wound up in a juvenile detention facility outside Helena."

"Thanks to my father."

"Best thing that could have happened to me," he admitted quietly. "It scared me straight. When I got out, I went back to rodeo and tried to forget all about my old man and the wife and the fair-haired, blue-eyed kids he'd never gotten around to telling me about." He braided his fingers with hers and lifted her hand to his mouth, kissing it. "Then I met you."

Kathleen closed her eyes and rested her forehead on his shoulder. "And your dad? Did he ever . . ."

"I hear from him now and again. The blonde ran off with a truck driver from Missoula a few years later, takin' the kids with her. My old man married again, and she seems nice enough. She sent a note and flowers when Pam died, and she remembers Jody on his birthday and all. They stopped by last year to show off their new baby.'' He gave an ironic smile. ''For a day or two there, we were almost like a real family.''

Like a real family.

No wonder he'd fought like a grizzly to get and keep his son all those years ago. And why he'd waited so long to tell her about Jody. He'd needed to be sure of her—of her feelings, her motives. Family. That was what it had been about. Just family.

Kathy was so silent for so long that Jett wondered if she'd fallen asleep. He eased himself out of her arms and turned to look at her, but she was just staring into the fire, a frown pulling her brows together.

She seemed to collect her thoughts, giving herself a little shake. ''What are we going to do, Jett? This is all such a mess—how are we ever going to get through it?''

''We'll work it out.'' He smiled and brushed a strand of hair from her cheek. ''It'll be all right, Kathy. You can see him whenever you want. And let's face it, he's going to pretty much do as he pleases, anyway.'' He gave a snort. ''Darn kid's as obstinate and hardheaded as you are.''

''Excuse me? If he's obstinate, he gets it from his Kendrick side, not mine. And I am *not* hardheaded.''

''Yeah, right.''

She smiled, then looked at him for a long, thoughtful while. ''You shouldn't be talking to me about this without a lawyer, you know. And you're not obligated to allow me visitation rights or anything else. You're being very... decent.''

Because I don't want to lose you, Jett nearly said. But he caught the treacherous words before they slipped out, knowing she would never believe him. Not sure he could believe them himself.

"I don't want a lawyer," he said evenly, knowing this *was* the truth. "I don't want to fight with you over this, Kathy. Jody's our son. We'll find a way to work it out."

"Just like a real family."

"Yeah." Smiling, he pretended to brush another strand of hair off her cheek again just for the excuse to touch her. He wanted to ask her to stay the night but had no idea how.

She smiled suddenly and rocked forward to cup his face with her hands and kiss him with satisfying thoroughness. "Thank you."

Then, before he could collect his wits enough to grab her and return the favor, the back door banged open.

"Hey, Dad? You around?"

"In here," Jett called in resignation. Another one of the unsung joys of parenthood Kathy had yet to learn—a kid's uncanny ability to know exactly when to interrupt.

"Angel says we should buy all them cattle and—" Jody hit the door to the living room in full stride and careened to a stop when he saw Kathy. "Sell what we don't want," he finished lamely.

He snatched his hat off, blushing furiously, and nearly fell over his feet. "Ma'am. Er, that is—I mean . . ." He stopped in an agony of indecision.

"Kathleen," she said gently. "I think, for a while at least, you should just call me Kathleen."

He nodded quickly, looking relieved at not having to call her *Mom,* and guilty at feeling relieved. He stood there, hat clutched in his hands, obviously not having a clue what he should be saying next. "You, uh, stayin' for supper?"

"You mean you hope she'll stay and *make* supper," Jett drawled. "Isn't it your turn to cook tonight?"

Jody gave Kathy a shy smile. "I do spaghetti pretty good, if you want to stay. . . ."

"I'd like that," Kathy said, almost as shyly. "If you're sure it's no trouble."

"Oh, it ain't no trouble." He grinned with delight. "It ain't no trouble, is it, Dad?"

"Nope." Jett found himself releasing a breath he hadn't even been aware of holding. It was going to be all right, he thought. Everything was going to work out just fine. "No trouble at all. And maybe I can give you a hand tossing a saddle on that paint of yours later, and you can show your mother what a hell of a bronc rider you are."

He didn't know which of the two of them looked more pleased.

"You know, I'm finally starting to think things might work out after all." Kathleen gazed happily around the freshly painted kitchen of her new home, then glanced around at Sherry. "I know you think I'm nuts to rent this place when all my furniture and stuff's still in Baltimore, but it *is* perfect, admit it."

Sherry rinsed off the glass she'd been washing and set it on a towel to dry. "I never said it wasn't perfect. I just said I don't know why you rented a house when we have wads of room at The Oaks. You know you're welcome to stay with us for as long as you want. Technically, the place is still half yours, anyway."

"I don't want it. And if I'm going to live in Burnt River, I need to start a real life, Sherry, not just camp out with you and Gord." A crash of thunder made her wince, and she walked across to check the catch on the window as a gust of rain hit the glass. The storm had been flirting along the edge of the mountains all day and now seemed to have settled in to stay. "Besides, you two need your privacy. Gordo told me you have plans for another baby."

Sherry grinned. "Just another addition to the dynasty." Her grin widened. "You've got some catching up to do, girl!"

"I think I'll leave the dynasty building to you and Gord and concentrate on figuring out how to be a mother to the one offspring I already have."

"I thought you two were getting along great."

"We are. But Jett and I had another wrangle this morning." She sighed and took another pot out of the box of

kitchen things they'd brought over from The Oaks. "Do
you and Gord argue over how to raise your kids?"

"All the time. But remember, we're raising ours together, and from scratch. We've spent a lot of time getting
the ground rules worked out. It's going to take time with you
and Jett."

"He's so damned stubborn!"

"And you're not, of course." Sherry smiled and set a box
of dishes on the table, then started unpacking them. "I'm
glad you have a use for all these extra dishes. I felt guilty
every time I saw them sitting in the attic."

"You were supposed to be using them," Kathleen said
dryly.

"Yeah, right, like I'm going to serve cornflakes to a two-
year-old in a china bowl that probably cost fifty bucks. Your
mother had exquisite taste, Kathy, but plastic is more my
style."

Watching her, Kathleen smiled. Then she sighed and
started unpacking the rest of the pots. She should just tell
Sherry the truth, she thought irritably. She should just stop
kidding herself and admit that this whole thing with Jett
wasn't working.

She'd thought after that day at his ranch that things really were going to be okay. Not easy, necessarily—she didn't
expect easy—but okay. It had been almost two weeks now,
and on the surface, things weren't that bad. Not between her
and Jody, anyway.

He'd taken to dropping by practically every afternoon
after school so she could help him with his homework, although more often than not they just kicked back and ate
cookies and talked until it was time for her to drive him
home. They went riding together now and again, and
watched video movies, and even went shopping in Indian
Springs.

But Jett. Well, Jett was a whole other matter.

They hardly ever talked anymore except to argue, and
then it was over the stupidest things. Like the time she
bought Jody a new shirt and Jett told her angrily that he

didn't want her spending Patterson money on his son. His son. As though she didn't really count. Or the time she'd stopped by the ranch to drop off a video Jody had wanted to borrow, and she and Jett had wound up arguing over which Jody liked best, orange juice or apple juice.

As though it mattered. And then there was the time she and Jody were having a hay fight in the barn and Jett had walked in. She'd tossed a handful of hay at him without even thinking, and he'd grinned and come after her, tackling her around the waist, and they'd gone tumbling into a pile of hay together, breathless with laughter.

She'd lain there in his arms, her mouth mere inches from his, feeling his breath on her cheek, the weight and heat of his body on hers, and for one moment it had been like old times. His eyes had held hers, as warm as toast and filled with memories, and then, in an eye blink, it was gone.

His face had gone all closed and cool, and he'd been on his feet in the next instant, brushing himself off and telling them in a surly voice that they were making a hell of a mess and had better get it cleaned up.

It had nothing to do with Jody, of course. It had to do with her. The fact that she was in Burnt River, in his life, in Jody's life. He was scared. She'd figured that out finally, although she still wasn't sure what he was scared *of*: her or himself.

"Want to talk about it?"

Kathleen looked up to find Sherry watching her with a thoughtful expression. She smiled. "It's nothing."

"Hah! Look, I know it's none of my business, but—"

To Kathleen's relief, the doorbell rang just then. "That'll be the pizza." Grabbing a handful of money from her wallet, she walked down the long hallway to the front door and pulled it open.

Jody was standing in the shelter of the overhang, the collar of his sheepskin jacket turned up against the pelting rain. He had a duffel bag in his hand, and he looked mad enough to char timber.

"Can I stay with you?" he blurted. "Me and Dad had a fight."

"Oh, Jody, I'm not sure that's a—"

"Please?" He looked at her pleadingly, teeth chattering. "Please, Kathleen? I ain't got no other place to go, 'cept a friend over in Indian Springs."

"Get in here!" Shaking her head at him, she pushed the screen door open. "How did you get into town?"

"Caught a ride with one of the ranch hands who was comin' in to see his girl." He edged past her in the narrow hallway, rainwater cascading off him and onto her newly waxed hardwood floor, mixing with the mud off his boots.

"Does your dad know you're here?"

"No." Jody's face was sullen.

"I'll give him a call and—"

"I ain't goin' back there!" Jody threw the bag down. "No way! He can do all his dang chores himself and see how he likes it."

"Hi, Jody!" Sherry appeared in the hallway just then, smiling brightly as she pulled on her rain slicker. "Kathy, I'm going to leave before this storm gets any worse."

"It's already startin' to clear in the west, ma'am."

"Well, Jody, that's not the storm I'm talking about. A truck just drove in that looks a lot like—"

A crash of thunder made Kathleen swear breathlessly, and she reached past Jody to push the door shut. It caught on something, and she gave it a shove, then gasped as it shoved back.

A gloved hand settled around its upper edge and pushed it inward, and in the next heartbeat something tall and wide stepped into the house, looking like part of the storm itself. Jett's face glowered down at her, as hard as stone.

"Where the hell is my son?"

Chapter 12

"Hi, Jett. 'Bye, Jett." Sherry smiled and edged past all of them the way she might a pack of rabid dogs. "'Bye, Jody. 'Bye, Kath."

"Sherry!" Kathleen looked at her sister-in-law helplessly. "You can't just leave me alone with this mess!"

"I'll drop by tomorrow and help you finish unpacking."

"I wasn't *talking* about the unpacking!"

Sherry waved a merry farewell, then scooted out the door before Kathleen could give a yelp of protest. Telling herself to stay calm, she turned to glare up at Jett, who was busy dripping rainwater over what remained of her clean floor. "Come in, Jett. Make yourself at home."

"What do you think you're doing, telling Jody he can stay with you any time he feels like—"

"It wasn't her idea," Jody cut in with a guilty glance at Kathleen. "She didn't know nothin' about it till I got here."

"Hey! This is *my* house! I get to ask the questions!" Kathleen looked from one to the other, hands on hips. "Okay, what's this about?"

"There's a PRCA-sanctioned amateur rodeo over in Indian Springs this weekend," Jody said angrily. "And I'm ridin' in it."

"The hell you are," Jett assured him just as angrily. "I've got a stock truck and driver headin' down to Butte on Saturday to pick up that herd of cattle, and I need your help loadin' and unloadin'. It's going to take all day—two trips, at least. You want to rodeo, that's fine. But you do it on your own time."

Jody's chin jutted out. "I'm goin' to that rodeo. Everybody worth competin' against is gonna be there, and the money's real good. You got hired hands to move those cattle!"

"They're going to be chasing down those cows and their calves that got out through that fence you never got around to fixing."

"I strung three miles of barbed wire last week. If those cows got through that fence, they done it someplace else!"

"*Stop it!*" Kathleen put a hand in the center of each male chest and shoved.

Jett stepped back, breathing heavily. "We'll finish this at home. Get your stuff and get in the truck."

"I ain't goin' home."

"Jett!" Kathleen put her hand on his arm as he took a step forward. "Let him stay the night. You could both use the time to cool off."

"Stay out of this, Kathy!" Jett wrenched his arm out of her grasp.

"Don't you talk to my mother like that!"

"Get in the truck." Jett's voice dropped dangerously. "Now."

Jody faced him belligerently; then he grabbed his duffel bag, shoved past Jett roughly and stormed back outside.

Jett watched him go, nostrils flared; then he pulled the door closed with a bang and angrily turned on Kathleen. "I got just about enough trouble with that boy without you butting in with all sorts of advice I don't need!"

"Jody didn't wind up on my doorstep tonight because of anything *I* did!" She caught her anger and turned away, heading down the hallway to the living room. "I'm not going to argue with you, Jett. It's all we do anymore, and I'm sick of it. If you have some issue with how I'm handling things, we can discuss it some other time, because I am not going to get into a brawl over child-rearing philosophies at ten o'clock at night."

"The only *issue* I have is him running to you every time I tell him something he doesn't want to hear."

"Maybe he comes to me because I talk with him instead of just barking orders." She looked at him impatiently. "And I *listen*. When was the last time you really listened to him? Do you ever ask him what his plans are? Do you know he has a girlfriend? Her name's Emily Pritchard, and she dreams of being a world champion barrel racer, and they met at a rodeo in Bear Falls last year. I'll bet you never knew that."

She could tell by his expression that he didn't. And that he wasn't too happy about the fact.

"When was the last time you told him you love him, Jett? Or the last time you took some time off to watch him ride rodeo and told him how good he is, how proud you are of him?"

Jett still didn't say anything, just watched her with that hot, angry expression in his eyes.

"He's still just a kid, Jett. He needs you to tell him how special he is."

"You don't know a damned thing about what he needs," he said in a tight voice. "I've been raising that boy for fifteen years, and I never had a problem with him until you turned up."

Kathleen drew a quick little breath, feeling as though he'd just slapped her. "That's not fair," she whispered.

Jett flushed slightly. "Kathy, damn it, this isn't—" He made an abrupt, angry gesture, as though not even knowing what he wanted to say.

"You're driving him away, Jett," she said quietly. "When he talks about rodeo, he has the same look on his face I used to see on yours. Keep fighting him and you're going to lose more than you win."

"Do you have any idea how hard the rodeo life is? For every cowboy who makes a living at it, there are a thousand who don't. You're on the road all the time, traveling from one event to the next, living in cheap motel rooms with three or four other guys, trying to make ends meet. You've got no time to build a proper life. And there's never a day when something doesn't hurt. You live with pain—pulled groin muscles, busted ribs, cracked collarbones, dislocated shoulders . . . you name it, you'll bust it."

"You loved it once."

Something crossed his face, a wistfulness, a memory, gone in an instant. "Once," he said hoarsely.

"I know you're doing this for all the right reasons, Jett, but you should know better than any man that you can't kill a boy's dreams."

"I'm not trying to kill his dreams! I'm just tryin' to—"

"Then back off and let him take his best shot. If it doesn't work out for him, he's got the rest of his life to be a rancher. But if it does, if he grabs that brass ring and makes the dream come true . . ." She smiled. "My God, Jett, you were *there*. I've seen all those trophies and championship buckles of yours that he keeps in his room. You had the dream right in your hand before you walked away from it. You *knew* how good you were. How can you possibly deny him the chance to prove just how good *he* can be?"

"This isn't any of your business," he said in a quiet, angry voice. "What gives you the right to turn up after fifteen years and tell me how to raise my son?"

"Your son. It always comes down to that, doesn't it? You'll let me play at being a parent, but he'll always be *your* son. I'll always be just the outsider."

"You are an outsider, damn it!" Then he swore and took a deep breath. "Look, I didn't mean that."

"Yes, you did." Kathleen clenched her fists at her sides, refusing to let him see how deeply those few words had hurt. "I was a fool to think you'd let me be anything else."

"Kathy—"

"Just stop, Jett. Just . . . don't say any more, all right?" She crossed her arms over her chest, chilled to the bone. So that was it. It hadn't been about her at all, but about Jody. He was scared of losing Jody. One more loss, one more betrayal, in a lifetime of them. "It's late. You'd better take your son home."

She turned and walked across the room to stare out the window, her back stiff with hurt, and Jett cursed silently.

What had happened between them, anyway? He'd been halfway in love with her once. More than halfway, if he was honest. And for a while there, he'd found himself thinking things he'd pretty much given up on. Things like a home. Family. Forever.

Then . . . well, then things had changed. It was his own fault, of course. He'd destroyed anything she might have felt for him. He saw the way she looked at him now, her eyes filled with wariness, as though she would never really believe anything he told her again.

And he didn't want it like this between them, damn it! Problem was, he didn't know *what* he wanted.

Thinking about this, he walked across to where she was standing, then bent and kissed her on the cheek. She turned her face away, and he swallowed a sigh of frustration, annoyed by his inability to do anything right these days.

"Look, I—" He swore wearily. "I'll give you a call."

"You do that, Jett." Kathleen walked away from him, the temperature in the room nearly subzero.

He wanted to say something to her, to tell her that he hadn't meant that crack about her being an outsider, that he'd shot his mouth off without thinking. But there was something about the set of her shoulders that made him think she probably wasn't interested in any of his excuses right now.

So he just left, figuring he'd done all the damage he could for one night. Jody hated his guts, and Kathy seemed to feel pretty much the same way. There didn't seem to be any point in hanging around.

Jody said exactly two words all the way home, and neither was one Jett wanted to hear. But he kept his own mouth shut, deciding there was nothing he could say that wouldn't just make things worse. It had stopped raining by the time they got home, and Jody got out of the truck and stormed into the house without a word, boot heels banging on hardwood, doors slamming.

Jett listened to the sounds wearily, knowing he was going to have to go up and make amends. Kathy had been right tonight. About a lot of things. Jody was growing up right in front of him, and he was missing most of it, too caught up in working ten-hour days to pay attention to anything but cattle, horses and the emptiness of his own life.

It had started right after Pam had died, he guessed. Before that, he and Jody used to go fishing nearly every weekend or play ball after school, or just sit at the kitchen table talking about things. Horses. Ranching. Rodeo. Even girls, now and again. They would rent old cowboy movies and cheer when the Indians burned the fort, read Zane Grey books out loud and wrestle in front of the fire. Jett had taught him how to saddle a horse and rope a calf and track a deer, and every summer they spent a few days camping in the mountains, just the two of them.

But Jody was too grown up for any of that now. Although Jett couldn't even remember when it had happened.

But if he wasn't careful, he thought with a chill, he was going to lose him altogether. Just like he was losing Kathy.

The Kicking Horse Ranch wouldn't tumble into ruin if Jody went to Indian Springs to test his mettle on some of the best rough stock the amateur circuit had to offer. He was good—probably better than he knew—and Kathy was right about that, too: he did deserve the chance to see how good he could be.

Billy could ride down to Butte with the stock truck and help load, and Angel could help unload at this end. And the cows and calves that had slipped through the fence up by Cougar Ridge would still be up there in a day or two. And even if a couple got picked off by a marauding bear or big cat, it would be worth it just to see Jody's eyes when he brought in the winning ride.

When Jett came down to the kitchen in the morning, Jody was already there. He gave Jett a hostile look from across the room, then downed a last swallow from the milk carton and tossed the empty container into the sink.

"We need to talk," Jett said quietly.

"No need," Jody said flatly. "I'm leavin'." He grabbed his duffel bag and slung it over his shoulder. "I thought about it all night, and I've decided. I'm goin' to live with my mother."

"What are you talking about?" Jett gave him an exasperated look.

"You ain't stoppin' me." Jody shoved the screen door open, then turned to level a defiant, angry look at Jett. "You know, it's no wonder Pam killed herself tryin' to get away from you."

Jett took a step back, feeling as though he'd been punched in the belly. And then Jody was gone. Out the door and across the yard, and before Jett could get himself moving, he heard the truck engine start with a roar.

For a split second, he didn't think anything of it. Jody had been driving the truck around the ranch for almost a year now, and Jett listened to it pull out a little numbly, still winded and half-sick with shock. Cougar Ridge. Jody would be heading up to Cougar Ridge to have a look at that damned sagging fence....

Except he hadn't said anything about fences and stray cattle. He'd *said* he was going to his mother's.

The reality hit Jett like another fist-blow and he swore with sudden, sharp fear and catapulted himself through the door and around to the side of the house. Jody had the truck in reverse and was backing out of the yard way too fast, tires slewing on wet leaves and grass. Jett bellowed at him to stop, then took off after his son at a dead run. But it was too late. Jody threw the truck into forward, floored the accelerator and went roaring down the lane toward the main road in a cloud of flying dust. And Jett stumbled to a stop and watched him go, heart pounding with fear. Remembering . . .

She'd always liked geraniums. But for some reason she'd never grown them in Baltimore. Baltimore had just never seemed like a geranium kind of place.

Kathleen smiled and moved the pot of brilliant red zonal geraniums a little to the left, then stood back to check the effect. Perfect. Five front steps, five pots of geraniums.

Then she let the smile fade and pulled off her cotton gardening gloves. Who was she kidding? This wasn't going to work. All the geraniums in the world weren't going to somehow magically make everything all right.

Jett had been right last night. She was an outsider. Maybe she had no right being here at all; maybe she should just go back to Baltimore. It wasn't too late. She and Gord hadn't finalized their partnership agreement yet. And she hadn't finished the paperwork that would allow her to practice law in Montana. So maybe . . .

The squeal of tires on pavement jolted her back to the here and now, and she looked around as Gord's Jeep Cherokee shot up the street and into her driveway, rocking to a stop.

He got out, and all it took was one look at his face for Kathleen's heart to stop. "What—oh, God, something's happened to one of the kids!"

"Jett called The Oaks looking for you. He's been trying to get you on the phone for over an hour."

"I—I've been outside," she whispered. "W-what's happened?"

"It's Jody, Kath. He's been in an accident. I'll take you to the hospital right now."

Kathleen didn't remember the drive to the hospital, aware only of the terrified hammering of her own heart and the sound of her own voice, urging Gord to go faster, faster.…

He stopped in front of the emergency entrance, and she was out of the Jeep and through the wide, swinging doors in a heartbeat. And in the next heartbeat she saw Jett, standing tall and solid as a mountain near the admitting desk, his face as grim as stone. She stumbled to a stop, trying to breathe, knowing it was bad. She couldn't go through this again, she thought numbly. She couldn't go through the pain of losing her baby again.…

Jett looked around just then, as though sensing that she was there. He looked gray and worn, and he just stood there for an eternity, looking at her. Then he strode toward her, reaching for her, and she was in his arms, sobbing and terrified.

"He's all right, Kathy," he said fiercely, as though needing to hear the words himself. "He's all right. He hit his head on the steering wheel, and they figure he's got a mild concussion, so they want to keep him until tomorrow, but otherwise he's fine."

"Oh, God." She gulped tears, trying to stop shaking. "A-are you sure? Y-you're not j-just saying that, are you?"

To her relief, Jett laughed. If Jody was hurt, if he was dead, Jett wouldn't be laughing, so it must be true. Jody must be all right.

"I th-thought I'd lost him again," she whispered, clinging to Jett. If he took his arms from around her, she would land on her backside in the middle of the polished floor, so she just hung on to the front of his T-shirt for dear life.

"He's got a lump on his head the size of Wisconsin, but he's going to be fine, Kathy, I swear it."

"H-how did it happen?"

"He drove the truck into the ditch just past Clover Corners."

"Drove?" Slowly, Kathleen stepped back from Jett's sheltering embrace, his words tumbling in her mind. "He was *driving* the truck?" She sucked in an outraged breath.

"What do you mean, he was *driving* the truck! He's fifteen years old, Jett! He doesn't even have his license yet! What on earth were you thinking, letting him—"

"I didn't say he was driving it with my permission," Jett growled defensively. "We had an argument, and he grabbed the keys, and before I could stop him, he was gone."

Just like Pam. Kathleen caught the words before she said them, knowing from the expression on his face that he was thinking the same thing. "Where...was he going?" Knowing that, too.

Jett hesitated. "It doesn't matter."

"He was running away again, wasn't he? He was coming back to my place."

"That doesn't matter now, Kathy."

It did matter, Kathleen thought with a sick, cold feeling somewhere under her heart. It mattered a lot. "Can I see him?"

"Yeah." He nodded toward a corridor leading off to one side. "He's in a room just down here."

Jody grinned when he saw her, looking pale and very young against the white linen. There was a patch of gauze taped to his forehead, and Kathleen swallowed when she looked at it.

"Hi, Mom."

"My God, what did you think you were doing?" Kathleen hugged him fiercely, dribbling tears down his neck. *Mom.* The word sang through her like a chorus of bells. "Don't you *ever* scare me like this again, you understand?"

"Sorry." He returned her hug a little awkwardly. "Scared myself, too."

"Good!"

"I asked the doc what he thought about you ridin' rodeo on Saturday," Jett said gruffly from behind her, "and he said he didn't know why not. Says you've got a head like concrete."

"You mean it? You mean I can go?"

Jett shrugged just a little too casually. "Word has it you're going to be the next Kendrick to make world champion. Can't do that if you don't get all the ridin' done you can. But the doc says he wants to have a look at you before we leave for Indian Springs, just to see that everything's okay."

"We?" Jody looked at him eagerly. "You mean you'll come and watch me ride?"

"Hell, yes." Jett pulled a chair over to the side of the bed and straddled it, reaching down to clasp one of Jody's hands in a firm victory grip. "You don't expect me to pass up the chance to watch the next up-and-coming world champion saddle bronc rider win his first big event, do you?"

"And Mom, too?"

Jett glanced around, but Kathleen wasn't there. He frowned, then nodded and gave Jody's slender shoulder a squeeze. "She'll be there, don't worry."

"Dad?" Jody flushed. "I'm real sorry about the truck. I guess I messed it up pretty bad, huh?"

"Bent the grill up some, but nothing a couple of whacks with a hammer won't fix."

"I, uh, I'm real sorry about what I said. About Pam. I—I shouldn't have said that. I was just tryin' to... to get even with you, I guess. Tryin' to say something ... mean."

"Look, Jody." Jett pinched the bridge of his nose with his fingers, eyes closed as he tried to get the words right. This time, damn it, he was going to get the words right. "I've been...wrong. I've yelled when I should have listened. I've told you what to do instead of asking you what you wanted to do. I've been treating you like a kid while expecting you to act like a man."

"I ain't been too good at listening myself," Jody muttered.

"Maybe because I haven't been saying much worth listening to," Jett admitted quietly. "I know I'm not much good at sayin' what I feel, Jody, but I don't know what I'd do if I lost you."

"You ain't gonna lose me, Dad," Jody whispered unsteadily. "Heck, I got a head like concrete, ain't I? And there ain't no horse that can kill me. So I reckon you're stuck with me for a while yet."

"Until you marry Emily Pritchard and move out to raise a whole batch of little rodeo champions."

Jody blushed right to the roots of his hair. "Heck, I ain't even kissed her yet!"

"You will," Jett said with a belly laugh. "You will!"

Kathy was gone when he came out of Jody's room. He looked around the waiting room for her and was going to head down the hall to where the vending machines were when one of the nurses called him over to the desk and pointed to the phone.

He grabbed up the receiver. "Kendrick."

"It's Patterson," Gord's voice growled in his ear. "Kathy made me drive her home. Now she's packing and saying she's moving back to Baltimore, and I figure it's all your fault. She won't listen to me, so unless you want to lose the best damn thing that ever happened to you, get over here. And make it fast. I don't think she's kidding."

"Baltimore? What the hell's so great about Baltimore?"

"You're not there, for one thing," Kathleen snapped. "Will you get out of my way!"

Jett stepped to one side so she could pull the closet door open. He was sorely tempted to slam it closed and sit her in a chair and damn well demand that she tell him what was going on, but he knew her too well for that. Jody didn't get *all* his obstinacy from his Kendrick side.

"I don't understand," he said finally, settling for halfway.

"In a few hours I'll be leaving, and you and Jody will have your lives back to normal. Is *that* easy enough to understand?"

"No," he growled. "Nothing about you is easy to understand. Never has been for as long as I've known you."

"You were right. I don't have a clue about being a mother. I've got him so confused he doesn't know if he's coming or going. You say one thing, I say another..."

"Heck, Kath, he's just testing you. And he's been playing the two of us against each other, seeing what he can get away with. That's what kids do. It doesn't have anything to do with whether you're a good mother or a bad one. It's got to do with a headstrong fifteen-year-old boy testing his limits, that's all."

"You make it sound so simple."

"Remember when you were fifteen?" His eyes held hers. "Seems to me you tested a few limits back then yourself."

He was relieved when she actually smiled, her eyes warmed with sudden memories. "For the first time in my life, I think I can actually feel some sympathy for my dad."

And for a moment he thought she'd changed her mind.

Then, "Tell Jody I'll stop by later to say goodbye."

"You still haven't told me why you're going."

"Because I can't stay here. I left Burnt River too many years ago. I just...don't belong anymore."

"You didn't seem to feel this way a couple of days ago."

"Things change."

"It's because of me, isn't it?"

Jett didn't think she was going to answer him. He could see her shoulders stiffen, then she shrugged carelessly. "Partly. You and I seem to be like fire and gasoline, Jett." She smiled at him. "I thought you'd be glad to see the end of me."

"And what about Jody? He still half believes you abandoned him once. How do you think he's going to take it this time?"

"I'll tell Jody the truth. That I love him, but that I can't stay. I'll explain that it doesn't have anything to do with him."

"Yeah, right. He'll believe that." He gave a snort and wheeled away from her, raking his fingers through his hair. This wasn't what he wanted, he thought despairingly. Damn it, this wasn't what he wanted at all!

"I can't stay, Jett." Kathleen's voice was soft, and he realized she'd come up behind him. She was standing there now, looking troubled and sad. "It's been staring me in the face for over a week. I've just been trying to ignore it. But this accident of Jody's..." She shook her head. "He could have killed himself, Jett. Because of me. Because I interfered." She lifted her head and looked up at him miserably. "You've been right all along. I can't just turn up in your lives fifteen years too late and think I have some say in things."

"Kathleen, this isn't—"

"If I stay, I'll destroy everything between the two of you. He'll wind up hating you, and he'll wind up hating me, too. And on top of that, *you'll* wind up hating me. And I... I love you both too much to let that happen."

Jett could have sworn he felt the earth tumble to a stop then and there. "Both?"

"Jody."

"You said both."

"I—" She looked away quickly. "Both."

Jett drew a deep, slow breath, waiting for his heart to start beating again. "You never said anything about... that."

"About loving you?" She smiled as she said it and looked up at him. "You can't even say the word, can you?"

"I can say it," he muttered stubbornly.

To his surprise, she just laughed. "Yeah, you probably can, at that. Love's a pretty easy word to use when you don't mean it."

He was thinking about that, trying to figure out what she meant, when she smiled again. "I've loved you since that day I saw you at the Indian Springs rodeo when I was fourteen. I think I knew right then that you were going to break my heart one day."

"Kathy..."

"Don't look so scared, Jett. I'm not trying to back you into a corner." She grinned. "Besides, I don't regret a thing. Every minute I had with you was worth the broken heart."

Then she turned and started putting things into the suitcase again as though nothing she'd said made any kind of difference. Jett stood there watching her, his mind gone as blank as a stone wall. Trying to grasp what she'd said. What it meant.

"I'd like to stay in touch," she said suddenly, her voice oddly rough. "I'd like to know h-how he's doing. Now and then."

Jett cut her a hard look, but she had her face turned away. "Why?" he finally growled. "Why bother with even that much? Seems to me if you were really interested in him, you'd stay."

She swallowed, and he saw her struggle to draw in a breath. "And how would you feel about that?" she asked after a moment, her voice just a whisper. "If I stayed?"

He wanted to tell her exactly what it would mean. He wanted to tell her that he couldn't sleep nights for thinking of her, thinking of what it would be like to have her in his life. Permanently, this time. Her and Jody and him. He wanted to tell her that he'd spent the last sixteen years wanting no one but her, with a hole inside him the size of the Rocky Mountains that only seeing her again had started to fill. He wanted to tell her that if she left again, it wouldn't kill him—not quite—but it might as well, because there wouldn't be much left to live for.

He wanted to tell her ten thousand things, all of which sounded like *I love you*.

But the words wouldn't come. He'd never needed words like that before, and now, when he needed them, they piled up in his throat like a logjam in a river, nearly ripping the breath out of him.

"Wouldn't mean a damn thing one way or the other," he finally managed to whisper, not wanting to say that at all, but knowing she expected it.

Needed it, even. She had to go, couldn't stay, and he had to be man enough to live with that. Man enough to give her the only thing she wanted from him. The only thing she'd ever wanted—her freedom.

She made a soft noise, not quite a word, not anything at all, really, just a soft, hurt sound that made him glance around. Her eyes held his for a split second; then she turned and walked away, and he just stood there and watched her go, knowing if he moved so much as a hair it would only be to throw his head back and howl like a gut-shot wolf.

He got through the rest of the day pretty well, all considered. He went back to the hospital to tell Jody what Kathleen had said, and discovered as he tried to explain her decision to the boy that he didn't understand it himself. Jody teared up and gave him a look almost as bewildered and hurt as the one Kathleen had given him, and Jett found himself standing there awkwardly, trying to comfort Jody and himself all in the same breath and failing miserably.

Then Jody got mad and said that if Kathleen was going back to Baltimore it must all be Jett's fault and why didn't he just go away and not come back. And when Jett said that Kathy herself would be up later to talk to him, Jody made it pretty clear he didn't want to talk to *her,* either.

On top of that, the two new hands Angel had hired the day before turned out to be pretty much useless. He yelled at them a couple of times and even fired one on the spot. But then Angel came stalking over and very softly told him in a handful of short, well-chosen words that the hands were doing their jobs just fine, that no one was fired, and that if he didn't back off, someone was going to lay him out colder than a mountain trout.

Jett shoved his face into the other man's and asked in words just as short and well-chosen who that somebody might be. Angel allowed as it might be him, and Jett sucked in a deep breath to tell him to take his best shot, when all of a sudden the fight went out of him. He mumbled something that might have been an apology and wandered off, fists clenched, feeling like he was six years old again and about ready to cry.

He went back up to the hospital to see Jody, but Jody wasn't having any of it. He turned onto his side with his face to the wall, so all Jett got was a good look at his back, as stiff with pride and hurt as a rail fence. He stayed a few minutes, not saying much, then gave up and went home.

Supper was a couple of stale biscuits and some leftover chicken, and he ate it right off the plate in front of the open refrigerator, then downed a couple of swallows of milk from the carton. Then he went to bed, deciding no one would mind too much if he called it a day.

Although if he'd thought he was going to get any sleep, he'd been crazy. Every time he closed his eyes he could see her, standing there with that look on her face.

The look that something small and vulnerable might give you after you'd kicked it in the ribs and sworn at it and told it to go away. The look that had told him he'd gotten it all wrong. That she hadn't wanted him to let her go at all. That if he'd asked—just asked—she'd be here beside him right now, tucked into the curves of his body where she belonged, and they'd be laughing quietly, belly to belly and legs all atangle, and every breath he drew would be filled with her.

How had he got it all so wrong?

Just like sixteen years ago, when he'd come back to Burnt River with a rodeo trophy and a hundred bucks in his jeans and had found her gone. He'd got it all wrong back then, too, thinking she didn't love him.

If he'd gone after her back then, he'd never have lost her in the first place.

A bath, Kathleen thought as she unlocked the front door of her town house. She'd spent the last hour in bumper-to-bumper traffic, breathing exhaust fumes and listening to cabdrivers exchange obscenities and reading the graffiti spray-painted along the sound barriers on the free-way...and all she wanted was a bath!

She closed the door behind her and secured the dead bolt, then kicked off her shoes with a sigh of relief. She wasn't used to this. Not the traffic, the noise, the smells, the dead bolt. And especially not the high heels she'd been wearing all day. She thought wistfully of her comfortable cowboy boots. She'd tossed them into the back of her closet the day she'd gotten back from Montana—nearly two weeks ago now—and hadn't seen them since.

But she didn't want to think about Montana. Because if she thought about Montana, she thought about Jett and the son she'd left behind, and the tears still came too easily.

Pushing the word and all it meant firmly from her mind, she pressed the replay button on her answering machine, then dropped into an easy chair. There was a message from her Aunt Leah, reminding her that she'd promised to drop by tonight, and another from someone wanting to shampoo her carpets. And one from Brice. There was *always* one from Brice.

But nothing from the one person she *wanted* to hear from.

She sighed and looked at the telephone, aching to call him. But calling Jody was tricky, because if she wasn't careful, she might get Jett. And she just wasn't ready for that yet.

She couldn't even think of him without a stab of anguish, remembering the impatience in his voice as he'd told her in that succinct, plain cowboy way of his that she meant nothing to him. Which shouldn't really have surprised her, of course. Love wasn't Jett's way. She knew that from hard experience.

But if she'd figured she was going to miss Jett, she'd had no idea—no idea at all—of how badly she was going to miss Jody.

She'd told herself that leaving Montana was the right thing to do. She'd told herself that it was for Jody's own good, that in the long run he was the one who mattered the most. She'd told herself she'd get over the pain of not having him in her life and that now-and-again phone calls and an occasional letter would be enough. That she only needed to know he was all right. And that he hadn't—entirely—forgotten her.

She'd told herself eight dozen things, but none of them took away the all-encompassing pain from around her heart. Even knowing he was coming out to stay with her for the month of August didn't take that pain away.

The fact it had been his idea, that he was giving up an entire month of rodeo to be with her before school started again, meant more to her than he could ever know. But under her joy was the realization that when he went back home—back to the ranch and school and rodeo and Jett—she'd be left alone with nothing but an empty house and some memories, and the ache around her heart would cut even deeper.

Just thinking about it made her chest pull tight and she had to take a deep breath, her eyes stinging with tears she refused to let fall. Crying didn't help. Jody and his father were part of a world that didn't include her, and there was no point in weeping for dreams that would never come true. She'd learned that sixteen years ago.

The answering machine finished nattering at her, winding up with another call from the second—and younger— Taylor of Taylor, Taylor, Greer and Leeds. It was one of the top law firms in the city, and they were doing their best to convince her to work for them. And one day soon she was going to have to make up her mind. Except the thought of going into big-city corporate law again was about as appealing as a broken leg.

There was a knock on her front door, and she got to her feet and padded back into the foyer. She unlocked the door, pulled it open and found her neighbor, Betsy Costano, glaring at her.

"You didn't check," Betsy said. "You gotta check the peephole before you unlock your door! There's all sorts of weirdos around these days. You're not in Burnt Creek anymore, remember?"

"You're right, Betsy. And it's Burnt River, not Creek."

"Whatever. I just wanted to return your casserole dish— and thank you very much for the use of it, and yes, now you ask, the wedding went off just wonderful!" She beamed.

"My little girl, she looked like an angel! That moron she married . . . well, that's another story. When you have a day or two, I'll tell you all about it." She rolled her eyes expressively.

Kathleen had to laugh. "I'm sure it will work out, Betsy."

"It does, it doesn't...who knows? You just gotta do your best and hope if he's a moron he dies young with lots of insurance, and if he's a good man, he goes old and quick. Like my Charlie, may he rest in peace." She patted Kathleen's arm. "Here's hoping you find yourself a good one, and soon." She started to turn away, then nodded toward the street. "And speaking of weirdos, that one's been there most of the day. I'm thinking of calling the cops, but you know what they're like. Unless you got a knife sticking out of you, they're too busy."

Kathleen glanced past Betsy to the curb. There were the usual parked cars, most of them belonging to local residents, and she had just about decided that Betsy was imagining things when she saw it. A blue and white Chevy pickup truck with a gun rack in the window, a couple of bales of hay in the back, and Montana plates.

She just gaped at it, wondering how on earth she hadn't seen it when she'd come in. Covered with mud, it was pretty hard to miss amid all the glossy Beamers and other highpriced rolling stock on the street.

Betsy looked at her sharply, then looked back at the truck. She squinted at the license plate, then looked at Kathleen again with a speculative expression. "Well, well. I think I left something on the stove." Then she was gone, grinning ferociously.

Kathleen stood there for an undecided moment or two, then took a deep breath and walked down her front steps and across the sidewalk to the truck, still barefoot. She peeked in hesitantly, breath huffing out when she realized it was empty.

Frowning, she turned to walk back to her door—and came face-to-face with the driver.

Jett was leaning against the wrought-iron railing in front of her town house, a paper cup of coffee from the café down the street in his hand, one booted foot planted on the bottom step. He touched his hat. "Ma'am."

It took Kathleen a moment to catch her breath. "What...what are you doing here?" she finally asked wonderingly.

"It took me sixteen years, but I finally made it." He grinned, looking about eighteen again and handsome enough in the bright Baltimore sun to make her heart do cartwheels. "I'm here to take you home, Kathy."

Epilogue

The moon would be up soon. Jett looked out at the night sky with a sense of subdued wonder, thinking he'd never seen the stars quite so bright. And why had he never noticed before how close the mountains looked on a night like this, rising in ragged silhouette against a sky that wasn't black at all, but navy blue? It was as though he'd been walking around in his world only half awake, blind to so many things.

The bathroom door opened, and he looked around. Kathleen stood in the doorway, smiling shyly at him, and he felt his breath snag on something in his chest. She looked like something heaven had sent, standing backlit with the light from the bathroom making her freshly brushed hair gleam like gold around her shoulders. She was wearing something white and lacy that left her shoulders bare and fell in an insubstantial drift to her ankles. He could see the faint outline of her body against the light, more imagined than real. But still enough to make a man's mouth go dry.

Still smiling, she turned off the light and walked across to him in a haze of scented steam, her eyes filled with star-light.

"My God, you are beautiful," he whispered. He reached out and ran his fingers down her cheek, then cupped her face and leaned over to kiss her very gently. "And damn, but I love you!"

Her shy smile widened, and she held her arms out and pirouetted gracefully. "Like it? It was Sherry's idea. I told her you'd be quite happy if I turned up in your bed on our wedding night in nothing whatsoever, but she insisted that even though this isn't the *first* time with you, it's still special enough to warrant a fortune in silk and lace."

"Your sister-in-law's a smart woman." He caught one of her hands and pulled her into his arms. "And it is the first time with you tonight, Kathy. The first time I'll make love to you as my wife. And I think that's pretty damn special."

Then he pulled back to look down at her again, not entirely sure he trusted his senses. "Mrs. Kendrick." He said the word deliberately, like an incantation. If this wasn't real, if she was just another dream, this was when he would wake up.

"Yes, Mr. Kendrick?" She laughed very softly and gazed up at him. "What can I do for you?"

Jett laughed out loud. "I can think of half a dozen things without even tryin' hard. But there's no rush. We've got all night."

"We've got our whole lives," she corrected gently. Then she laid her head on his shoulder and looked out the window. "It was a wonderful wedding. Thank you."

"Well, it took us long enough to get around to it. I figured we should do it up proper." He kissed the top of her head. "I just wish I could take you on a long, long honeymoon. Somewhere hot and tropical, with palm trees. And a beach. Maybe this winter, when things quiet down."

Kathleen looked up at him. "I don't need a honeymoon or tropical beaches or palm trees," she whispered. "I have absolutely everything I ever wanted, right here in this house."

Jett kissed her again, taking his time. Reminding himself that this was for good now. "God, I love you!"

Kathy gave a merry laugh. "You keep saying that."

"I have a lot of time to make up for." He kissed her again, and then once more for good measure. "Did you see Jody today?" He grinned, his arms tightening around her. "He looked proud enough to bust. Guess it must be something, to be fifteen and finally see your parents get married."

"And handsome!" She laughed. "The girls were flocking around him like they used to flock around you. If that boy figures out how irresistible he is, we're in for some rough times!"

"Your brother looked as though he couldn't quite make up his mind whether he wanted to give you away or not—to me, anyway."

"Are you kidding? He could hardly wait to hand me over! Gord has turned into an incorrigible romantic."

"He seems to walk the walk. He told me Sherry's pregnant."

"They're starting a dynasty."

"So's my old man, obviously." Jett gave a snort of laughter. "That's what—three kids now? Not countin' me and God knows how many others I don't know about."

"I really like his wife. And the kids are wonderful." She smiled and nestled against him. "Quite a little family you've got there, Mr. Kendrick."

"Yeah. Yeah, it is."

Kathleen heard something in his voice that made her look up at him. "Jett?"

He smiled at her, dark eyes as warm as chocolate on a winter's night. Then he reached into his pocket and took out a small square of paper. "My dad gave this to me this afternoon, just after the ceremony. It was tucked into my blanket when my mother dumped me off on my grandmother that day. He said he forgot all about it until the other day." Jett gave his head a tolerant shake. "Dad never was much good at remembering stuff. But he managed to find it and figured this was a good time to give it to me. Sort of a wedding present.''

Kathleen took it almost hesitantly. The paper was yellowed and brittle, and she held her breath as she carefully unfolded it, praying it didn't fall apart in her hands.

It was lined notepaper, obviously torn from a book, and there wasn't much written on it. Just a few blurred lines in pencil in a schoolgirl's scrawl.

My name is Beth. I'm only fifteen and my ma and dad say I can't keep the baby on acount of he's half white and they don't want him. But I don't want no strangers raising him. When he's growd up, tell him I loved him. Take good care of my baby.

"Oh, Jett." Tears welled in Kathleen's eyes. "Fifteen!"

"Just a little younger than you were when Jody was born."

"She must have loved you desperately to bring you all the way to Montana to make sure you'd be raised by family."

"Yeah." He took a deep breath. "Yeah, I guess she did. And this was with it." He held out his hand and dangled something from his fingers.

Kathleen reached out curiously. It was a narrow thong of braided leather, maybe ten inches long, with a dozen multicolored glass beads inexpertly strung in the center. Kathleen took it from him and turned it in her fingers. "She made this herself." Then, smiling, she wrapped it loosely around his left wrist and knotted it securely. "I think," she said softly, "that she'd like that."

"She feels real," Jett said, almost in a whisper. "For the first time in my life, my mother feels like a real person."

Kathleen refolded the paper. "Your dad was right. This is a wonderful gift."

"It made me think about that blue-eyed kid of his, for some reason. The one from the trailer park."

"The one you punched in the nose?"

"Yeah." He managed a flicker of a grin. "My half brother. I asked Dad about him. His name's Nick, and the baby was a girl, Karen. Dad admitted he lost track of them years ago, but the last he heard, they were living in New Mexico. Santa Fe, he thought."

"Maybe," Kathleen said quietly, "this winter, instead of going somewhere with a beach, we could go to Santa Fe."

"You think?" He smiled then, and ran the back of his hand down her cheek. "You're something else, lady, you know that? And God, I love you!" He wrapped both arms around her and hugged her ferociously, face buried in her hair.

Laughing, Kathleen slipped both arms around his neck. "And you know what I'd like?"

"I know what I'd like," he growled, as though just discovering she was naked under all the silk and lacy bits. He started delicately unraveling ribbon.

Kathleen gazed at him, unable to believe she could feel so much love and still be able to breathe. "In a while, say six months or so, what would you say to starting an addition to our own little dynasty?"

Jett grinned slowly. "I'd like that a lot. I wasn't sure if you'd want...I mean, with your career and all. And Jody."

"Not right away, because it's important that I spend some time alone with Jody, to get to know him and to let him know me. I think he needs that." She smiled. "But I missed all those first fifteen years with him. I want that. I want to have another baby with you, and this time be the mother I never got to be."

Jett grinned. "Two o'clock feedings. Colic. Diaper rash. Toilet training. Oh, yeah. All that *good* stuff."

Kathleen laughed. "I'm game if you are, Sundance."

"Old Gord's got a pretty good lead on this dynasty-building thing," he drawled.

"Well," Kathleen said very reasonably, walking backward to the bed with Jett's hands in hers, "I guess that means we'll just have to work a little harder."

"Amen to that." His shirt sailed across the room, landing in a heap, and a moment later, Kathleen's lovely silk and lace negligee floated through the air to land beside it.

And Jett, tumbling back across the bed with his arms full of soft female flesh and Kathy's delighted laughter ringing around him, could have sworn he heard the singing of angels. Or maybe it was just his own wild heart....

* * * * *

*Coming in 1997,
don't miss Rafe and Nick's stories
as Naomi Horton's WILD HEARTS
miniseries continues.*

The first book in the exciting new
Fortune's Children series is

HIRED HUSBAND

by *New York Times* bestselling writer
Rebecca Brandewyne

Beginning in July 1996
Only from Silhouette Books

Here's an exciting sneak preview....

Minneapolis, Minnesota

As Caroline Fortune wheeled her dark blue Volvo into the underground parking lot of the towering, glass-and-steel structure that housed the global headquarters of Fortune Cosmetics, she glanced anxiously at her gold Piaget wristwatch. An accident on the snowy freeway had caused rush-hour traffic to be a nightmare this morning. As a result, she was running late for her 9:00 a.m. meeting—and if there was one thing her grandmother, Kate Winfield Fortune, simply couldn't abide, it was slack, unprofessional behavior on the job. And lateness was the sign of a sloppy, disorganized schedule.

Involuntarily, Caroline shuddered at the thought of her grandmother's infamous wrath being unleashed upon her. The stern rebuke would be precise, apropos, scathing and delivered with coolly raised, condemnatory eyebrows and in icy tones of haughty grandeur that had in the past reduced many an executive—even the male ones—at Fortune Cosmetics not only to obsequious apologies, but even to tears. Caroline had seen it happen on more than one occasion, although, much to her gratitude and relief, she herself was seldom a target of her grandmother's anger. And she wouldn't be this morning, either, not if she could help it. That would be a disastrous way to start out the new year.

Grabbing her Louis Vuitton totebag and her black leather portfolio from the front passenger seat, Caroline stepped gracefully from the Volvo and slammed the door. The heels of her Maud Frizon pumps clicked briskly on the concrete

floor as she hurried toward the bank of elevators that would
take her up into the skyscraper owned by her family. As the
elevator doors slid open, she rushed down the long, plushly
carpeted corridors of one of the hushed upper floors toward the conference room.

By now Caroline had her portfolio open and was leafing
through it as she hastened along, reviewing her notes she had
prepared for her presentation. So she didn't see Dr. Nicolai
Valkov until she literally ran right into him. Like her, he had
his head bent over his own portfolio, not watching where he
was going. As the two of them collided, both their portfo-
lios and the papers inside went flying. At the unexpected
impact, Caroline lost her balance, stumbled, and would
have fallen had not Nick's strong, sure hands abruptly shot
out, grabbing hold of her and pulling her to him to steady
her. She gasped, startled and stricken, as she came up hard
against his broad chest, lean hips and corded thighs, her face
just inches from his own—as though they were lovers about
to kiss.

Caroline had never been so close to Nick Valkov before,
and, in that instant, she was acutely aware of him—not just
as a fellow employee of Fortune Cosmetics but also as a
man. Of how tall and ruggedly handsome he was, dressed
in an elegant, pin-striped black suit cut in the European
fashion, a crisp white shirt, a foulard tie and a pair of Cole
Haan loafers. Of how dark his thick, glossy hair and his
deep-set eyes framed by raven-wing brows were—so dark
that they were almost black, despite the bright, fluorescent
lights that blazed overhead. Of the whiteness of his straight
teeth against his bronzed skin as a brazen, mocking grin
slowly curved his wide, sensual mouth.

"Actually, I *was* hoping for a sweet roll this morning—
but I daresay you would prove even tastier, Ms. Fortune,"
Nick drawled impertinently, his low, silky voice tinged with
a faint accent born of the fact that Russian, not English, was
his native language.

At his words, Caroline flushed painfully, embarrassed
and annoyed. If there was one person she always attempted

to avoid at Fortune Cosmetics, it was Nick Valkov. Following the breakup of the Soviet Union, he had emigrated to the United States, where her grandmother had hired him to direct the company's research and development department. Since that time, Nick had constantly demonstrated marked, traditional, Old World tendencies that had led Caroline to believe he not only had no use for equal rights but also would actually have been more than happy to turn back the clock several centuries where females were concerned. She thought his remark was typical of his attitude toward women: insolent, arrogant and domineering. Really, the man was simply insufferable!

Caroline couldn't imagine what had ever prompted her grandmother to hire him—and at a highly generous salary, too—except that Nick Valkov was considered one of the foremost chemists anywhere on the planet. Deep down inside Caroline knew that no matter how he behaved, Fortune Cosmetics was extremely lucky to have him. Still, that didn't give him the right to manhandle and insult her!

"I assure you that you would find me more bitter than a cup of the strongest black coffee, Dr. Valkov," she insisted, attempting without success to free her trembling body from his steely grip, while he continued to hold her so near that she could feel his heart beating steadily in his chest—and knew he must be equally able to feel the erratic hammering of her own.

"Oh, I'm willing to wager there's more sugar and cream to you than you let on, Ms. Fortune." To her utter mortification and outrage, she felt one of Nick's hands slide insidiously up her back and nape to her luxuriant mass of sable hair, done up in a stylish French twist.

"You know so much about fashion," he murmured, eyeing her assessingly, pointedly ignoring her indignation and efforts to escape from him. "So why do you always wear your hair like this...so tightly wrapped and severe? I've never seen it down. Still, that's the way it needs to be worn, you know...soft, loose, tangled about your face. As it is, your hair fairly cries out for a man to take the pins from it, so he can see how long it is. Does it fall past your shoulders?'' He quirked one eyebrow inquisitively, a mocking half smile still twisting his lips, letting her know he was enjoying her obvious discomfiture. ''You aren't going to tell me, are you? What a pity. Because my guess is that it does— and I'd like to know if I'm right. And these glasses.'' He indicated the large, square, tortoiseshell frames perched on her slender, classic nose. ''I think you use them to hide behind more than you do to see. I'll bet you don't actually even need them at all.''

Caroline felt the blush that had yet to leave her cheeks deepen, its heat seeming to spread throughout her entire quivering body. Damn the man! Why must he be so infuriatingly perceptive?

Because everything that Nick suspected was true.

* * * * *

To read more, don't miss
HIRED HUSBAND
by Rebecca Brandewyne,
Book One in the new
FORTUNE'S CHILDREN *series,*
beginning this month and available only from
Silhouette Books!

There's nothing quite like a family

REUNION

HANNAH · MICHAEL · KATE

The new miniseries by
Pat Warren

Three siblings are about to be reunited.
And each finds love along the way....

HANNAH
Her life is about to change now that she's met
the irresistible Joel Merrick in **HOME FOR HANNAH**
(Special Edition #1048, August 1996).

MICHAEL
He's been on his own all his life. Now he's
going to take a risk on love...and
take part in the reunion he's been
waiting for in **MICHAEL'S HOUSE**
(Intimate Moments #737, September 1996).

KATE
A job as a nanny leads her to Aaron Carver,
his adorable baby daughter and the
fulfillment of her dreams in **KEEPING KATE**
(Special Edition #1060, October 1996).

Meet these three siblings from

Silhouette SPECIAL EDITION®
and
INTIMATE MOMENTS®
™ *Silhouette*

Look us up on-line at: http://www.romance.net

REUNION

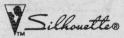

Silhouette's recipe for a sizzling summer:

* Take the best-looking cowboy in South Dakota
* Mix in a brilliant bachelor
* Add a sexy, mysterious sheikh
* Combine their stories into one collection and you've got one sensational super-hot read!

Summer Sizzlers

MEN OF Summer

Three short stories by these favorite authors:

Kathleen Eagle
Joan Hohl
Barbara Faith

Available this July wherever Silhouette books are sold.

Look us up on-line at: http://www.romance.net

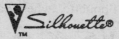

Silhouette®
™

SS96

FORTUNE'S Children™

New York Times Bestselling Author
REBECCA BRANDEWYNE

Launches a new twelve-book series—FORTUNE'S CHILDREN
beginning in July 1996 with Book One

Hired Husband

Caroline Fortune knew her marriage to Nick Valkov was in
name only. She would help save the family business, Nick
would get a green card, and a paper marriage would suit both
of them. Until Caroline could no longer deny the feelings Nick
stirred in her and the practical union turned passionate.

MEET THE FORTUNES—a family whose legacy is greater than
riches. Because where there's a will...there's a wedding!

Look for Book Two, *The Millionaire and the Cowgirl,*
by Lisa Jackson. Available in August 1996 wherever Silhouette
books are sold.

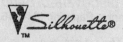

This exciting new cross-line continuity series unites five of your favorite authors as they weave five connected novels about love, marriage—and Daddy's unexpected need for a baby carriage!

Get ready for

THE BABY NOTION by Dixie Browning (SD#1011, 7/96)
Single gal Priscilla Barrington would do anything for a baby—even visit the local sperm bank. Until cowboy Jake Spencer set out to convince her to have a family the natural—and much more exciting—way!

And the romance in New Hope, Texas, continues with:

BABY IN A BASKET
by Helen R. Myers (SR#1169, 8/96)

MARRIED...WITH TWINS!
by Jennifer Mikels (SSE#1054, 9/96)

HOW TO HOOK A HUSBAND (AND A BABY)
by Carolyn Zane (YT#29, 10/96)

DISCOVERED: DADDY
by Marilyn Pappano (IM#746, 11/96)

DADDY KNOWS LAST arrives in July...only from

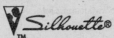